Sunrise at the American Market

To Richard & Brua —
With great
affection. Best,

Andy Popper

3/2-7/2016

Sunrise at the American Market

Andrew F. Popper

CAROLINA ACADEMIC PRESS

Durham, North Carolina

Library of Congress Cataloging-in-Publication Data

Popper, Andrew F.
  Sunrise at the American market / Andrew F. Popper.
     pages ; cm
  ISBN 978-1-61163-818-9 (acid-free paper)
  I. Title.

PS3616.O658S86 2015
813'.6--dc23

                            2015034439

CAROLINA ACADEMIC PRESS
700 Kent Street
Durham, North Carolina 27701
Telephone (919) 489-7486
Fax (919) 493-5668
www.cap-press.com

Dedicated
to
Cherished Family and Friends
and to
Sparky, McGee, Tao, and Camden

Contents

"It is one of the blessings of old friends that you can afford to be stupid with them."

Attributed to the Journals of Ralph Waldo Emerson

~

"I count myself in nothing else so happy
As in a soul remembering my good friends…"

William Shakespeare, *Richard II*, Act 2, Scene 3

Sunrise at the American Market

Chapter 1

Coffee and Flynn
2006

In the time before I knew I would never have the wealth and position my family enjoyed, I allowed myself a station in life suitable to my best hopes. As I think back, I realize I sorted people based on my superficial impression of their prosperity and standing, and a simplistic sorting it was. Construction workers and those who delivered packages had uniforms, and no one of means or consequence, I thought, wore a uniform.

There were other signs — old winter coats, heavy boots, and, of course, the coffee. It was ordinary and inexpensive. And so in the beginning, before the odd and lovely friendship I found in the American Market, a companionship unlike any I had ever known, I stood back, aloof, superior, and thoroughly wrong.

Given my observations of status and class, you might wonder why I opted to get my morning coffee at the American Market, the convenience store at the center of all that follows. Like most of us, I am a person of rituals, and getting a quick cup of coffee before walking my dog has been a modest daily indulgence of mine for many years.

I learned long ago that dogs will wait in the car for as long as it takes to get a cup of coffee. Perhaps they spend the time contemplating the grander things in life or trying to remember the location of a particularly disgusting tennis ball, but in any case, they are disinclined to complain, content that at the end of the vigil there will be time in that best of all places, the park. I, on the other hand, worried about time, mostly the summer heat — which in Washington is not all that bad if one longs for August in Mumbai. And then there is February, a meteorological anomaly when everything

3

and everyone freezes to a greater or lesser extent. For my ritual to work year-round, the coffee had to be quick, and in the beginning, the coffee at the American Market, if nothing else, was just that.

Satisfied with the idea of fast coffee of uncertain provenance, I became a regular at the American Market, steering clear of long lines at the gourmet coffee shop down the street. During the first few years, I barely took in my surroundings but after a time, even the dullest among us can't help but notice repeating patterns and behaviors, the soothing cadence of familiarity.

And so it was one rainy March morning I uttered a greeting to the man behind the counter. I later learned he had chosen for himself the name Henry DuChamp not long after entering the United States with his wife, Simone, on the freighter *The Jersey Jane*, docking at the Port of Baltimore, hidden in a metal container packed with men's black socks made in China.

Henry responded to my greeting with unexpected warmth. I had turned from the counter, when he said: "It's cold and wet today. Why not stay until the rain lets up?"

"Thank you. I need to walk my dog and get to work."

"You need an umbrella. I have one you can borrow."

I set down my briefcase. "That's nice of you to offer but my car is just a few blocks away."

"Then you will get wet."

"I suppose so." I turned and faced him. "I'm Charlie—Charlie Pratt."

"I'm Henry." We shook hands.

"I come in every day."

"I know," Henry nodded. "You must like my coffee."

"It's fine." Henry leaned forward, expecting more, but I was hesitant to share its unmemorable characteristics: it was consistent, simple, modest, neither bitter nor weak.

His eyes narrowed as he waited. Finally, unable to think of anything better, I asked: "Are you thinking of changing it?"

He shook his head as if I had suggested something harsh. "No, of course not," and then more quietly, "you might not come back." He scanned the area near the counter, insuring our privacy. "You talk to newspapers. Sometimes I listen."

Henry was right. Some mornings I stood by the newspaper rack and read headlines muttering things like: "What's the matter with our Congress?" and, "They lost—again?" and, "Oh, those poor people." I made these comments to no one in particular.

You might think these are stage whispers designed to be overheard and engage the world around me, and perhaps at some subconscious level they were, but as I see things, they were a voice of my circumstance. I lived alone, spoke at length with my dog, and despite the security I enjoyed at work, felt on uncertain ground.

"You live a solitary life?" Henry asked quietly.

It was an oddly framed but timely question. As a rule, I am at peace with the mundane and solitary nature of my existence. Recently, however, I'd felt a discomforting sense of incompletion. It was as if the normally benign hollows within me had been occupied by an interior shadow, an inchoate, incorporeal ectoplasm, a constant, spectral reminder of the most obvious fact in my life: I lack a true home.

As I'm sure you know, my reference to true home is not about a roof over my head—I own a perfectly respectable house—but in the more important meaning of the term. I no longer had the best promise of home: the assurance there is a place you are always welcome. I missed the familiarity born of essences from a properly roasted chicken, a couch that anticipates and welcomes your every angle, of calming and anticipated resonant sounds, voices in harmony without the requirement of substance or meaning.

This unmet, primitive need flows from the obvious: I was and am a self-initiated transplant. With full knowledge of the consequences, I left my childhood home twenty years ago, and while I live in physical comfort, I am without that potent embrace, that essential base, true home.

I considered sharing this self-indulgent monologue with Henry but thought better of it. Instead, I made a series of linguistic and cultural assumptions—ultimately all incorrect—and decided to give the question and the term *solitary* its most common meaning. "In some ways," I said. "My family lives in Brampton, Maine. I don't see them that often."

"Ah," Henry said, nodding, and then, "No family here?"

I shook my head and took a long sip of my inconsequential and happily noninvasive coffee. Before I could say anything further, I became aware of a customer standing next to me waiting to pay for a roll of paper towels, a newspaper, a donut, and a cup of coffee. "Excuse me. I hate to interrupt but...."

"I am so very sorry," Henry said. It was more of an apology than necessary and when he was gone, Henry turned to me. "Everyone is in a hurry in this store. I hope one day you are not in a hurry." Without saying more, Henry pushed his umbrella across the counter and there it sat. He turned to another waiting customer.

I cannot tell you why that umbrella, a simple and unexpected gesture, touched me but it did.

Beyond the expanse of windows nearly covered with advertisements for phone cards, soft drinks, and the lottery—and there shall be more about the lottery later—I could see it was raining harder than before. I picked up Henry's umbrella, put a lid on my coffee, and walked to my car. My dog, Flynn, made no mention of the fact that I had been gone longer than usual. In that sense, he is a remarkably tolerant dog.

His previous owners, a couple in the diplomatic corps, believed they'd been assigned permanently to Washington, but war and politics interceded. On short notice, they learned they would be spending at least two years in Baghdad, and Flynn—the name they chose and I kept—ended up in the Jackson Park Animal Shelter. Their rapid departure coincided fortuitously with my decision to get a dog, and Flynn, then barely a year old, ambled into my life.

I had owned Flynn for two years at the time I introduced myself to Henry. It was March 2006 and while the events that form the backbone of this story do not begin until the fall of 2012, I want to make sure you know how things started.

~

After our first encounter that March, Henry and I hardly spoke beyond the normal pleasantries—often little more than greetings and comments on the weather.

One preposterous August morning, as yesterday's stale and sodden heat flooded the city before sunrise, I parked in the shade under a tree, opened all the windows of my car and started toward the

Market. After a few steps, I turned back and let out Flynn. It was simply too hot for Flynn or any other breathing being to be left in a car, regardless of open windows. We were both panting by the time we reached the Market.

I tied his leash to a bike rack shaded by the awning that ran the full length of the Market and asked Flynn not to bite anyone. This was not an idle wish.

Almost all dogs, given sufficient provocation, are quite capable of a well-placed, litigation-inducing bite, and the lazy, loving, mostly affable, faithful Flynn was no exception. Flynn had a list. He was not good—and by that I mean ill-tempered, lunge-prone, and risky—with certain small children (I never knew which ones he favored and which ones were in jeopardy), people in hats, bicyclists, loud noises, bells, ice cream trucks, mailmen and mailwomen (Flynn did not discriminate based on gender), cats, small dogs, and men with beards. I caution this is a partial list.

Henry was at the door. "He looks like a bear," he said.

Flynn looks nothing like a bear as far as I can tell, but he is a big black dog with an admirable paunch.

"He's big-boned," I responded.

"He's of the fat lab family." This statement—Flynn is indeed a fat black Labrador Retriever—came from a woman standing by the newspaper racks. Thus began my first encounter with Claire Beaumont.

I had been unable to classify Claire. She was usually well-dressed and alert, but there were days when things were not perfectly in place. Every now and then, I'd notice a stain on her skirt or blouse, and from these momentous bits of evidence concluded (it pains me to admit this) she was a waitress at a fancy hotel who worked late nights or early mornings.

That Claire held a demanding job—she was the manager of the Jackson Park office of the investment firm of Baker and Duval—and had endless, draining responsibilities at work and at home, never crossed my mind.

I tell you this about Claire because, while it was impossible to miss those many qualities in her appearance that made her powerfully attractive to me, I failed to see in our first few exchanges her fundamental decency, a virtue I later came to realize exists in far more people than I could have imagined.

I don't want you to get the wrong impression of Claire based on our initial interaction—orchestrated by Henry—but it did not go well. I started with, "Fat lab is about right." I hoped there was a touch of bravado in my response but Claire simply nodded and continued to look at a newspaper.

Henry, for reasons known only to him, jet-whispered to me from a distance: "That's Claire Beaumont. You'll like her. She might be a little older than you but she is smart and handsome—and I think unmarried."

There must be a formula to calculate the distance a whisper can travel and remain unheard by all but the intended recipient. Assuming such a formula exists, Henry did not do the math. The distance and volume of this particular whisper rendered it audible on the sidewalk in front of the Market. In less time than it took for me to glare helplessly at Henry, Claire spun around. "What?"

Henry turned to the wall behind him, to the phone cards and cigarettes, the magazines with innocuous plain brown covers and busied himself as Claire walked to the counter and repeated her question.

In what he saw as a moment of inspiration and I saw as understandable cowardice, Henry turned to the rear of the store and said, "Yes, Simone—I'll be right there!"

Henry's wife, Simone, shared responsibilities with him and was in the Market most days. Sadly for Henry, everyone in the store, including Claire, could see Simone was nowhere to be found.

Apparently deciding Henry was too easy a target, Claire turned to me: "I see you in here every day—were you and Henry talking about me?"

I am capable of neutral gestures but the pose I assumed was much closer to nitwit than neutral. She shook her head slowly. "Curiosity getting the better of you? I don't know how many times I've seen you and never a word. Now you want to know my age and marital status?"

"Of course not, and sure, yes … well, my dog is … I didn't want to ask.…" It was a conversational collapse of some magnitude.

She allowed the smallest smile. "You just looked at my left hand—no ring." I had. How is it that this common male maneuver, thought surreptitious, is almost always evident? She continued: "So it's a fair guess I'm single. Want to guess my age? How about my weight?"

"Please, no, I had nothing like that in mind."

She stepped closer toward me. "What is it with you, anyway? You never say hello, except on occasion to Henry. Maurice and I talked about you the other day. He said you drive a nice car and had a dog—but didn't seem like a convenience store guy." She looked at Flynn who was sprawled outside on the warm sidewalk.

Recovery from dumbfound is a slow process, but I was on the mend. "Who's Maurice?"

Claire pointed to a large, red-haired man who at that moment was pouring himself a second cup of coffee. I had seen him many times and, in my silent world, dubbed him *l'homme de tricot*—which I think means sweater man. I confess a crush on my high school French teacher, Madame Glickstein, though more than a quarter century ago, still lingered and from time to time, I treat myself to a word or two, imagining how she would pronounce it.

In any case, my French was weak then and is more so now. Over time, I wondered whether the words I chose for Maurice, my sweater man, suggested he knit his own sweaters but it no longer mattered. Henceforth, he would simply be Maurice, notwithstanding his impressive and immense collection of sweaters, some themed (for example, he had a New Year's Eve sweater with an embroidered ball drop) and some un-themed but spectacular ... his Jackson Pollock cardigan comes to mind.

"Maurice," Claire called, her voice barely raised, "this is Charlie—not Charles, right?" She'd listened carefully to Henry.

"Yes, just Charlie."

Apparently, my parents liked the name Charlie but chose Charles to honor Charles Westminster Pratt, an uncle my father favored who died in the Second World War while commanding a Marine ground infantry unit on Tarawa. With due deference to my revered namesake, I cannot remember ever being called Charles though I am denominated on my birth certificate Charles Emerson Pratt.

Going back in time, there were others in the Pratt familial line with more enviable names—Moses Great Oak Pratt, Eagle Pratt, Thunder Pratt, Harrington Washington Pratt, Wyatt Pratt, and my favorite, William Mad Mountain Pratt (whose great grandfather was said to own most of northern New Hampshire at one point—but none of us believed that).

Maurice nodded at me.

"Join the human race, Charlie," Claire said. "You can say hello now that you know us." She picked up her coffee from the counter and took a sip. "It's really none of your business whether I'm married or not." Another sip. "I was married—and I have two children, a son and a daughter ... my son is married and now lives in France. My daughter is grown-up ... well, grown-up is a reach." She stopped. "What about you?"

"I'm not married—not that I have ... at this time...." I was slipping quickly. "I don't mean that I once was. No, I've never been ... and children ... well ... yes ... that...."

"What?" Claire asked.

Henry, who'd been watching this catastrophe, issued another whisper loud enough to be heard by Maurice and everyone else in the Market. "Introduce yourself properly."

I shhh'ed Henry and announced: "I'm sorry. My name is Charlie Pratt."

"And I'm Claire Beaumont." She shook my hand and then let it slide away slowly.

Most handshakes are impersonal, barely remembered touchings, but this was alive, strong and warm, and lingered briefly in my palm. While speech was failing me, at least I had the presence of mind not to turn my hand to my face to see if anything of her hand remained.

"It's really quite ... today ... and my dog...."

"I'm sure he's thirsty—Henry?" Claire was not shy in dealing with Henry. "Do you have a bowl of water for the bear?"

A bowl was found, Flynn slurped happily, and with another stumbling apology for nothing in particular, I untied Flynn and fled. Flynn waddled more than fled but you get the idea.

~

One morning in late September when the weather had calmed, I stood at the counter as Henry counted out my change. Without looking up, he said: "You'll like him. He comes here most days." He nodded in the direction of a uniformed deliveryman I'd seen often and about whom, as you already know, I'd drawn dire conclusions. Relegated to life in a truck, inhaling exhaust fumes, handing over the prized possessions of others, returning periodically to a loading dock where a mountain of packages awaited. "Did you know he teaches piano and poetry at the Beardsley House?" Henry asked. I shook my head.

Beardsley House is a large assisted-living and nursing home almost in the center of Jackson Park. Henry continued: "It is a nice place for some—people who can live at home no longer. When I am too old to work, I wish to die quickly. I don't want to live in a place like Beardsley House, surrounded by those near death." He lowered his voice. "Life is given with hope unlimited. Then comes the expectations of others. We balance everything, do with it as we can—but the ending is fully ours and ours alone, don't you think?"

My answer bordered on meaningless. "I suppose for some that's so." I decided not to explore further Henry's statement because, and I tell you this in all honesty, I am not one to contemplate the necessity of having direct dominion over my death in more than the most superficial manner. I considered and rejected responses to what seemed Henry's expectation for his last days and instead asked, "Piano and poetry? When?"

Henry accepted my demurrer to his deeper query and turned to my question: "In the late afternoon. He finishes his delivery route and then teaches for a few hours."

"Do you know him?" I asked.

"He knows Claire—and he talks to the newspapers. Like you. His name is Alex. He's knowledgeable about many things—particularly the lottery."

"What's there to know? You buy tickets and hope."

Before Henry could answer, Alex, who had heard his name used, walked to the counter. "Just coffee today, Henry."

"Do you know Charlie?" Henry asked.

"No—I recognize him. Should I know him?"

"I think so," Henry said.

I had the same awkward feeling I used to get in law school. Each time I was called on in class, particularly during my first year of law school, I was sure nothing would come out of my mouth that made the slightest sense; humiliation was inevitable. My answers were rushed, wrong, and embarrassing—and not even close to what I knew, on reflection, was probably the correct answer.

After a time, I perfected the art of being physically present in class and on the cusp of invisibility. Any professor looking for an eager or anxious student would pass me by. It worked and I became more and more quiet.

"Henry and I met this spring." I held out my hand. "I'm Charlie Pratt."

He leaned forward. "Alex Roman. Nice to meet you. And there's a lot to learn about the lottery." He shook my hand, put a couple of dollars on the counter, told Henry to keep the change, and walked out.

"Maybe you and Alex can be friends," Henry said.

At the time, friendship seemed most unlikely. I had no idea how one went about befriending a uniformed deliveryman. Do you ask about his route? Were there particularly heavy packages today? How many of those brown uniforms do you own? Does your company clean them for you? How is it possible that a deliveryman teaches senior citizens to play the piano or write poems?

At this point, so early in this story, you might think me detached and, frankly, supercilious. If so, and I am not arguing with you, perhaps this will help you understand how some of those traits came to pass.

We all come into the world with one hand already dealt. For most, the hand has at best two jacks and an assortment of unmatched other cards. For me, it was a full house, a deep and expansive family hand centered in Brampton, Maine, with relatives and offshoots throughout New England and Upstate New York, that—I tell you this knowing the implications—had been there for centuries.

My family was nothing I deserved or worked for. It was heritage:

elitist and unfair, tenacious, with broad, deep, diversified, compounded wealth that spanned the entire history of this country. We were and are the beneficiaries of massive, multiple public land grants that became our private property, followed by lucrative investments in banking and agriculture, beginning in the eighteenth century and continuing to the present.

With that fiscal depth, it should come as no surprise that my parents and grandparents and their brothers, sisters, aunts, and uncles were the force that pushed me through the whole of the educational system, from a few months past infancy to a law degree and from there to a job at a law firm. After all, as my father said when I finally passed the bar, one needs something to occupy the day.

My work at the firm was predictable and reasonably paced. You may know lawyers who work long hours, sacrifice family, putting mind, heart, and soul into their profession. I admire those lawyers—but I was not one of them. I knew my field—everyone in the firm did at varying levels. I was on decent terms with most of my colleagues, on a first-name basis with certain clients, but little more.

I had not set foot in a courtroom since an uncomfortable moot court experience my first year of law school. I was, however, connected. It was by family of course, and those connections brought in clients who retained the firm because I worked there. They paid massive amounts of money for a range of legal services, some a complete mystery to me. If you are expecting to learn what those darker services entailed, you will be disappointed. I never learned and was not particularly interested.

I knew enough to write client letters, memos, and draft interrogatories, all in the area of electric utility law. It's more interesting than you might think ... well, perhaps not. I knew the cases, statutes, and regulations that affected one particular group of our clients (large, private, investor-owned utilities), and that was about it.

What I will share with you (and this is a bit embarrassing and may irritate you) is that I could not be fired. The lucrative clients I mentioned a moment ago stayed with our firm only because of my family. It was that simple.

And so, at least professionally, I was secure, though that neither explains nor excuses the quiet snobbery I brought with me to the Market.

When the weather was right, I jogged in the evenings (without Flynn, as I'm sure you've realized—Flynn is many things but a jogger he is not), and, once or twice a month, played golf at a country club in Potomac, Maryland. A long-deceased great uncle of mine, a defense contractor who made an unspeakable fortune during the same war that took my namesake, joined the club shortly after he moved to Washington. The Pratts have been members ever since. I have privileges at the club with all costs covered by my family.

Beyond work and occasional golf outings, I had a series of marginally promising relationships that failed for one reason or another. As it turned out, on the evening of the day I met the brown-uniformed Alex, I had plans to go to dinner with Elisa Ravel.

Elisa was a marketing specialist working with a small group hired by my firm to help form better client development strategies. Client development was the firm's benign way of describing the means by which we identified, courted, and on occasion locked in clients. Elisa was professionally astute, attractive, and thoroughly uninteresting. It was time to bring things to a close and—you won't be surprised by this (I wasn't)—when I picked her up that night, after an obligatory kiss on the cheek, she said, "Charlie, this isn't working out." She beat me to the punch. So much for Elisa.

~

As long as I have raised my past, it would be irresponsible to leave unmentioned my relationship with my unending, cherished echo, Jennifer Strong.

Apparently my tendency to what Henry characterized as a solitary existence became evident even before I left for college. My solitude (and its downstream financial implications) was unacceptable to my parents who, in response, undertook the challenge of marrying me off to the beautiful and bright Jennifer Strong. Jennifer's parents, openly co-conspirators in this effort, were our neighbors and, importantly from my parents' perspective, an extraordinarily wealthy family in Brampton.

When I say neighbor, I should add that the Strongs, like my family and many of those with whom we associated, lived on large tracts of land. Some had driveways that stretched half a mile or more, guest houses that rivaled small and elegant Parisian hotels, stables, heated pools and tennis courts with retractable roofs so that one could play year-round. In Maine. In blizzards. When you think about it, it was just preposterous.

For many years, the Strongs and my parents pushed the relationship—and I confess it was in no way unpleasant. Jennifer was unlike any girl I had known. She was stunning in every sense of the word, in every aspect of her being.

We dated on and off in high school and, as per her gentle insistence, were in an extended "off" period our entire senior year until a short class trip to Wellfleet on Cape Cod late that spring. After a visit to a whaling museum, an afternoon on the beach, and lobster served on picnic tables, we headed to our hotel. I turned from the reservation desk after checking in and there she was. She took my arm as we walked through the lobby and asked me the one question every 18-year-old boy away from home hopes to hear: "What's your room number?"

She was in my room before midnight and in bed with me moments later. I think it's fair, though not particularly dignified, to say simply that we had sex. I know I should say we made love, but in this instance and to my profound disappointment, love was neither made nor suggested.

When it was over, Jennifer told me that she decided long ago that if she did *it* with anyone, it would be me, thanked me warmly, dressed, and explained she was wildly in love with another girl in our high school class. "I wanted to see what it would be like—just once," she said.

I was, Jennifer explained, her shield against her parents' efforts to pair her with a male from a good (meaning generational wealth) family. "But we can't do *that* again, Charlie," she said.

We sat on the bed and talked and after a time she asked, "Why don't you have a girlfriend?"

It crossed my mind to say, "I was hoping it would be you—and hoping we would do just what we just did, often, and of course not as an experiment," but thought better of it. "I've had some girl-friends," was where I ended up. Frankly, at that moment, it was all I could muster.

"You'll find someone," she said. "Until then, we can hold hands at the holiday party at your house, exchange quick greeting kisses, and make vaguely suggestive comments about each other. My parents are not ready to hear who I am and, at least for now, I'm not ready to deal with their craziness."

"On the lips?" I asked.

"What?"

"The greeting kisses."

"Sure, Charlie—occasionally," and, anticipating my next question, continued, "but no tongue."

So it was that Jennifer and I went through a long and consistent faux courtship that flourished for years. I enjoyed these interactions far more than I should have.

To me, she was always the amazing Jennifer, notwithstanding her happy whisperings about her girlfriend who, for reasons that were not clear, she would not name. I saw her whenever we were home from college and maintained the charade until the Strongs—and my parents—finally gave up. "You two were so right for each other," my mother said with some resignation after a family party held the Christmas following my graduation from law school.

"We're just friends," I said. "Good friends ... that's all we've been for years," and after a pause continued, "We'll never be anything more."

At some level I think she had always known—and that was the end of it, at least for my mother.

~

Henry picked up the coins Alex left on the counter and dropped them in a jar marked: "Children's Fund."

"Next time, you can talk more with Alex. He is an interesting man."

I followed Alex's exit a few minutes later. As I walked to my car, I found the sidewalk partially blocked by a cement truck preparing to deposit a slurry of concrete into forms at the base of a recently dug excavation. The building to be constructed, a six-story apartment building with retail shops on the main floor, had been the subject of debate both in the Market and with the Town Council of Jackson Park.

The view of some in the Market, expressed passionately by my new sweater-wearing friend, Maurice, was that Jackson Park had a rare, personal, welcoming, small-town feel that connected its inhabitants with a better and simpler time. We had all heard Maurice's lament: Throughout the country, communities like Jackson Park are being transformed into small cities, assimilated into their large contiguous urban centers, disappearing from the regional metropolitan landscape. He was certain—and dedicated to the proposition—that such suburban villages are worth preserving.

For Maurice, a six-story building was one more step toward unwanted urbanization. That view, however, did not prevail in the Town Council (as the presence of the cement truck demonstrated), though there was an ugly public fight regarding the permit for this particular building led by Councilwoman Celia Bell, the voice of opposition to almost all changes in Jackson Park.

Jackson Park sits on the northwest border of Washington, D.C., and like a few close-in suburban communities in this area, can trace its roots to events just after the Revolutionary War. Notwithstanding its history, Jackson Park's political structure is somewhat vague. There is no mayor—the highest elected official is the Chairman of the Town Council. We are aptly and fully represented in the Maryland House and Senate and governed more by the actions of the county government than by our Town Council in all but one important way: The Town Council controls zoning and building permits. It is a unique power, ordained by state law and jealously protected.

I stepped around the cement truck and was soon at my car. I hope you are not worrying about Flynn—though my digression with you regarding Jennifer Strong and my family has taken time, my stay in the Market the morning I met Alex was actually quite short. When I got back to the car, Flynn was snoozing and, once awakened, happy to see me. We drove to the park and walked for twenty minutes.

At the far end of the park, some distance from the road, I let Flynn off the leash. He gave half-hearted chase to a squirrel (at least

I think that's what it was) and returned, panting, ready for the air conditioning in the car and a nap.

Chapter 2

The Table
2008

One October morning in 2008, almost three years after Henry and I first met, I walked into the American Market and stopped short. Gone entirely was the rack of dry goods that faced the front window. On these most visible shelves had been the high turnover/high profit-margin items, in that place of marketing prominence for that reason.

In place of the rack was a table covered with a yellow plastic cloth surrounded by a half-dozen folding chairs. Four or five newspapers sat in the center next to a bowl of Prairie Spy apples dappled with tan and green hues.

Henry leaned over the counter. "Get your coffee, Charlie. Sit." As they came in, Claire, Alex, and Maurice received similar instructions. Simone joined us at the table with a tray of still-warm pignoli and sesame cookies. "So," Henry said, "Now everyone can sit and talk."

Henry took a step back from the counter to watch. He was barely breathing, waiting to see if the discussions floating throughout the Market for three years would descend from flight, gliding with purpose, landing softly on the table.

Up until that October morning, we had been speaking with each other while leaning on the counter, huddled by the coffee machine in the rear of the store, standing in twos and threes out of earshot on the sidewalk in front of the Market, holding forth near the newspaper rack, pressed up against the few sections of wall not covered by shelves or displays.

To be seated at a table was a new experience—and to stay seated was something else entirely. I was not sure what our presence would imply to others who came into the Market that day or thereafter. I suppose some would assume we had nowhere else to go. Others might be troubled or offended, wondering why they were not asked to join us.

On that morning, in fact all that fall, there was plenty to discuss—and slowly, far too self-consciously and seriously, we started. Claire's opener, a dire prediction, set the initial tone: "We're spiraling into a recession—it could be the worst in our lifetime." While there were a few comments evincing vague hope that the recession would not be as bad as she implied, it was hard to argue with Claire.

Maurice followed Claire with panicky, unhappy facts: "The stock market is in near free-fall. Did you know the Dow dropped nearly 800 points in one day last month?" No one nodded as if affirmation would insure further devaluation of this measure of confidence in our fiscal vitality. The lack of a response pushed Maurice to another example. "Just look what's going on in Detroit. The U.S. auto industry is on the brink of collapse."

"Our lives haven't changed," Alex said. Everyone seemed to agree.

"I suppose," Maurice countered, "but as a country, we're on a slippery slope." This time, there were knowing nods, tacit acceptance of a bleak future that would inflict untold harm on many, and so we turned to blame. Wall Street, we all agreed, had failed to control its inhabitants, and the Securities Exchange Commission stood by, inert and complicit by its inaction, while wildly unreliable derivatives imploded and mortgage-backed securities toppled, setting into motion a domestic and international economic catastrophe.

The darkness of the discussion did not lift as we shifted to foreign policy. Maurice and Alex were skeptical of headlines in the newspapers on the table reporting expansive campaign promises to end the wars in Iraq and Afghanistan. "Those are hollow claims," Maurice asserted. Alex nodded in agreement but when Maurice followed up with, "Quite simply, we can't leave those countries in worse shape than when we found them," their commonality shattered.

"The longer we stay, fighting their fights, the worse things will get," Alex said softly. "Time to leave."

Maurice countered: "That would be a terrible thing for both countries. The governments will collapse."

"Alex is right," Claire said. "We can't prop up leaders who won't survive on their own."

Henry joined from behind the counter. "Extremists will destroy all that is worthwhile—I've seen it." This was stated with such certainty that any thought of further argument disappeared and the topic deflated.

I'm sure Henry had hoped for discussions on these topics but thus far our dark discourse was far from animated. We sounded like a group of depressed amateur political commentators and while Henry listened carefully and even added his piece to these sorry projections, I would understand if, at that point, he was a bit disappointed.

As customers lined up in front of him, he turned away from the table, his grand creation, content to ring up a two-pack of toilet paper, can of tuna, packet of notebook paper, and a phone card for calls to Honduras.

It was just before 7:00 when I finished my coffee and reached for my jacket. "Flynn is in the car and I can't keep him waiting too long." This was not entirely true. Flynn, still the fat lab Claire dubbed him three years ago, was quite content to spend hours snoozing on the back seat of my car. This was particularly so on fall days when open car windows became ports of entry for the perfumes of life in Jackson Park, airborne essences only dogs can decipher.

"Sorry, Henry," Maurice said, "I should get going as well."

Before Claire or Alex could proffer similar excuses, Henry leaned forward. "Wait!" He paused. "Please?"

Alex, still seated, picked up a Prairie Spy from the bowl in the center of the table and took a loud bite. Following his lead, I took a couple of Simone's cookies (and you must try these unreal and divine creations if ever the opportunity arises), sipped from a cup of freshly poured coffee, and settled back into my chair. Claire, Simone, and Maurice refilled their cups as well and we continued.

The political discourse had worn thin. After a time, Alex leaned forward and, as if questioning his own recollection, said quietly, "A couple of days ago—no maybe it was last week—I delivered two boxes of unshelled walnuts to a customer in Great Falls, Virginia." Speaking to no one in particular, he concluded: "You don't see that very often."

Henry's anxious response, "I'll bring walnuts tomorrow," implied the Market table was incomplete in the absence of walnuts. Claire shook her head. "I wouldn't do that. Ask Charlie—he's our lawyer—if you crack a nut at this table and part of the shell goes flying into someone's eye, you'll get sued."

"I suppose it's possible," I said, hoping to shift the discussion away from lawsuits and lawyers. After all, I am neither her lawyer nor the lawyer for anyone at the Market. The bland nature of my response to Claire's question, however, is a consequence of something you have probably realized. I confess to being part of a nondescript but substantial segment of my professional cohort: I am a reluctant lawyer. Outside of my work at the firm, I am hesitant to give direct legal advice or take on the painful legal problems of anyone else. Whether this is due to laziness, lack of confidence, fear of being sued for malpractice, or some less admirable trait, I cannot say. Thus, instead of legal analysis, I went with: "I'd be more worried about allergies. Adverse reactions to nuts can be deadly."

This prompted a challenge from Maurice. "That's peanuts—no one is allergic to walnuts."

"Nonsense," Alex said. "If you're allergic to one nut, you're allergic to them all."

Claire was incapable of passing up these misstatements. "That's not true—you might be allergic both to walnuts and peanuts but it's not a certainty. They're different foods. Peanuts are tubers. They grow underground—and walnuts grow on trees."

Between restorative sips of coffee, a ragged consensus began to form regarding the inadvisability of nuts, wal- or otherwise, at our table in the Market—and everyone had a story. Claire told of an uncle who, one Thanksgiving, enjoyed a piece of homemade Maryland pecan pie (the family recipe inexplicably called for a sauce that contained, among other things, canned sour cherries and dark chocolate) and ended up in the emergency room. Maurice contributed a narrative centered on a childhood visit to a restroom at the National Zoo where peanuts he had consumed played a central and most unpleasant role. (You'll have to trust me on this—the details of that day were predictable and would be indelicate to discuss further.) All of us knew cautionary unverified tales about allergic reactions that occurred in classrooms, on ball fields, at office picnics, and on the sidewalk adjacent to the House of Representatives. By the time that discussion played out, there was no way Henry would consider placing walnuts, peanuts, cashews, or any of their close or distant relatives on our table.

You may think that such things never happen, that seemingly busy adults would be disinclined to take time in the morning, sit on folding chairs in a convenience store, and chat. Until the Market entered my life, I would have agreed. There was, however, something magical about this group.

Each morning that followed had characteristics of that first day. On occasion, the apples in the center of the table were replaced by shortbread, biscuits, grapes, and on one unfortunate morning, a variety of egg rolls appeared. Henry claimed they were suitable as a morning snack. They were not.

I will share with you that polite disposal of partially eaten distasteful food is surprisingly difficult while seated in the openness of a convenience store—hopefully this is advice you will need only sparingly.

Over time, there developed an intimacy at our table that was extraordinary given the lack of any connection between us external to the Market. Soon, and with only rare exceptions, mornings at the American Market were the best part of my day.

In the beginning, we were loosely bound by unstated guidelines that kept our discussions free of the normal milestones and battles of life. Our table (though technically Henry's) was not the place to discuss and solve problems about jobs and finances, children and weddings, grandchildren and aging parents, divorce and related family disturbances.

Friendships can degrade and take on a journalistic quality, becoming little more than reporting on work and home, coupled with a modicum of demonstrated sincerity that the receiver of this momentous information actually cares. At some point, what is real about friendship gets lost. Our relationships were not exactly like that. It's not that there was a lack of caring—it was more a commitment simply to being yourself in its most fundamental and least constructed form.

We were not in the Market as employees or parents, brothers or sisters, as mothers, fathers, lovers, partners, sons, daughters, supervisors, victims, patients, customers, or sellers. We did not gather to harness resources or use our professional skills or contacts. In this zone of potential neutrality, we sought to exist in a manner disconnected from the entanglements of life, to just *be*.

For me, it turned out that simply *being* was a demanding discipline. To remove judgment and guilt, ambition and assessment, accusation and accomplishment, and just *be* was no small task. Who among us, beyond the age of ten, can just be without considerable effort?

Realizing that simple existence, in its raw form, is an underappreciated gift of life meant that all else could, for that short time each morning, be suspended. It did not always work—and over time, became less and less possible, and then it was impossible—but we tried.

Of course we touched on the news every day. Henry set out newspapers and expected us to glance at the front pages of papers from Washington, New York, Chicago, London (always a few days late but fascinating), and beyond. In addition to running a very traditional convenience store, Henry carried an assortment of papers that rivaled any modest urban newsstand. I'm sure he lost money on the papers—but their presence evinced Henry's interest in a worldly discourse.

Perhaps you think the lack of personal and professional exchanges made the initiation of our friendship more possible. I'm not sure. In the beginning, for all I knew, earlier in life Claire won medals in an Olympic sport—or spent a year in reform school; Alex lived in his truck—or was independently wealthy, owned a fleet of private jets, and delivered packages to break the monotony. Perhaps Maurice ran the men's department at a clothing store—or sang in the opera at the Kennedy Center. Our lives beyond the Market really didn't matter back then—for all but Henry.

Henry, who loved to listen, who imagined his convenience store, his source of economic vitality, a salon where the goodness of a few people could emerge and be sustained, had a story. We were drawn to it, sucked into his world by way of his unanticipated history.

Chapter 3

Apples and Walnuts
2012

Three more years passed. It was August, 2012, six years after I first met Henry.

Both the domestic recession and U.S. involvement in Iraq seemed to be drawing to a close while the situation in Afghanistan was increasingly confusing and, on horrifying occasions, deadly. These events and the presidential re-election campaign dominated the headlines — and with decreasing frequency, were part of our discussions at the table. At a certain point, one needs a break from war, politics (and I am fairly sure those are separate topics), and international relations. That August morning was no exception. We were mid-stream in a discussion about the decline in the popularity of quiche when Alex looked up at Henry. "DuChamp — that's French, right?" He nodded. "Do you speak French?"

The answer came from Simone. "Neither of us can." She was at the far end of the counter cleaning the glass cabinet that held the donuts. "But we loved the Paris Opera."

Henry let Simone's comment pass. "I picked the name DuChamp when we were in France. My name by birth is too long and we thought one day we might end up in Paris." He hesitated as if a confession was to follow. "As it turned out, we weren't in France very long." And then looking at Simone, continued, "I don't think we had quiche." She nodded and he stopped his explanation rather suddenly to ring up a customer buying a large coffee, a box of cookies, and a lottery ticket.

"And a number 12," the customer said looking at the plastic box holding the scratch-off tickets.

"That's a $20 ticket," Henry said.

"I know—but if I win, it's a million dollars," he replied.

Henry tore off the ticket from the display and watched as the customer rubbed the coating off the ticket. "Nothing," the customer said and left.

"The guy is out $20 and he's smiling," Maurice said quietly.

"I have no trouble understanding that," Alex said.

I didn't understand it at all and it must have showed on my face. Alex turned to me. "For a moment," he said, "for just a small moment before he rubbed off the surface on the ticket, he was able to think how everything would change if he had a million dollars. He paid $20 for that moment."

As the quiche and scratch-off discussion dissolved to nothingness, the store began to fill. Henry was off his stool, ringing up canned cat food and ginger ale, toothpaste and manila envelopes, and a package of undershirts, three for $9.99. Just how undershirts made their way to the shelves of the Market remains one of the mysteries we never solved. They appeared one morning a few weeks earlier and, after the last packet was sold a month later, vanished into American Market commercial history.

It was the end of the first week in October. Even with the midterm election only a month away, while I won't say we'd lost interest, there was little left to say. Claire attempted a brief comparison between President Obama and his opponent, Governor Romney, concluding that they were both decent people but so different that comparisons served no purpose. In a moment lacking insight or linguistic originality, I agreed with Claire: "Like apples and oranges."

Maurice seized the moment to get away from the worn-out political rhetoric. "I meant to say this earlier—these apples are absolutely beautiful." It was all we needed. Candidates Obama and Romney vanished and in their place were a dozen magnificent rose-hued Ruby Frost apples Henry brought to the Market that morning.

In the six years we'd gathered at the Market, I thought we'd consumed every variety of apple on the planet—but this one was new and spectacular. Still, as much as I admired the Ruby Frost, I saw no reason to change the apple I took with me to work each day—the venerable McIntosh—as part of my lunch.

Unlike most of my colleagues at the law firm, I brought lunch to work each day unless something at the firm compelled me to dine out with clients. Co-workers at the firm who knew the circumstances of my family and had some idea of our resources must have wondered why I would deny myself the pleasure of their company or, at a minimum, lunch at a decent restaurant—and Jackson Park had a number of them. However, as with most things at the firm, no one questioned my practice of dining alone. After all, clients that retained the firm because of the Prattian connection, namely me, were far more valuable an asset than my company at the noon meal.

My friends at the Market were not as passive as my co-workers when it came to my lunch routine. It was the content of my lunch, and my apple of choice, that bothered them … though there were other complaints as well.

"Have you tasted these, Charlie?" Claire asked, pointing to the Ruby Frost apples left in the bowl on the table. "Take one to work with you." The demand that I remove the McIntosh from my briefcase and substitute it for the Ruby Frost was not the end of her bill of particulars. I barely had a chance to get my second cup of coffee that morning when Claire looked at me. "What's with that briefcase? It looks like something you found in an alley."

"It's not very impressive," Henry chimed in. "You should have something more dignified. Lawyers have leather briefcases."

"Not all lawyers—and I don't have to worry about coffee leaking from my thermos and ruining the leather."

"That's ridiculous," Claire said—but then came that wonderful forgiving laugh, a combination of soft throaty tones and warmth that would stay with me all day.

I turned from the pleasure of watching and listening to Claire and stared at my briefcase, a gray-green rectangle of plastic-covered puckered aluminum with two worn clasps and a cracked and taped plastic handle. I've used the same briefcase for years. Its contents vary rarely: a thermos of coffee, a bologna and cheese on white bread (if I'm feeling indulgent, I substitute mortadella for the bologna) with yellow mustard wrapped in a piece of wax paper, a

McIntosh apple, and today's paper. I don't bring work home, in large part because I have no work worth bringing home.

Beyond the attack on my briefcase, Claire also questioned — repeatedly over the years — my use of wax paper. "Why can't you use cellophane or a plastic bag? Doesn't the sandwich get stale? And McIntosh?"

My response, "I've been making the same lunch and wrapping it in the same way for years," was limited and I considered adding that I was not about to change anything, but thought better of it.

Claire shook her head. "I'm not sure what to say about that sandwich — but I think we all know apples. McIntoshes taste like wet cotton, Charlie."

I felt certain this was about more than apples but before I could test my hypothesis, Alex challenged. "The plural of McIntosh is McIntosh — not McIntoshes."

Claire's response, "Hooey," was enough to slow down Alex. "The point," Claire continued, "is that Charlie is afraid of change — in this instance, apples."

What does one say in response to such global criticism? I was not even close to a rejoinder when she continued. "I don't understand why you won't try something else."

"I like McIntoshes," I said, siding with Claire in the debate over plural form. Despite that alignment, my comment was unconvincing and Claire marched on.

"No one likes McIntoshes." I expected others to jump in but no one came to my defense. "Maybe for applesauce or an apple crisp, but to bring to work every day?"

Claire stopped her critique and looked at me, as if taking in some part of my interior. Her eyes crinkled and a small smile surfaced. You may think this odd but as the smile warmed, I had the sensation that Claire and I had known each other forever. Then softly: "Oh, Charlie, really, I'm sure you can do better."

Alex nodded as if he'd been thinking the same thing — and I wondered if he was — and I wondered if I could.

Over the last six years, my clothing has taken a similar beating — white shirt (the kind you don't need to iron), dark gray tie, blue blazer, charcoal or khaki pants. Even Alex, who wears an identical brown uniform every day, has taken shots at my clothing.

"This is a perfect opportunity, Charlie," Claire said. "Take that horrible apple out of your briefcase and put in this one from Henry." She turned to Henry. "Where do you get all the different varieties of apples?" It was a legitimate question. Henry brought in apples for our table on a regular basis. They were almost always fresh—in stark contrast to the apples Henry sold in the Market, some variant of Golden Delicious that were neither golden nor delicious.

"A roadside stand not far from my house," Henry said. "They charge too much but have such good fruit."

As the discussion rambled along, I had to place one foot on my briefcase to keep Claire and the others from forcing a change of my apple.

When I arrived at 6:15 the next morning, Alex was standing outside. "Henry's not here yet," he said.

"How long have you been here?"

He shrugged. "Maybe five minutes. Simone must be having a bad morning."

Claire walked up to us. "She's sick." She hesitated. "Simone told me last week that she was having some tests."

"She's been under the weather more than usual," Alex said. "I hope they have good insurance." He peered through the glass door as if he expected to see some activity within and, without turning away, continued: "Depending on the kind of tests, you could be talking about thousands of dollars for lab and doctor bills, x-rays, and blood work. Of course, Henry and Simone work enough hours a week to require the parent corporation owning the Market to provide health insurance."

"There is no corporate owner," Claire said. "The Market is not part of a chain. I think Henry and Simone are the owners."

"Do they own the building and the lot?" Alex asked.

We were still speculating on just how much of our Market they owned when Henry came up the sidewalk. "I'm so sorry. Simone…."

After he unlocked the door, we lugged the bundles of newspapers inside. Maurice, who arrived a moment after Henry, turned on the overhead lights. I put the newspapers in the rack while Henry got the coffee going. Claire placed a box of Danish pastry on the table. Henry switched on the lottery monitor and, after a moment, reported: "No one won last night—the jackpot is up to seventy-five million dollars."

Alex shook his head slowly. "It's definitely time to get a ticket." Each of us gave Alex two dollars which he, in turn, gave to Henry. We have done this dozens of times over the last six years.

Once the ticket issued from the terminal, with some formality Alex stated: "I'm writing 'Group ticket—Henry, Simone, Maurice, Claire, Charlie, and Alex' in pen, on the 'name and address' lines of the ticket." Years ago Alex explained that this required the winnings to be split among us, eliminating any thought or temptation that Alex, as holder of the ticket, would cash it and disappear.

Sometimes, as part of the ritual, Henry would ask to see the ticket, tilt his chin upward, hold the ticket in front of him, squint, read our names out loud as if taking attendance, nod affirmingly, and hand the ticket back to Alex. Occasionally, this would be followed by a coffee toast ("To the liberation of soul wealth provides," or "To paid bills and the best of times," or something similar) with raised cups and a "Here, Here!" or two.

Instead of the ticket inspection, public reading, and toast, Henry stayed behind the cash register and turned, looking out onto the street. Claire walked casually to the counter. "Are you all right?"

Henry said nothing and continued looking out beyond the glass door at the empty sidewalk, his face a hunter's scan.

Inexcusably, that we were concerned about or missed Simone went unsaid. An uncharacteristic quiet followed. Sensing the need to get beyond the awkwardness of the moment, Alex held forth: "I painted my bathroom last night." He leaned forward, looking at his hands. We all looked. There were a few gray blotches on his fingers and wrist.

Maurice examined the spots, squinting knowingly. "You'll need mineral spirits or turpentine to remove those."

After a couple of comments regarding the questionable recommendation of mineral spirits, Alex shifted in his seat: "Did you know a gallon of paint costs almost $50?"

I sympathized with Alex. "That's a lot of money for a bucket of paint," and then added, "Of course I haven't painted a room in years." Actually, I don't think I've ever painted any room of any kind—but that was not something I chose to share.

Claire walked to the counter and stood in front of Henry. "Any news on Simone?" He was nonresponsive. "Will we be seeing her on Monday?"

Henry shrugged. "But you will see me this weekend." Henry rarely misses a day at the Market. Claire turned back toward the table but Henry called after her and she stopped. "I want to tell you something." He hesitated and then: "You should know why I'm here."

"Where?" Claire asked.

"Here. In the United States. Not back home."

He spoke quietly now. "We tried to live as if nothing was happening, but it ended up spreading across everything until there were no safe places left."

Henry stopped to ring up two magazines and a large soda. When the customer was gone, he continued. "You have heard of this time in my country." I wasn't sure what country Henry was describing. When I first met him, I thought he was from India but some years later when I mentioned that to Claire, she said she wasn't certain but assumed he was from Thailand or Vietnam.

A group of high school students crowded around the counter. Four more large drinks, chewing gum, a pen, a package of sweet rolls, and another magazine were purchased. There was a failed attempt to buy cigarettes by a girl who could not have been fifteen. They left and Henry continued, his tone entirely different.

"These so-called soldiers—religious fanatics with fascist fantasies, others claiming to follow antiquated communist values, always yelling about the people's government. In the end, they were nothing but thugs."

Henry stopped again. This time it was a newspaper, coffee, and a donut—perhaps the most common morning acquisition.

"Simone and I were imprisoned." Henry stopped abruptly and, strange as it sounds, his look was one of distrust. We waited and after a time he continued. "This is not to be discussed with anyone." We stumbled over each other assuring Henry we would not mention a word he said. He nodded, but I am quite sure he was not comfortable finishing the story. After what seemed an endless pause, he said: "In the end, we lived. I guess that makes us luckier than many."

More sales of coffee, more candy and newspapers, and finally there was no one in the store but us. Henry spoke more quickly than before. "It took months but finally we arrived in Paris. We stayed several weeks and then headed to Le Havre. We boarded a freighter and crossed the Atlantic. They locked us in a shipping container a few hours before we landed in Baltimore. The crate was taken off the ship, put on a truck, driven a few blocks from the harbor, and opened. They said, 'This is where you get out.'" Henry smiled. "What does one say under such circumstances?"

"Maybe a prayer," Maurice said.

Henry paused, checking to make sure no one else was listening. "I told them I needed a bathroom." Henry held his serious, secretive expression for just a moment and then lightened. Alex, who'd been suppressing his reaction, gave in and laughed. Claire followed suit when Henry said, "Really, I wasn't kidding," but caught herself as Henry continued. "We still had money hidden in Simone's clothing—enough to get started. We hired a lawyer and worked our way through the asylum process. It took five years and all we had."

Claire tried a follow-up question. "What about your relatives?"

Henry's features began to shift as if a neurological tick had repositioned his face. The result was a small, autonomic, indecipherable smile—and that was the end of it.

As you can imagine, there were unanswered questions about Henry and Simone's flight from their home country—whatever it was—but after a few attempts, we stopped. It was as if he had completed his end of the bargain and in exchange, we owed him discussions about politics, walnuts, and a hundred other topics.

Simone came back to the Market the following Monday. She sat erect in a chair at the far end of the counter, working on bookkeeping, tabulating receipts spread across the glass, entering numbers in a notebook.

After a time, Maurice, decked out in a bold yellow cardigan and neatly pressed green cargo pants, circled slowly to the back of the

Market and surveyed the limited selection of off-brand ketchup, mustard, and mayonnaise on display. Out of the corner of my eye, I watched him conclude his marginally coincidental wanderings and come to rest at the counter across from and close to Simone.

Back at the table, we were midstream in a discussion about the lack of change in the design of flashlight batteries when Maurice returned. He called us to a tabletop huddle and whispered, a quarterback determined to keep the next play secret. "She says her health is improved—but I don't believe her," he breathed, "and she's disgusted with Henry."

I tried to digest this unsettling news and looked at Simone who was peacefully absorbed with receipts and her calculator. "She's worried he's not taking care of the business end of the Market," Maurice concluded. The report of Simone's indictment of Henry hung over our table while Henry chatted happily with two customers, one buying two large bags of ice and a sleeve of plastic cups and the other a can of ravioli (dinner in a can for $3.99) and a box of tissues.

~

"We miss the winter holidays every year," Simone said one morning in late November. "We should offer wrapping paper, more tape, small gifts, cards...." She looked at Henry. "Are you listening?"

Henry nodded and went back to checking out a customer, another purchaser of lottery tickets—this time eight plays of "Pick 4" tickets that cost $5 each.

When the customer left the Market, Claire started in. "This guy just blew $40. That's insane."

"Unless he wins $100—or a million," Alex said. "He's looking for a quick way out of whatever predicament he faces."

Maurice turned to Henry. "How much do people spend on these tickets in the Market in a year?"

"He has no idea," Simone said.

"Do you know?" Alex asked Simone.

"Of course."

"And?" Alex continued.

"I know," Simone said, ending her involvement in the lottery discussion.

We spent another few minutes on the allure of the lottery and somewhere in that discussion, floating just outside our table, I heard Henry say, "Holiday inventory is a terrible idea. We can't store what doesn't sell," to which Simone said, "It's a miracle we don't go bankrupt."

Whatever ailed Simone apparently had abated for the moment and the following morning, she was back at the table. Her skin had more color and her black hair was pulled back, revealing an appealing angularity. In the six years I have been coming to the Market, I do not recall Simone ever pulling back her hair. She wore a silver silk blouse that hung loosely. The folds accented subtle variations in the silk giving the appearance of movement. Instead of a skirt hanging well below her knees, her standard attire, she wore dark gray slacks that suited her blouse perfectly.

At least three different times that morning, Maurice mentioned to me Simone's outfit and finally, not long before he left, he turned to her. "Are you going to a meeting or event later today? You look lovely."

The comment startled me. Henry was at the counter and did not look up. I'm sure he heard Maurice. I'm sure everyone heard Maurice. It was impossible to miss.

As it often did, our time at the Market passed quickly and around 7:15, Claire left with Alex close behind. By 7:30, having explored the ineptitude of the city planners who, Maurice explained, had authorized the demolition of a building at the end of the next block so that yet another high-rise apartment could be built (considered by him an abomination), I put on my coat and waited for Maurice.

"Go ahead," he said. "I'm going to have another cup of coffee."

"Have a good day."

Flynn was snoozing comfortably on the back seat. Some mornings, waking Flynn was not unlike waking a teenager who had stayed up too late. On the way to the park, I drove slowly past the Market and saw Maurice and Simone still seated at the table. Henry was alone, behind the register, a mechanical figure in the otherwise empty Market.

From that point forward, Simone and Henry said nothing more

about their past. Just how that experience played on them, what death-driven images intruded on dark, uncertain memories, tracking them as they navigated the aisles of the American Market, we never knew. No one experiences horror unchanged.

Most of us see life through the prism our intellect and experience concocts. People like Simone and Henry have a second prism, an alternative way of seeing all that was around them. When the continuation of life is dependent on the whims of adolescents with automatic rifles, fate has a different tone. Life and death are fluid, detached, and random. Henry's transition from refugee to proprietor, a shift from inconceivably mystifying hazard to simple, controlled, and steady, might be seen in just those terms.

Part of what made Henry's transition possible was the reality of the American Market. The Market meant reliable revenue, a stable and predictable daily routine that, over time, restored his sense of security—but now there was a need for more. His goals had expanded. He sought stimulation and community, something to replace all that was lost when he fled his homeland, and we were that community—and Henry was our founding member.

I don't know how he picked each of us. We were an odd group, a small and closed world and, when you think about it, unproductive. We made nothing, neither focused on nor wrote great ideas, contributing in no meaningful way to the human condition, and yet there was something about us that I loved and Henry craved.

~

An unexpected wet snow fell in early December, not long after the revelation of Henry's life before the American Market. As you know, I grew up in Maine where the first snow was a celebrated event. It purified the omnipresent gray-brown palate and gave assurance of the expected winter to follow. Not so in Washington— here, snow congests and snarls traffic while the federal government contemplates shutting down, leaving workers confused, until finally an announcement is made giving employees unscheduled or liberal leave, usually far too late. This puts everyone but Flynn in a bad mood. If it's not too cold or too deep, Flynn is capable of frolicking in snow. It's quite a sight.

In any case, on the morning of the first snow, Alex lost his glasses and Maurice sported a seasonally themed sweater that was more a mural than a garment.

Alex was in a less-than charitable mood, perhaps because he had to drive his truck on snow-covered streets—and certainly because of the absence of his glasses, and was more critical of the sweater than seemed fair. In defense of Maurice, I questioned his ability to see the majesty of this woolen masterpiece in the absence of his glasses.

"I can see colors just fine," he said, his tone short of militant.

Simone listened to this exchange and disappeared into the store-room at the rear of the store, emerging with several pairs of reading glasses. "We have not put these out in a while," she said. She turned to Henry. "You should go into the storeroom—you might be surprised by what's there." A pause. "You really don't listen to me, do you?"

Henry was absorbed in ringing up a customer and when he looked at Simone and said, "What?" she shook her head and walked away.

Alex tried a couple of pairs and settled on one with a thick, black-rimmed frame. Claire made an attempt to be reassuring: "You look scholarly in those," but she was unable to stay with the compliment and started to laugh. Claire's laugh began suppressed, a series of swallows that sounded more like throat-clearing, then the dead-giveaway of shaking shoulders. When she finally surrendered to the fullness of it, it was honest, loud, and took her over.

The thick frames might have been a trend years ago but not now. Still, in the world of dry goods—and a portion of convenience store products are dry goods—unsold items are stored and not discarded. Inventory that does not spoil or rot can stay with a seller for generations.

To everyone's surprise, Alex wore the glasses for several weeks after his new prescription glasses arrived. I believe he wore them with the hope they would make Claire laugh.

I would not blame you for thinking the obvious: here is a group of three middle-aged males who frequent a convenience store, say little about their lives outside of the store, and seem interested—more than just interested—in Claire. I can't speak for Maurice and Alex, but I assume they found Claire appealing. At a minimum, as Henry said, she was a handsome woman.

As you may have guessed by now, in my heart and mind, Claire

Beaumont was far more than handsome. She was that rare combination of strength, wit, and compassion, blessed by intellect and values that resonated with my best hopes. I was drawn to her, taken with her every glance. Her just-above shoulder-length hair, a complex brown, like well-rubbed cherry wood reflecting hints of light, framed a smile just below the surface, at times revealed only by those remarkable eyes, telling and caring eyes that welcomed me each day.

I kept these feelings to myself in part because nothing had happened thus far to suggest that Claire found me appealing, at least not in that way. Moreover, I was not sure an intimate relationship could thrive in this setting. Relationships are complicated and complicating. Henry and Simone were our only couple, and even for them, time and circumstance had taken an obvious toll.

And there was this: As fascinating as she was, after six years I did not know much about Claire's life outside the Market. I did know — in fact we all knew — one surprising fact. In the last year, just before her forty-second birthday, Claire became a grandmother.

She told us about her launch into grandmotherhood one morning while we were deeply involved in a discussion of pencils. Beyond filling in bubbles on standardized tests, high school art classes, the occasional waiter in a rural diner, and carefully drawn lines of older carpenters, does anyone use pencils? I don't recall how Claire moved from this compelling discourse to her new status as a grandmother but I remember what happened next. Out of nowhere, Claire announced: "My son and his wife had a child."

"They live in France, right?" I asked.

"Good memory, Charlie. He and his wife moved to Bordeaux some time ago. I'm going to visit them as soon as I have time." She hesitated. "They're young — but they're ready."

Simone came out from behind the counter, hugged Claire, spoke with her softly, hugged her again, and returned to her stool behind the cash register.

Maurice, Alex, and I sat there, unsure what one says under these circumstances, quietly contemplating pencils. "What's wrong with you?" Claire said to us. "You look almost guilty."

After a time, Maurice said, "I hope the baby is good ... you know, healthy."

In substance, Maurice's statement seemed accurate and I was going to sign on but decided to stay quiet. "Thanks, Maurice," Claire said. "Any interest in knowing about the mom? My grandson's name?"

We nodded. "Three tools," Claire said shaking her head and turned to Simone who glanced sympathetically in our direction and then returned to her bookkeeping. In this context, I'm sure you know *tool* is not a particularly flattering label and does not refer to hammers and pliers.

While I was contemplating just why I had been designated a tool, Maurice let the comment disappear and turned to Simone. His was a look of undeniable affection and Henry and I both saw it.

The moment was broken when Alex, shifting gears decisively and entirely, noted that in some ways, the Democratic Party had faltered politically even when it had control of the presidency and both houses of Congress. When Claire and I immediately disagreed, Maurice, unwilling to move into a discussion of that nature, countered with a comment about the demise of incandescent light bulbs. Apparently at that moment, Claire was not all that enthusiastic about politics because she responded to Maurice, criticizing fluorescent bulbs and LEDs, which, she said, felt like blinding construction klieg lights. Frankly, the light bulb discussion may have been more illuminating than anything pertaining to Capitol Hill.

Most of our discussions did not live beyond the last word, much less beyond the day they took place. For the past six years, no grudges were held, no balance sheet kept. Still, over time, I began to feel something different, a protectiveness about us—and we had definitely become an us.

Us—or we—reflects an advanced stage in relationships. Things are serious when one person says: "*We* don't like that music," or "That restaurant just isn't right for *us*." In that sense, we had become familial.

Chapter 4

The Invitation
2013

Not long after I spent an uneventful New Year's Eve with Flynn saying farewell to 2012, I got an invitation to attend Jennifer Strong's wedding. The RSVP did not go to Jennifer's family home in Brampton but rather to "The Wedding Collective" in Burlington, Vermont. I had to read the invitation twice to be sure: Burlington would be the venue for the wedding, not our hometown in Maine.

Jennifer was marrying Samantha Eckington, daughter of Isaiah and Faye Eckington, owners of a spectacular oceanfront manse just outside of Brampton Harbor. The mystery was finally resolved: Jennifer's lover in high school (and obviously thereafter) was Samantha, an attractive classmate I knew well—but, with this news, apparently not that well.

When we were in high school, Jennifer, Samantha, and I played tennis—usually doubles—on the Eckingtons' private court. The fourth in our sets was Jennifer's younger brother, Carter.

I liked Carter Strong. While not one of my closest friends, he and I spent a good deal of time together, perhaps because it increased the probability of being with his sister. He was a more than willing companion in various high school beer drinking episodes, several ending with me getting sick and Carter happily staggering home.

Years later, and to my amazement, Carter became Dr. Carter Strong. He was a psychiatrist and some time ago was embroiled in a scandal when a patient with whom he was having an affair—one Brittany Dunblane Parsons (mother of three, wife of banker H. Lawrence Parsons, marginally promiscuous socialite from one of Brampton's oldest families)—was badly hurt in a car accident. It happened along the Maine Coastal Highway. Carter had been driving and, it turns out, was thoroughly and completely intoxicated. It was the end of a predictably bad run for Carter. He had become a drug provider to those passing time in search of anything that thrilled, to the arrogant, hungry, unemployable successors adrift in wealth beyond measure. Carter was the host of wild secret parties (once contracting a jazz trio flown in from New Orleans for unrehearsed music), late night soirées where the least disciplined over-privileged heirs of Bramptonia explored dark fantastical limits of debauchery fueled by pills provided by one Dr. Carter Strong and served generously in heirloom silver bowls.

All that came to an end when criminal charges were brought against Carter after the accident and his license to practice medicine was suspended. To no one's surprise, the charges were later dropped when Carter went into a pricey rehabilitation hospital where he stayed long enough to allow time to dissolve the sensation, luminosity, and intensity of the matter. I'm still not sure if he's regained his license to practice—but I am sure that practicing medicine was in no way necessary. Like most people in my parents' circle of friends, Carter has a trust fund that produces more annual income than his practice possibly could generate.

Until her death some years ago, my mother relished in such details and when we spoke, which was not all that often, would provide me news of Brampton's elite. She followed closely Carter's saga, speaking in crisply toned whispers, loud enough for me to hear but sufficiently muted to prevent the scorn of my father, who believed that matters of the Maine patricians—even those of Dr. Carter Strong—were not to be discussed.

As I tell you this, it strikes me that my predilection to insularity and classification of people was environmental and derivative of my father. My mother was more open, even marginally tolerant, of those less fortunate.

When my mother died, my tearless father delivered an eloquent, elegant eulogy, went home, and resumed his life as if he had lost nothing more than a pair of cufflinks.

About a week after her funeral, as I was packing to return to Jackson Park—and very, very ready to leave—my father informed me that I had inherited from my mother a guest house on our property. It overlooks wide, well-kept lawns and stone walkways, and beyond that hundreds of acres of pristine Pratt-owned Maine forest that have been in my family since the early 1800s. The guest house is larger and more elegantly furnished than any place I've lived since graduating from law school, but I have not used it once after leaving home.

~

I cannot tell you why, several weeks after receiving the invitation, I asked Claire to join me at Jennifer Strong's wedding. We were at the table in the Market involved in a discussion of pretzels that began when Maurice mentioned that he had a corned beef sandwich at a well-known delicatessen the day before and was given the option to have it on white, rye, whole wheat, pumpernickel, a Kaiser roll, or pretzel bread.

Maurice picked rye—who wouldn't?—but that did not resolve the matter. What need was served in civilized society by the addition of pretzel bread? Closer to home, was there any relationship between pretzel bread and those thick, dry-as-dust pretzels Henry sells? Alex wondered aloud why anyone would buy something that, when eaten, puffs tastelessly all over the inside of your mouth, when, as if possessed by a force from beyond, I said: "I've been invited to the wedding of an old friend. Claire … want to go with me? I hate going to these things alone."

Everything stopped.

Alex pulled back his chair as if someone had spilled a vat of coffee on the table and he wanted to protect his uniform. Maurice, sedate, adorned in gray cashmere, folded his hands prayerfully and turned to Claire. Henry popped up from his stool behind the counter. The pretzel discourse had held his attention, but this turn of events was far more sensational. "What a nice invitation," he said.

Claire looked at me, turned her head slightly, started to speak, and then stopped.

"You should go," Henry said.

"Maybe this is a bad idea," I said.

"Is it?" Claire said so quietly I barely heard her.

The silence continued as I contemplated the hazards of pursuing the invitation and the even greater hazards of withdrawing it.

An odd fluttering sensation started in my knees and worked its way into my lower abdomen.

Two customers, complete strangers waiting to check out (newspapers, coffee, donuts, and a pair of brown cotton gloves for $3.99 — a small price on a cold day when either you've left your gloves at home or lost one somewhere in your car) turned to the table, caught up in the moment.

Simone broke the silence. "Are you going to ring up these customers?" she asked Henry. Her voice was coarse.

Henry turned away from the table, apologized for the delay, and with the sound of money moving into the cash register, the moment was about to pass until Claire, who regained her bearings, said: "Were you serious, Charlie?"

More silence. Finally I said, "Of course." I told her the wedding was in early March and then added: "It's in Vermont. I plan on driving up on Friday before the wedding."

Three implications of this fact were immediately evident. First, at least a day would be missed at the Market and probably two. Second, such a trip meant spending two nights — in beds, possibly in pajamas — somewhere other than home. Third, the regularity of my life and hers, home, work, walks with Flynn, would be changed and even though it was temporary, the potential was there for a re-ordering in ways I could not predict.

"Let me think about it," Claire said after an excruciating pause.

Nothing caught on the rest of that morning. No one raised the matter of the wedding and none of the topics that ordinarily held us seemed worth pursuing.

Simone walked next to Henry's stool and whispered to him something that provoked him to say, quite audibly, "It's impossible — we will never sell them."

"You don't listen — you should pay more attention to my ideas."

Henry protested but Simone rolled her eyes and came out from behind the counter. She straightened up the candy in the front display cabinet and made fresh coffee.

The following morning, no mention was made of the wedding and life seemed more normal. Yet something was different, tentative, out of balance.

Several days later, Simone passed out in the rear of the Market. She hit her head as she fell, but her descent was so quiet that neither Henry nor any of us saw it. A customer found her unconscious on the floor behind the last rack of dry goods, a small, round, dark red pool near her ear.

Maurice was first to her side. In the ensuing chaos, Claire called an ambulance, Henry stared at Simone with uncharacteristic uncertainty, and for a brief time, I stood behind the counter while we waited for the ambulance. The fact was and is, I do not know how to operate a cash register and, while I offered to stay, Henry ignored my comments.

Maurice pressed paper napkins against Simone's head and the bleeding stopped. She regained consciousness as the paramedics arrived. Henry said he would accompany Simone to the hospital and apologized to us for having to close the Market.

Alex wrote a sign for the door: "Closed for the morning." The lights were left on and, as Henry locked the door, he said, "I will see everyone tomorrow." I had no idea what to make of Henry's departing comment and turned to Maurice who shrugged and shook his head.

We wished Simone a quick recovery, offered to do anything when we knew there was nothing we could do, and left.

When I got to the car I could tell Flynn was dreaming. His black legs were twitching and, if I didn't know better, I'd swear he smiled. Dogs give many signs of happiness — the tail being the most obvious. Flynn, once convinced we are heading out for his evening walk, turns circles and almost seems to tap dance. As much as I study him, however, I can't actually confirm that I've seen him smile.

Our walk was longer than usual and, to be frank, he walked me more than the other way around. I thought about Simone and Henry and replayed in my mind my invitation to Claire. Once we were alone, I let Flynn off the leash — but instead of running around and getting some much needed exercise, he sat down on the cold ground, dropped the tennis ball he was holding, and waited for me to throw it.

I neglected to tell you that, whenever possible, Flynn carries a ball in his mouth the entire time we walk except when he allows me to toss it so that he can earn the nomenclature of his breed. Flynn is, and this is not particularly complimentary, a ball dog. By comparison, however, and at the risk of offending a meaningful number of dogs, I confess to the following prejudice: In my view of things, ball dogs are a bit more sophisticated than stick dogs. Granted, dogs requiring sticks in their mouths as a precondition to a decent walk provide more visual humor than ball dogs—but being laughable is not necessarily a mark of superiority.

Just what specific comfort Flynn derives from having a ball in his large mouth is known to him only. What I know is that the ball matters. When I forget to bring it, the walks are, quite simply, nowhere near as pleasurable for him. I don't know what to make of that except I know it is true.

As I do every morning, I dropped Flynn off at home and drove to work—where I got almost nothing done. I had planned on making my way through a pile of recently arrived documents that required commentary—and truly, their content is of no moment other than to say I get paid to write up those comments—but it was hopeless. I was distracted and anxious and nothing seemed in place.

I called Jackson Memorial, the closest hospital, to see if they had a patient named Simone DuChamp and was told they had no patient of that name. I considered calling Claire but did not know her phone number. Strange, isn't it? To be part of a group that meets every day—for more than six years at this point—and not know such a simple piece of information.

I left work earlier than normal knowing no one at the firm would question why and drove back to the Market. It was late January and what snow remained was tarnished and reconfigured.

The Market was open again. No one was sitting at our table. I asked the afternoon proprietor, a dark-haired man, if he knew how Simone DuChamp was doing.

"Who?"

"Henry's wife, Simone."

"Don't know," the dark-haired man said.

"You do know Henry?" I asked.

"Sure—he was here as usual when I got here—left around four—why?"

The implications of the comment were startling. Unless I misunderstood him, Henry had stayed at the hospital only briefly and then come back to the Market. I was going to tell the afternoon clerk about Simone but realized that if Henry wanted him to know, he would have said something. Instead I said, "I'm one of the people who comes here each morning."

"Well," the man said, "we appreciate your business."

I turned to walk out and said, "I sit there on most days," pointing to my chair.

"I wondered why Henry had that table in the middle of everything," the man said. "You just sit there every morning?"

"We talk," I said and walked out.

The following morning Henry would say only that Simone was resting. Perhaps to emphasize normalcy, he brought to the table a pan of freshly baked cornbread and butter. He cut the bread into generous squares and placed one on a napkin in front of each of us. It was still warm and the butter melted across the top of the bread, soaking slowly into its interior, merging perfectly with hot coffee.

There was one other difference that morning. Instead of the daily fare of barely evident elevator music playing in a continuous inconsequential loop, Henry selected a decent rendition of Brahms' Symphony No. 1 that played as we worked our way through the cornbread and coffee. I don't know just why Brahms fit so neatly in our Market—but he did. Mahler, on the other hand, would be a colossal mistake.

I left that day quietly embarrassed by my failure to express to Henry my sincere concern for Simone. It's not that I should have gushed—but I said nothing. While I was truly concerned and scared that something was terribly wrong, my sympathetic repertoire was limited. What does one do or say under such circumstances? A vacuous, 'Please tell Simone we're thinking about her,' borders on imbecilic. My father's response under these circumstances, almost uniformly, was something along the lines of, 'That's unfortunate'— and if the illness or accident was life-threatening, he'd add, 'Hope they have good insurance.'

As I do with far too many things, it would be easy to blame my lack of a compassionate lexicon on my inaccessible and icy father—but this was and is my problem and I felt it directly that morning.

The next day, Maurice pulled me aside as I was getting my first cup of coffee. "I called the hospital and there is no sign of Simone." Like me, Maurice assumed Simone was at Jackson Memorial.

"She's probably home," I whispered, worried Henry would hear us.

"I don't think so," Maurice said quietly. "I went during the day— while Henry was here. There was no one at their home."

That Maurice called the hospital was nowhere near as interesting as the fact that he knew where Simone and Henry lived. "Did you follow Henry home? Did he know?"

"No. Of course not. I shouldn't have said anything to you."

"Maybe she's in a rehabilitation facility. We don't know much about her condition." I was still whispering.

Henry, who had been busy at the cash register, was walking toward us. "Coffee run out?" he said.

"No—there's plenty," I said.

"Enough for you, Maurice?" Henry asked. I could not see Henry's face but his tone, at first monotone, was accusatory.

"Sure," Maurice said quietly, his narrowed eyes focused on Henry. "Plenty. No problem."

Henry turned his back to Maurice, took two steps, and then stood still, hands met behind his back, eyes forward, assuming a formal 'parade rest' stance. He was motionless for several seconds and then walked back behind the counter where several customers were waiting to check out.

My arrival at the Market the next day came on the heels of a difficult night. I want to go back and tell you what happened.

I'm not a sound sleeper and from time to time take a sleeping pill, a blend of a hypnotic and a sedative that has an atypical effect on me. I often wake up with vivid recollections of the bizarre images that form the factual context for my nocturnal subconscious. The dream from that night was particularly unsettling.

Henry and I were in an old station-wagon driving northwest on Interstate 70 with Maryland's Catoctin Mountains off in the distance. In a slow, deliberate maneuver, Henry veered off the highway, across the shoulder, steering onto an unplowed field. We bounced over underbrush and came to a stop surrounded by wild grasses sprouting from uneven lumps on uncertain ground.

In retrospect, Henry's decision to leave the highway was easily understood: Had he stayed on course, we would have slammed into a small herd of deer—behind whom stood their shepherdess, Simone. She was calm and attentive throughout, a placid guardian in unity with her ruminant flock. Simone nodded, apparently confident in what would transpire. While Simone seemed quietly unfazed, my terror at the near catastrophe was expressed in the form of a silent dreamscream that did not abate until we were clear of the deer and Simone.

Once stopped, Henry made a declaration that, to this day, leaves me off-balance: "Simone and I—you—everything and everyone— come from and go to the All of Alls." He made a skyward gesture. "We exist only because we are in the embrace of the All that lies beyond." He reached for the handle to the door. "Charlie, this is about fate, peace with life and death. Why must you try? It can't be understood."

Having proclaimed a universal theory encompassing life, death, eternity, and beyond, Henry marched off, his dreamscape gait military, eyes front, back straight as a platoon sergeant on the drill field at Quantico.

Once awake, I tried unsuccessfully to make sense of the dream and then tried, also unsuccessfully, to put it out of my head. At one point, I had the odd sensation that the dream was Henry's, not mine, and then let that thought slide.

It did not take much analysis to conclude that Henry's "All of Alls" was a reference to a—or the—deity (in my mind, translucent) who surrounds us and everything in an embrace, keeping all things from blasting apart, transformed to incorporeal fragments of eternal nothingness.

I understand you might be taken aback in a tale centered on a convenience store by any reference to a deity or god. If so, I understand. Frankly, I found it unsettling that my subconscious imbued Henry with the power to envision the whole of everything, including eternity.

Going back to sleep was hopeless. I reached across the covers and patted Flynn who snorted lightly, stretched, yawned, rolled on his back, sneezed magnificently, and morning began. I had a bowl of cereal with milk and blueberries, marginally convinced that the antioxidants in a few blueberries mattered, while Flynn ate a cup of dry dog food and a can of clumpy food for Dogs with Sensitive Stomachs. Between bites, I told Flynn about my dream. He finished his food long before I finished mine and walked to me, lying down on my feet as I rambled on about Henry and the nature of the universe. I realize Flynn probably did not understand the language in the dream—but he knew I was troubled and his warm body across my feet on a cold kitchen floor was conscious comfort.

I drove to the Market, going more slowly than normal, playing and replaying the dream. I've known Henry for many years and cannot remember ever discussing any aspect of the universe, religion, much less a translucent deity of any sort. The closest he came to theology was early in our relationship when he expressed distain for the notion of festering in an assisted-living facility like the Beardsley House.

I was about a mile from the Market when I remembered one discussion several years ago regarding meteorites that at least touched on the universe. Maurice had read a piece in the *Post* involving a woman in North Dakota who found a baseball-sized black meteorite in her backyard and sold it to a collector for over a thousand dollars. Maurice speculated that meteorites, like comets, orbit in the solar system. Alex disagreed, sure that meteorites are random, free-flying objects. Claire followed with a theory that the whole of the universe was shaped like a figure-eight in constant motion. "How could anyone know that?" Maurice pressed. "We can see only the tiniest part of space, much less some figure-eight—and if that's everything, what's beyond it?"

"That's all there is, Maurice," she said.

Based on my dream, the All of Alls was within and beyond the galaxies and interstellar dust, the great force that held it all together—which was and is something worth considering for anyone (and that includes me) seeking a locale for their divinity.

I arrived at the Market with images from my dream passing privately and uncomfortably through my mind and, once comfortably in place with my coffee, listened as Alex described the difference between taking a lottery grand prize in cash all at once as opposed to taking annual payouts from an annuity. "I'd take the cash — always," Alex said. "They can promise you annual payments but what happens if they go bankrupt? You get nothing."

"I'd take the annuity," Claire said. "Not even a close question. Income security for twenty-five years is more valuable to me than a large cash payout that could be poorly invested, stolen, or wasted."

Normally, I would weigh in on this topic. It is not a new discussion for us. Instead, my thoughts were elsewhere — in the Catoctin Mountains to be precise, those rolling ancient hills that once stood high as the Rockies, geological offshoots of the Blue Ridge, home to Camp David, state parks and summer camps, a mountain zoo, family restaurants, and cheap motels.

"What about you," Claire asked. "Charlie?"

"I'm sorry," I replied. "What?"

"The lottery — cash or annuity?"

"I don't know — it would depend on when we won. Needs change." The truth is — and I have alluded to this before — when one is the beneficiary of a well-funded trust and holds a well-paying job and cannot be fired, regularity of revenue is not an issue.

Similarly, when one comes from wealth, a large influx of cash isn't the stuff of dreams. Just so you know, it makes me as uneasy to share this as it makes you to read it. Only a tiny number of us can lay claim to a life in which money does not play a dominant role. For the rest, my financial situation may generate envy or resentment, particularly since my finances are the consequence of heritage. Naturally, I could have left out this detail of my life — but you would have wondered: why doesn't he have an answer to the cash vs. annuity question? Well, now you know.

For Claire, Maurice, Simone, Henry, and Alex, there is a shared belief that winning the lottery would change everything. For me, it would not. I doubt most people examine closely the promise of the lottery. It's not just the completely preposterous odds that are ignored. It is the bitter fact that difficult parents, troubling children, bad marriages, illnesses, and a host of other problems are not solved by money. Perhaps you disagree — if so, I hope one day you win — and I am wrong.

It was time to leave. I bought a copy of the *Times* to take with me (a bit of an indulgence—I usually limit myself to the *Post*) and opened my briefcase. I had come to understand that Alex and Claire looked forward to a brief glimpse—and the harangue that would follow—once I revealed in public my bologna and cheese sandwich. Moreover, I knew with certainty that Claire has her sights on my apple.

That may sound to you like a euphemism—but it's not. By apple, I mean, for better or worse, apple.

It was one week after Simone's fall. As our discussions wandered from donuts to demagogues and back, I tuned out, listening instead to Henry as he transacted business with the endless variety of customers who came to the Market. While it is tempting to call it an American parade in deference to the name of the store, it was more than that.

Although Henry and Simone were at least bilingual, they were no match for the range of languages and dialects that formed the morning counter song. On one day alone, I heard people speaking Spanish, Russian, and Portuguese. As you might suspect, this is just a guess.

Convenience stores are comfortable and familiar places for almost anyone from almost anywhere and exist, in one form or another, almost everywhere. Everyone needs something—coffee, band-aids, tissues, a candy bar, or chewing gum, and, when the jackpot is high enough, lines for lottery tickets form around the block.

In France, they might be called *épicerie* or *supérette*, and in those French-speaking parts of Canada, such a store is *dépanneur*. As to my presence north of the border, my father had businesses in Ottawa and Québec and on rare occasions, let me tag along.

As I look back on it, I realize my comfort with convenience stores was not new. They are everything my family is not—open to all and without an overt class structure. In Japan they are called *konbini*, something we learned from a customer who spent a brief time at our table about a year ago. He had been stationed at a U.S. military base in the Kanagawa Prefecture outside of Tokyo and told us, in some detail, about his *konbini* as if he owned a controlling interest in the store.

Towards the tail-end of that discussion, Alex said, as if it was common knowledge—and it was not—that he had been to Japan while in the Navy, notwithstanding his propensity for seasickness.

"How did you handle it when you were at sea?" Claire asked after the *konbini* customer was on his way. "I've been seasick—it's awful."

"Parts of it were most unpleasant," Alex said and then added: "Early in my tour of duty, I knew the Navy would not be in my future."

"Why the Navy?" Maurice asked.

Alex smiled. "To see the world—that was the recruiting pitch when we were kids."

"Did you?" I asked.

"A bit."

"I had no idea," Claire said. "Did you go to Iraq?"

"The combat in Iraq took place several years after I was discharged. Frankly, I was lucky. There were critical military engagements while I was in, including Kosovo, but I was never within 1,000 miles of harm's way. My focus was on evolving computer technology. That became the basis of my next career."

"As a truck driver?" Maurice smiled and then backed off.

Alex continued, seemingly unconcerned with Maurice's comment. "I enjoy my job—I know you think that's odd—but I like the feeling of getting to the end of my route knowing I did something tangible, something that matters to a few people." I thought the end of Alex's day involved piano lessons and poetry but chose to remain quiet.

Claire sipped her coffee. "In my work, the end product ..." Claire looked at me as if I would understand best. "There is no end product ... everything simply goes on, day after day." Her barely perceptible smile touched me, even as it accompanied a modest resignation of an unpalatable truth. "That's normal in my business—but I understand what you're saying, Alex. You start with a full truck—and when you're done, it's empty. That emptiness must be reassuring."

"That sounds like a lawyer's lament," I chimed in. "Some trial lawyers experience catharsis; someone wins, someone loses, sometimes money changes hands ... my work is nothing like that. It's routine, remote, occasionally theoretical, and, if our managing partner has his way, goes on forever."

Alex, not taken with the existential career critique, continued his narrative. "When I left the Navy, I went into business with an old friend, used what I learned and came up with a new product—a good one. We secured a patent, promoted the product online, word spread, and sold the company in a few months. I split the proceeds with my partner and we parted ways. I took a long vacation … and that's when I saw the world, Maurice."

Maurice nodded. He was capable of and generous with that simple silent reassurance of friendship and it pleased Alex. It pleased all of us. Maurice had the capacity to affirm friendship with a squint—but this smile was more than that and Alex continued. "I met a woman in Mexico and got married," he paused for some time, forming words not shared, and took a long sip of coffee. "Then I got my job as a driver," and he was done.

We all must have wondered: Alex had been in the Navy? Was he married? Did he have children? Was he wealthy—a millionaire born of the revolution in information technology? If so, why did he drive a delivery truck? And what about the piano and poetry—how did that fit in? Why the interest in the elderly? And why was Alex buying lottery tickets in increasingly large quantities? I'm sure these questions were common to all seated at our table, but no one said a word.

Chapter 5

Auditions

As I was pouring my first cup of coffee the next morning, Henry came out from behind the counter and stood next to me. "You should speak with Claire today. The wedding date is approaching, isn't it?" He gave me a small piece of paper. "This is her phone number, just in case."

I put the paper in my pocket. "I don't want to talk about the wedding. It's still more than a month away."

"You made an invitation. You need to work out the details."

His comment irritated me, but I let it pass. "Listen, my old friend, I have not asked you for anything over the years."

I was not sure where "my old friend" came from but let that pass as well.

"Get some coffee—no charge today."

"This isn't about free coffee, Henry, is it … and I assume this isn't about the wedding."

He took my arm and led me to the back of the store. "You will be my lawyer, Charlie. There are things that will happen I cannot resolve."

The nature of this declaration was so out of character that it almost seemed comical. I half-expected to see Maurice, dressed in a sweater with Themis, the blindfolded Lady of Justice, embroidered on the front but no one emerged from the storeroom or anywhere else.

"What's going on?" I whispered carefully.

"Simone and I will have legal problems, Charlie—so you will be our lawyer."

"My firm does not take on clients under these circumstances. I cannot do this, Henry—but I can find someone who can represent you. I have a good friend in private practice in Wheaton...."

He held up his hand. "If I wanted you to refer me to another lawyer, I would have asked."

"You can't simply proclaim that I am your lawyer," I said.

"Can't *proclaim*? Of course I can proclaim, my old friend. I just did. You are my lawyer. It's a small thing that I ask."

"No, Henry. It's not a small thing. It changes my life—my firm does not do this kind of work."

"Then leave the firm." Henry was strident. "You don't seem happy about your work."

I hesitated. The observation was partially correct. While I wasn't uniformly content with the work I did, I wasn't unhappy at the firm and I certainly wasn't about to set up my own practice. "That's ridiculous," I said. "That is how I live."

"What kind of life is it, Charlie? Aren't there other things you'd rather do? Start with this case—my case—maybe you will find it better than doing work with no beginning and no end." He lowered his head. "We are going to need some ... family help."

"Don't tell me any more, Henry—please."

"But even the little bit I just said—you will not repeat it to anyone?"

"Of course not," I said.

He smiled. "Then you are my lawyer and this is confidential."

"I will maintain your confidence as a friend, not as your lawyer."

The late-January chill blew through the store as Maurice and Alex stepped inside. "My two best customers," Henry said. I looked at Henry and wondered how he could possibly think them better customers than I. After all, he hadn't asked them to quit their jobs and serve as his lawyer.

As Alex walked to the coffee pot he said: "How's Simone, Henry? It's been awhile since we've seen her." What happened next was not what any of us expected.

"Why not ask Maurice?" Henry said. "He seems to know much about my wife."

Claire arrived in the silence that followed. "Isn't anyone going to say hello?" she asked.

"I am sorry, my dear friend," Henry said. "Good morning."

In the second silence that followed, I contemplated how I could be an old friend and Claire a dear friend. It was a petty concern—but every now and then I am not above self-pitying pettiness.

Maurice placed his coffee cup in front of him and stared at Henry. "Henry," he began, "I haven't seen Simone in a long time. None of us have. That's why Alex asked. She is our friend—and it's normal to wonder how she is doing."

Through a dry clay smile Henry said, "She was sick. You know that. If there is more to say, I will tell you. Simone is aware of how much each of you cares for her."

A half-dozen hard-hatted construction workers walked in, several with yellow vests, and emptied the coffee pot. Henry was suddenly busy with making coffee, running the cash register, selling commercial pastries so full of preservatives that they could fairly be considered dry goods. The workers bought new Pick-5 tickets (drawing set to take place at 11:00 pm that evening). They next checked the results on the tickets they bought yesterday ... everyone lost but one—and that one hard-hatted worker won $200 on a $5.00 ticket.

"That," Alex said, "is why people play." The victorious worker was laughing, surrounded by his friends who watched as Henry counted out his winnings.

"Of course that money will be gone in a day or two," Alex said. "Unless he puts it in the bank, it will find itself back into Henry's cash register."

"I don't ask people to buy these tickets," Henry said defensively. "It is their choice."

"No one is blaming you," Claire said.

Henry nodded and while looking down at something on the counter said: "When is that wedding you and Charlie are attending?"

"Charlie and I need to talk about that," Claire said.

For a moment, I had the distinct feeling that Claire and I were a couple dealing with an overly inquisitive older relative, much as Jennifer Strong and I had teamed up to quiet our parents, a charade I enjoyed far, far more than Jennifer imagined.

The rest of the morning faded to a series of quiet exits. I could not wait to reunite with Flynn, scratch under his neck, and take in the morning air as we walked to the far end of the park. I benefit from his love and laziness. He is always happy to stop for a prolonged head rub followed by a lethargic roll on his back. Occasionally he is overwhelmed by the temptation of a passing rabbit or squirrel but, for the most part, he is a natural-born ambler.

That evening, for the first time since I met her, Claire Beaumont called me at home. I had given Henry my number some years ago and he must have shared it with Claire much as he had shared hers with me.

It was time to talk about the wedding. As soon as I realized it was her, I said that it was just fine for her to call me at home. This was before she asked whether it was a problem for her to call me—and I heard her muffle a laugh.

"So what do you think?" she asked. "Should we go?"

This was not a real question. I had asked her. It happened with and without thinking, a spontaneous moment—and by this point, Claire was certain I was not given to spontaneity. "Sure—yes—of course—but can you take time off from work? It's a long weekend."

"Why are you making excuses for me?" she asked.

"I'm just thinking out loud," I said.

I must have sounded desperate. "I can take the time, Charlie."

As if someone else was speaking I heard: "We should go to dinner this weekend and go over the trip in more detail."

"A dinner date, a weekend in New England—this is all so sudden. After all, I've only known you for six or seven years." She laughed and continued. "Sure—dinner is fine, Charlie. Going to the wedding together will be an adventure. Henry, Simone, Alex, and Maurice will be possessed, wanting every detail. Imagine how much fun that will be, holding back, not telling them the details of the weekend. I'm not saying there will be much to tell, but it will be our weekend, our details."

For some reason I took this comment to mean that if I had hopes of intimacy, of Claire sharing more than good food and the remarkable gossip this wedding would generate, they had ended before they could take root. A wildly regrettable comment followed:

"Well, sure—yes—something involving sex—now that wasn't even vaguely—and well, it would be very personal—not that anyone...." In the predictable silence that followed I added: "I'm not saying—it never crossed my mind...." And finally, "We would sleep ... of course not together ... but who would think that would happen?"

This collection of words was up there on the list of completely idiotic things I have said in the course of my adult life.

"Of course," Claire said. "Why would you think that? As you were told at the outset, I am older than you."

"That has nothing to do with it," I said, but the damage was done. There are undoubtedly clever and upbeat ways to conduct these kinds of discussions but I do not know them and wanted the call to end. "Let's talk about this tomorrow."

"Charlie, you and I can't talk about this tomorrow—not with the others trying to hear every word. I would be happy to have dinner with you. There's a restaurant not far from the Market—Pauline's. Do you know where it is?" I mumbled and she continued. "Meet me there around seven on Sunday and we can figure out what we want to do."

The call ended and I called Flynn who was snoozing under my desk. With some effort, he got up on the couch next to me, circled on the cushions twice, then collapsed in a heap, burying his head against my back. It was the perfect antidote.

Claire was at the table speaking with Maurice when I arrived the next morning. Maurice looked at me, his face scrunched in a frown.

"Claire told you we're going to the wedding?" I guessed.

"What? You are?" He looked at Claire. "Really?" She nodded. "Actually, Charlie, no. That's not what we were talking about. Claire told me, too late," and he leaned forward and whispered, "that the coffee is awful this morning and not to drink it."

Delighted with the subject, I called: "Henry?" He was at the cash register ringing up lottery tickets for Alex. "What did you do to the coffee?"

I was smiling—but Henry was not. "It's old—from yesterday," he said. The moment he had finished with the customer, he rushed to the coffee counter, poured down the drain yesterday's dregs, washed the pot, and started brewing a new pot. "You don't have to pay for that," he said. "I forgot to make a fresh pot this morning." I expected a "Can I talk to you?" from Claire, but she decided to let me marinate.

About 45 minutes later, I joined her as she was leaving the Market. "Are we still on for dinner?"

"For God's sake Charlie, do you have any idea what you sound like?"

I did and I didn't. My words made sense but only in a phonetic manner. "Sure," I said. "I just wondered...." I actually hadn't wondered. I had hit a dead end.

"Yes. You owe me a decent meal." She walked away in that unmistakably certain manner that conveyed an end to our discussion.

The next few days stand out in my memory as unique, not because of my upcoming dinner date, but because of the number of other people who came and sat at our table. I cannot explain just why this happened—we weren't looking to add to our numbers, but weren't completely opposed either. Accordingly, from our insular perspective, these were auditions.

Paul McMahon, a mason from North Carolina, told us he had been asked to come to Washington to work on a special project to repair a wall in a historically preserved building. Apparently he was highly regarded—his story left no other interpretation. We concluded that he was a short-term visitor.

Harold Leeman, a retired teacher from Upper Sandusky, Ohio, sat with us as well. He was chaperoning a group of students visiting from his hometown, making a little bit of extra money to cover the costs of a vacation to Florida he was planning with his wife, Madeline, also retired from her job as a guidance counselor. Again, just a visitor.

A county police officer, Scott Greenberg, wondered about the change in the tax laws. No one knew anything about the change but, not surprisingly, Henry announced that I was a lawyer and could help them if needed. Officer Greenberg had potential—but he made Alex uneasy and no invitation was extended.

The most surprising of our visitors, at least for me, was Elisa Ravel, former consultant to my law firm and recent entrant in my compendium of misguided relationships. A friend had told her I spent mornings at the Market and she decided to check it out. She was as I recalled—attractive, articulate, and not particularly nice. "I'm moving to New York, Charlie," she said. "New job and...." She held out her left hand displaying a garish engagement ring.

"Let me guess," Claire said, "there's a lucky guy waiting for you in New York."

Elisa nodded and turned to me. "How's it going?"

"Fine, Elisa. No complaints."

"What are you doing here?"

"Having coffee," I said.

She looked around the Market and shook her head. "I had to see this for myself." She bid a "goodbye" to no one in particular, and left.

"Ex-girlfriend?" Alex asked after she left.

"I went out with her a couple of times. It was nothing serious."

"It would have been serious if it lasted longer." Alex was smiling. "Definitely not your type."

"And what type would that be?" Claire asked. Apparently this was such a perplexing question that it rendered Alex—and everyone else—mute.

Leslie Finster, an artist born in downstate Illinois (she chose not to disclose her hometown), had moved to Washington after graduating from college and shared stories about her career with the *Post* in their computer graphics department. Leslie had table potential but when we asked if she was often in the area in the morning, she explained that she lived some distance from here and was in Jackson Park for an appointment with her podiatrist.

Oscar Casillas, the owner of the place down the street that sold roasted chickens, asked if we met in the evenings. He said he could place a table for us in his store and offered us coupons for roast chickens. (Obviously, a one-time visit.)

An upright woman with a British accent, Aubrey Collins, joined us one morning and asked if I owned a large black dog. I acknowledged that I did and worried briefly that Flynn had done something terrible. She explained that she had seen me in the park a number of times while walking her dog, a rare Norwegian hound called a Dunker. She'd kept her distance, unsure if my dog was safe.

"We could let them play. That could be quite fun," she said. I told her Flynn was probably no match for a Dunker. She assured me that her dog was considerably smaller than Flynn but, in my view, that really wasn't the point. Flynn was simply too unpredictable to mix it up with the likes of a Dunker. I ended the inquiry explaining that walking from the lot to the end of the park and back drained Flynn of resources such that a nap was needed. Frankly, playing with her Dunker simply was not in the cards.

Once again, just so we are clear, *playing with her Dunker* is not a euphemism for anything—and, to be honest, Aubrey was a bit too proper for us.

As the flow of visitors continued, we discussed why it was that so many people had auditioned. In the years since we first convened our group in the Market, nothing like this had happened before. One or two people a week would pull up a chair but almost always would leave shortly thereafter. Just what forces encouraged this collection of visitors to surface remained yet another mystery of the Market.

It rained hard Saturday morning. Claire, Maurice, and I were on our second cup of coffee and discussing the weather when we noticed a dark-haired and rather attractive woman nodding at Maurice as she stood by the door, coffee in hand. "She wants you to walk her to her car—go for it," Claire whispered.

"She's right—have at it, Maurice," I added.

"She wants me to hold her umbrella, get my feet wet, help her get in her car without ruining her shoes, and then she will drive away and I will be drenched and without her name or phone number," Maurice said. After a moment he added. "You must know she is not my type."

"Weenie," Claire whispered.

"You walk her," Maurice said turning to me.

The woman must have heard some part of this. When I looked up she was gone.

Flynn and I got soaked on our way to the car before I went to the Market and re-soaked during our walk in the park. The drive back home left no doubt—my car reeked of Flynn.

It is a sad fact that most dogs, and Flynn was no exception, have a distinct smell. It is enhanced when they get wet. Knowing I would have a soggy Flynn in the car guaranteed that my car would have that smell for days to come and also limited my options in terms of my dinner with Claire. I did not want her in my car when it smelled as badly as I knew it would. As it turned out, it was not a problem.

On Sunday night, Claire was seated in the restaurant and had in front of her what appeared to be a martini when I arrived. Before I was seated, she said: "If you don't want me to go, just say so. We will still be friends. Go, don't go—I don't care. Just make up your mind."

I was prepared this time. You probably think I practiced with Flynn. If so, you're getting to know me. "I would very much like to have you join me. It should be quite an event." And then, with some effort: "I already made reservations for us at the New Marlow Inn. It's the closest place—and they have a wedding rate for guests."

Claire took a sip of her drink and smiled. "Fair enough, Charlie. I'm game."

What she didn't ask, perhaps because there was no reason, was whether I had reserved one or two rooms probably because she knew that there was no possible way I would force this by reserving just one.

A small salad, a decent piece of rockfish, a baked potato, a second martini for Claire, and a first for me, and the evening was almost over.

"I would give you a lift…." I started.

"My car is out front, Charlie—but thanks for the offer." She took out her wallet.

"Please, no—I'll take care of the bill." She thanked me and excused herself, saying she had a long day tomorrow, and left.

On Monday, the collection of newcomers—I suppose we could have called them *hopefuls* but that assumes too many unknown and unexplored facts—continued.

A man named Hilbert Stanley told us he was a rare disease researcher at NIH, the massive U.S. National Institutes of Health located ten minutes from the Market. When he left the table, Claire said that people named Hilbert were destined to be researchers and that his career was entirely predictable once he announced his name.

Alex disagreed. "Hilberts are invariably debonair and worldly—and I think the coffee was forced. Hilberts are tea drinkers."

"That's nonsense—and even if you're right about that particular Hilbert, tea doesn't disqualify him," Claire said—but the looks around the table suggested otherwise.

Before we could expand the discussion of all things Hilbert, a buyer for an appliance store, Alison Everhart, sat down and asked us our preferences in toaster ovens. She could not have known how intriguing her question was, how consistent it was with our normal discourse.

"Who uses toasters anymore?" she asked, as if conducting a focus group. Apparently, she was out to convince us that the traditional pop-up, two-slice toaster was outdated. As you know, I am loathe to change much of anything. I have had the same traditional toaster for the last two decades.

Out of nowhere, Henry said: "I love my toaster. It's fast and makes perfect toast." Maurice and I nodded in agreement. Alison Everhart, the buyer, seemed disappointed.

"Why not get a toaster oven? They do so much more." She appeared momentarily desperate.

Maurice countered: "They take longer and don't make toast the way I like it. It's that simple." Everyone agreed except Alison.

The discussion of toast took some time and Ms. Everhart appeared, well, disheartened until Claire allowed that she had both a toaster and a toaster oven. This seemed to inspire Ms. Everhart and gave her the strength to leave with some modicum of grace. We never saw her again.

Later that morning, we were joined by an aide to State Senator Wellington Norris, who heard there was a morning political colloquy at the Market. This was clearly not an audition. The aide wanted us to know that Senator Norris would be happy to join us some morning—and would we mind if there were press present to memorialize the informal chat.

This absurd request unified the group almost instantly. "That's a kind offer," Alex said, leading the charge, "but I am afraid it would be completely out of the question." Everyone nodded. "I have a better idea," he continued. "Tell the Senator that the residents of the

Beardsley House would be happy to have him speak with them one afternoon."

Apparently the prospect was not all that compelling — that interaction would be full of real questions about health care, insurance, and taxes, not some happy media moment generating pictures and video clips to be used in the next campaign.

Before he left, Maurice asked, "By the way, how did you learn about our table?"

"They are talking about it at Café One," the aide said. Café One is the gourmet coffee shop down the street from the Market.

"Do they have a table?" Henry asked.

"Not like this," the aide replied. "But they have free Internet access."

Henry smiled. "That sounds *so* very nice." Up to this point, it was as close as Henry got to satire.

Even though there was resistance to these interlopers, they kept coming. Somehow the word was out and people wanted to see just what was so special at the American Market.

A dentist sat with us for two days and said little about his work and much about a general store in his very rural hometown. When he left, we decided he was lying ... perhaps that is why I've forgotten his name.

The minister from the local Methodist church, Reverend Mike (I have a hard time believing that last names are no longer important to Methodists), showed up. Reverend Mike turned out to be a delightful person who wanted to understand how we came to know each other and spoke, very briefly, about the abstract concept of community.

While the discussion with Reverend Mike was underway, we were joined by Town Councilwoman Celia Bell. Councilwoman Bell was known to us politically — her "no" votes on just about any building project were discussed often in the *Jackson Park Gazette* and, on occasion, in the Market.

She introduced herself and seemed to enjoy the discussion about the abstract notion of community but became quite stiff when questions were raised about yet another large apartment building taking form two blocks from the Market.

"Those are not rental units," Maurice said, his tone uncharacteristically sharp. "They are condominiums selling before the building is half-finished for well over a million dollars each. This is for Washington's elite, lobbyists and bankers who want the benefit of a short commute, not for the people who have lived in Jackson Park for years."

Councilwoman Bell agreed: "I think it's a disaster. Jackson Park is growing too fast. We are squandering our greatest asset—our small-town character. My colleagues on the Council think this kind of building will bring revenue and residents who will frequent our shops, dine in our restaurants—but they are incorrect."

"You are absolutely right," Maurice said and then, with no consultation whatsoever, blurted out: "You're welcome to join us any time."

Before any of us could say a word, Councilwoman Bell responded. "You are an interesting group. Perhaps if I'm in the area, we can talk more."

While this was close to a rejection, Maurice seemed to hear only the potential for more interaction with this kindred spirit. "Once that monstrosity is built down the street, the idea that the residents will frequent local restaurants is wrong." He paused. "I doubt we will see them in the Market."

"I disagree." Henry, who normally listens happily as these battles take form, was animated. "You know nothing about my customers." He looked only at Maurice as he spoke. "I know them. I learn about them. Many are executives." Henry's comments were followed by an unpleasant silence and he continued. "Claire is an executive. Charlie is a respected lawyer. Alex is an inventor. And what are you?"

Maurice shook his head and looked at Alex who nodded and held up one hand, an unmistakable gesture directing Maurice not to engage with Henry.

Not surprisingly, both Reverend Mike and Councilwoman Bell backed away from the table moments later, mumbled about wishing they could stay, and made a quick exit.

As Henry left the counter and went to the coffee machine in the rear of the store, Claire leaned into my shoulder and said: "What the hell was that about?"

~

Reverend Mike and Councilwoman Bell were the last to audition and while we neither extended invitations nor discouraged future visits (other than Maurice's unauthorized encouragement to Councilwoman Bell), the membership in our group remained unchanged. Looking back, I wondered what it was about our interactions that suggested we were looking for new members. After all, as Alex pointed out, there were times when we weren't particularly nice.

You might think one or more of us would quickly disagree with Alex—but no one said a word. It was true. We were different, one to the next, but we were honest with each other—or as honest as one can be as an adult. That meant both fundamental decency and an unfiltered bluntness.

In that blunt vein, the absence of Simone was impossible to ignore. Claire finally cornered Henry before she left the Market. "She is my friend, Henry—it's not like her to disappear—and it's not like you to be this evasive."

In fact, Henry *was* evasive when it came to his personal life. He seemed unprepared for the directness of Claire's question. "She is fine, Claire. Stop worrying." The answer was not helpful and did not quiet fears that something truly awful had happened. However, speculation regarding Simone's fate finally ended the following Tuesday morning.

Simone was behind the store cash register and greeted each of us as we came in. Her green silk blouse was complemented by a pale yellow scarf and pearl earrings, her hair, nails, and makeup all in good order. In a way, her outfit, her entire presentation, reminded me of a person about to be interviewed for a job. I'm not saying Simone ordinarily came to the Market unkempt, but her attire that morning was more elegant, more attractive than we had seen, perhaps ever.

Henry sat on a stool in front of the lottery terminal a few feet away handling all matters pertaining to lottery tickets. The value of the game (for which we'd bought a ticket, of course) was now in excess of $100 million.

Huge jackpots were not unusual—with tickets sold in nearly every state and jackpots *starting* at $40 million, the grand prizes grow quickly—but the odds do not improve. For each game they are roughly one in 180 million. Roughly. This does not dissuade the millions upon millions of buyers. If you are not a ticket buyer, you might be surprised to learn that you are in the minority. Alex once told us that more than half the adults in the U.S. buy lottery tickets either periodically or regularly—and no one at our table disagreed.

Large jackpots bring customers and therefore ancillary business to the Market, and that day was no exception. Even though all stores selling these tickets make only a tiny amount of money from sales, even with bonuses (if they happen to sell jackpot prizes), there is a spillover effect. As long as one is at the store to buy a ticket, why not pick up a newspaper, a bottle of soda, a cup of coffee, or a pack of gum?

On this day, Henry took more time than usual, chatting with complete strangers, asking them what they would do if they won. He made it seem like an important part of his job and yet I believed, at least then, that Henry immersed himself in lottery sales to avoid discussions with and about Simone.

The large number of lottery ticket purchasers could not be ignored and we watched. Some of the hopefuls promised that if they won, Henry would be rewarded. Some even said they would split the winnings 50/50 with him, a complete stranger. Henry smiled, encouraged their faint hopes, and took his time as he took their money.

The buyers, all part of the most common "what if" gamblers' fantasy, were well-behaved and prematurely magnanimous. This, they would tell themselves, is how I will be, generous to a fault, even to strangers, so long as they are possessed of decency. You could almost hear their interiors quietly assuring that in a matter of days every major issue in their lives, all of which they believed related to money, would be resolved.

They bought tickets for the infinitesimally slim chance of fiscal redemption and what I know to be the false hope that money would bring absolution and remission of all that was hard, harsh, lonely, loveless, insurmountable, impossible, and uncontrollable. Of this I am quite certain. I began this tale with the qualification that while I will never have anything resembling the assets some members of my family enjoy (though I am not sure *enjoy*, with its root term "joy," could ever be applied to my family), I am the beneficiary of a well-funded trust and have a job from which I cannot be fired. I understand what money and financial security can buy—and what it can never acquire.

My father is still around, in his early 70s, healthy, wealthy, and remarried to a woman named Priscilla Coughlin who will doubtlessly fight to hang on to his substantial resources when my father takes up residence with that great translucence, the All of Alls, to whom you have been indirectly introduced.

The marriage to Priscilla Coughlin guaranteed that our family resources would be further divided—my share diminished by the mere fact of their union. I hope you understand I am not that bitter about this. Among other things, I am confident that any financial interest I might have on the demise of my father will be advocated with frightening intensity, certainty, and ruthlessness by my one and only sibling, my brother Wesley, a Bostonian fourteen years my senior. Other than genetics and money, we have little in common and rarely speak beyond a passing greeting. You might assume this is a feud—but that's not the case. Beyond the punctual arrival of a Christmas card every year on which he scribbles something like, 'You really must come to Boston and visit Sally and the kids one of these days,' we do not have—nor have we ever had—a real relationship. After all, I turned four the year Wes began college.

I met Sally, his wife (and the daughter of George and Matty Ross, half-owners of Becker Metals, an enormous company that trades silver, copper, and of course gold) at their wedding. She seemed nice enough, but one can never really tell from a wedding. They have two children who, my mother had complained, have been in fancy boarding schools since they were barely two. I hope that is not true—but it might be.

~

When customers approached Simone with items to buy and also the wish to purchase a lottery ticket, she checked out their other purchases and passed them along to Henry for the lottery transaction. Although she did not engage in the kind of idle chatter taking place a few feet away, she seemed warmer and more welcoming than usual. Something had changed in her. While the circumstances would suggest otherwise, she seemed at peace.

When there was a lull in the action at the counter, we asked questions about her health. Simone acted as if nothing had happened, dismissing every question with, "I decided to take some time off," or "It was nothing—certainly nothing to worry about," and, "I thought Henry told you—I'm sorry you were worried."

Henry added nothing of substance to this denial. He smiled and nodded, a practiced gesture suggesting he didn't quite understand English when we all knew he understood precisely what was being asked and why.

Chapter 6

The Painter from Acumbaro

The following morning I stood next to Alex as he poured his coffee. He hummed a melody I recognized but could not identify. "What is that?"

"The Sixth—the *Pastoral*."

"Of course," I said and then added, "Do you perform that piece when you play the piano at Beardsley?"

"I teach piano for the most part. I don't perform very often. The point is to get senior citizens to engage, appreciate, and even play music ... not to sit passively and listen." I nodded and Alex continued. "I've composed some short pieces." He paused. "I play every now and then—but no, not Beethoven. I can't imagine one person playing the Sixth—that requires an orchestra." Alex took a long sip followed by an "*Ahhh*."

The quality of the coffee had not changed, but real milk, a new arrival at the Market, made a difference. Some weeks earlier, we had asked Henry to provide milk, not just the chemical creamer one often finds where cheap coffee is sold. His solution was uncharacteristically elegant: a good-sized ice bucket with a half-gallon of real milk. We took responsibility for keeping the milk iced and letting Henry know if it was running low.

"You know I teach piano and poetry?"

"Yes," I said quietly. "Of course."

"It's something I wanted to do for a long time. Just because one is older does not mean the ability to play, appreciate, or even create music is lost. Aging slows one down, fades memory, hearing lessens, and aspects of our physical abilities decline. Music, however, lives on so long as one is open to trying. However, before you can create, you need to know the fundamentals of your instrument—and at Beardsley House, it's the piano. Actually, it is four Kelleher pianos."

"Kelleher?"

"Master piano builders—they have a small factory outside of Wilmington."

"I haven't heard of them—I know Steinway and Kawai...."

"Of course you do," Alex said. "Your family probably has a Steinway—and no one ever plays it."

"You're right. How did you know?"

Alex looked at me. "You've let enough slip over the years. Old money—New England—a Steinway is a prerequisite. It goes along with the four or five complete sets of fine china, silver settings for 60, Waterford crystal, a few Chippendale hutches...."

"All good guesses," I said, careful not to defend myself with an "but that's not me." To an extent, as you know, it is me and Alex seemed to know that as well.

"I won't tell the others. Claire already has a good sense of you— and probably will learn more at that wedding ... and Maurice is not interested in anyone's past except Simone." He was speaking quietly. "And Henry—Henry knows all about you. Don't underestimate him."

"You know more about this group than I do," I said.

He cleared his throat, and in a more normal voice said: "Henry, we're running low on milk."

"Take one of the containers from the cooler." Like most people who run convenience stores, Henry is careful about money—and Simone more so. As to the milk, the day he brought out the ice bucket and announced the plan to make real milk available, the cost of coffee went up ten cents a cup. Before the first hour of fresh milk ended, Henry had made a profit on his cleverly calculated commercial conception.

As we walked back to the table, Alex took hold of my elbow and whispered: "Claire is a special person. I have known her longer than any of you. She is not as tough as she seems."

This was a warning I had not expected. "You're talking about the wedding trip?" I said and he nodded.

I looked closely at Alex—was this an admonition from a friend or was there more? "You and Claire—were you involved … ?"

Before I could finish, in a most matter-of-fact way, Alex said: "No—Claire and I are just old friends. That's all we've ever been." He let go of my arm and sat down at the table and joined in a discussion about trees.

Jackson Park has several parks with beautiful oak, elm, and maple trees. The park Flynn and I use almost every day has a huge white oak with a plaque explaining that it is one of the oldest trees in the state. I have seen people from the National Park Service and an arborist from the University of Maryland work on that tree, trimming and feeding it.

Street trees are another matter. As the township grew and new buildings burst out of the ground, we lost trees. In an effort to replace them, the Town Council decided on Zelkova Serrate, hardy street trees that are disease resistant, grow quickly, and, according to the Council, are used successfully in Tokyo and on Beijing's crowded and polluted thoroughfares. "They are not oaks, that's for darn sure," Maurice said. Maurice told us he had been part of a "Save the Oaks" movement at one point.

"Aren't they elms?" Claire asked.

"Elm family," Maurice said authoritatively.

"The ones they planted on Central Avenue years ago don't look healthy," Alex said. "Their bark is peeling off, leaving these orange patches. They are on a route I drive fairly often."

"That's normal," Maurice said. "Zelkovas slough off bark as a normal part of their maturation."

"I don't think something *sloughs off*," Claire said. "I think it just sloughs. The off is part of the sloughing."

"It's like molting," Alex added. "Something doesn't molt off."

And on it went.

The table cleared and I was still reading the paper when Henry walked up to me. "You and Alex were having a serious discussion. I hope he is not in trouble."

"Why would he be in trouble?" I asked.

"People seek out lawyers when they need help—just as I have done with you."

"Henry, we really need to talk about this. I am not the kind of lawyer you think I am. I work on regulatory cases involving private investor-owned utilities."

"I know," Henry said. "You are smart or they would not hire you at a firm like that." I had no idea how Henry knew about my firm but in one sense he was right. The firm is very selective and hires proven lawyers, only laterals, never recent law school graduates— except me. I was hired—or more accurately told I had an office in the firm—in the middle of my last year of law school. I was never interviewed. While Henry could not possibly know that detail, he would, with some research, be able to find out that I started with the firm immediately after graduation.

"I appreciate the kind words, but I am quite sure you need a lawyer who is an expert in fields I know nothing about."

"You will learn what you need to know—isn't that what lawyers do? No one is an expert on everything." Henry was right. The best lawyers know what they need to learn, what questions they need to ask, to research.

"I believe you when you say you do not represent people like me, Charlie—but I know you can." He paused. "And Alex—does he need your help?"

I could not suppress a laugh. "If I am such a good lawyer, you know I can't tell you what has been said to me."

"By a client—is Alex your client?"

"I need to walk Flynn and get to work. Have a good day, Henry."

The following morning came and went without talk of law and lawyers. As was the case yesterday, Simone dressed elegantly and seemed remarkably calm.

Claire left early saying she had an appointment. When I asked with whom, she shook her head without turning around and said: "I don't think you could handle it if I told you," and walked out.

I asked Alex and Maurice what that was all about. Maurice shrugged but Alex leaned forward. "Don't be an ass, Charlie. Women have appointments for their … special parts … and are unlikely to announce that in a convenience store—or anywhere else."

Maurice and I worked on this answer briefly and, almost simultaneously said, "Oh. That." Alex nodded and Simone, who had been witness to our density, sighed.

It was time to head to the park with Flynn. As I walked out, Maurice grabbed his coat and joined me. "Can I walk with you?"

I had come to like Maurice more and more. It was obvious he enjoyed our morning dialogues and it was, at least from my vantage point, fairly clear that his life was, like mine, solitary. As you know, I am given to assumptions about people, and Maurice was no exception. I imagined he lived alone, had some form of reliable employment, owned shelves and shelves of sweaters, and both enjoyed and felt incomplete by virtue of his circumstances.

"Some years ago," Maurice began, "before I met you, I came to the Market one morning before anyone else had arrived. While I knew Claire and Alex, there was not even the pretense of a group at the time. Simone was at the counter, alone."

It was not all that unusual for Henry to be in the Market without Simone, particularly as she healed from whatever mysterious illness ailed her. It was unusual, however, for Simone to be in the Market without Henry.

"Simone explained that Henry had to renew his driver's license. She told me he always gets to the Motor Vehicle Administration at least an hour before they open so that he will be first in line and miss as little time at the Market as possible." This small piece of information added to my sense that Henry, who for some years I thought to be an innocent, floating on the winds of uncertain fate, was rather calculating and determined to control variables in his life.

"I walked to the counter to pay Simone for my coffee and a newspaper. She reached out to me, taking both hands. Her head tilted to one side and she said to me, 'I would like to be your very special friend,' and then squeezed my hands in that way we all understand to have meaning beyond assurance. Before letting go, she pulled me toward her and I thought for a moment she would kiss me but that did not happen. Instead, she breathed these words: 'I know I can trust you.'"

We were still more than a block from my car but I stopped walking and turned to Maurice. "I assume more has happened since then, but I am not sure I want to know. What you and Simone do is your affair."

"Interesting choice of words—I'm not sure I would characterize my relationship with Simone as an affair. I like her very much and liked her even before that morning. However, if you are wondering whether we are lovers, the answer is no."

Of course that was exactly what I wondered but said nothing and Maurice continued. "I am going to tell you something, Charlie, and given what I've just said about Simone, it will help you understand more about me."

I was fairly sure that Maurice was about to tell me something about the intimacy in his life but what he said instead, while related to sexuality, was not what I expected. "I have not had a sexual relationship with anyone in the last 20 years."

His comment hung in the air like a small puff of smoke. I wanted to ask him whether this was his choice or a tragic lack of opportunity. Everyone, I assumed, as part of the human experience, seeks out some form of intimate relationship, something more than the casual interaction that comes along with work or friendship. Before I said anything, however, I was possessed of this thought: What if Maurice had some type of illness or injury that prevented him from functioning? I looked at him and realized this was a question I could not ask; fortunately, it was unnecessary.

"This is a choice I made a long time ago," he said. "I was involved with a woman with whom I worked. We had a sexual relationship and she got pregnant. She did not tell me until after she had terminated the birth." His eyes rimmed just slightly and, had I not known him so well, I might have thought it was the glare of the morning sun.

"I never knew if it was a boy or girl—never had a chance to offer to raise my child." He looked into my eyes. "That was the end of it for me. I didn't want to go through something like that again and made the decision, quite consciously, to forgo sexuality." Maurice turned and began walking down the sidewalk and I followed. "It has been a surprisingly easy decision for me," he said as we got to the corner and then repeated, "Surprisingly easy."

His eyes were clear now. I looked at Maurice and sensed I'd never really seen him before. His curly reddish-brown hair was neatly trimmed, short but not lacking style. I noted the round-ness of his stomach pushing against the red and grey pattern of his sweater that, on closer inspection, turned out to be a carefully woven brick wall.

Much as I wanted to ask about Simone and his life as an asex-ual, the first question that found its way out of my mouth was: "You must have a hundred sweaters. Do the sweaters fit somehow into your decision?"

"Not to have sex? Are my wardrobe choices affected by that?"

I realized at that moment that I was not particularly interested in Maurice's sweaters and so I recovered, though only slightly. "I don't mean to pry."

"Given what I've told you, I wouldn't worry about prying. I wear the sweaters because I like them. I'm not saying I don't care how I look. That honor, I'm sorry to say, goes to you. When it comes to appearance, one consequence of my decision is that I am not con-stantly on the hunt. I get to experience men and women without contemplating whether I am appealing or whether they would be a suitable match."

"Is this what you wanted to tell me?"

"In part," Maurice said. "I wanted you to know that my interest in Simone is, in some ways, no different than my interest in you."

"I am fairly sure Henry doesn't see it that way."

"I agree," Maurice said, "and I wanted to make sure that you knew that as well." He stopped on the sidewalk and took a step closer to me. "In the beginning, I believed there was an undeni-able purity in Henry — the humble refugee, a victim seeking sanc-tuary, a simple and courageous man with a good heart ... and I still see most of that, but there are other parts to Henry that are troubling. If he reacts with some jealousy towards me, ultimately, that should benefit Simone."

"How could you think that? If anything, he seems angry at Si-mone and distant from her."

"Of course I understand that, and there are two explanations. Either he is jealous of the attention Simone pays me—and I pay her—because of the depth, expanse, and power of his relationship with her ... or he has ceased to view Simone as anything other than a possession, a player in the life he has orchestrated. I think it will come out, one way or the other, and frankly I hope Henry's reactions are based on his love of his wife and not on his need to control everything around him."

Maybe Maurice was right—for years, I envisioned Henry as a heroic figure—I still do—but after listening to Maurice, he seemed slightly less so.

"I am assuming that no one else is aware of your decision...."

"To be a voluntary eunuch?" Maurice finished my sentence and then quickly added, "Though not in the physiological sense of the term?" I nodded and Maurice went on. "It's not the kind of thing that one readily shares. Everyone has secrets, even those who claim to be an open book."

I grew up in a world where one did not tell tales out of school. I still pride myself on that capacity. "I won't say anything."

"Particularly to Henry," Maurice said. "I want him to think that my interest in Simone is sexual. Let him wallow in that for a while. There is something satisfying about watching someone marinate in their pettiness."

"I would not characterize Henry's concern as petty," I said. "He believes you're having an affair with his wife."

"Perhaps," Maurice said, "and perhaps he is upset because I am tampering with his possession."

"How much of this does Simone know?"

"Simone has no idea about my self-imposed asexuality."

"Then it is quite possible she misinterprets the interest you show," I said. "Why lead her on?"

"Simone is not well. That I show her that I care, pay special attention, convey that she is appealing, desirable, wanted—those are positive things," Maurice said. "Everyone wants to be wanted and needed, and I'm not sure Henry plays that role for Simone."

Maurice put his hand on my shoulder. "There is one other thing—it's personal, Charlie...." He took a long time, looked away from me briefly and seemed to be experimenting with what he was about to say. Finally he said: "Why Claire?"

"You too?"

"What do you mean?"

"Alex wanted to talk to me about Claire—he was concerned about her."

"They go back," Maurice said. "Nothing romantic—just friends."

"So what's your interest in Claire?" I could have added 'isn't Simone enough?' but thought better of it.

"Other than friendship, I have none—I was asking about you." He stopped again, exhaled, and without meeting my eyes, said, "She's kind of tough on you—critical ... sometimes a bit harsh, you know? I'm not sure how she feels about you."

The sweetness of this comment may be hard to see at first—but I felt it immediately and decided to say the one thing I felt sure about Claire's sense of me. "She thinks I can do better ... that I am capable of change."

"And you see that as affection?"

"I see it as caring—that I'm worth her time."

"Fair enough," Maurice said. His hand was still on my shoulder. "For your sake, I hope you're right." And then, with a big smile, "I believe you are besotted, my friend."

Through these disclosures and observations, I began to feel an even greater fondness for Maurice. I waited to see if he was going to say anything further and when he neither spoke nor moved I decided to shift gears. "For as long as we've known each other, it's odd that we know so little. Take Alex—in many ways, a complete enigma. I don't know if he is a technology millionaire or living on the economic edge. I do know that he spends hundreds of dollars a week on the lottery."

"I know a few things about Alex, but you'll need to ask him if you are interested in learning more." Maurice said. "He is desperate for a heavy dose of good luck."

"Shouldn't we intercede and try to get him to slow down? I don't care how much money he made with his invention, whatever it was, he is going to go broke."

"I wouldn't say anything," Maurice said, and then added: "One last thing, Charlie. Despite all that I've said, if the right person comes along, I would reconsider my decision. Do you understand what I'm saying?"

"Of course." I paused and smiled. "You're a romantic."

"I hope so," he said and with that walked off smartly as if I had kept him from being on time.

Back at the car, I apologized to Flynn for the delay and drove to the park. As was sometimes the case this time of day, ours was the only car in the lot. That may seem to you a small thing but it meant we would have the blessing of solitude in this public space. Small, barely visible snowflakes fell through gray light. Flynn and I were alone, in communion with the quiet of a winter morning in Jackson Park.

~

An elderly couple came into the Market the following morning and bought a newspaper and coffee. As they were leaving, they exchanged greetings with Alex.

"Friends of yours?" I asked after they were gone.

"They live at Beardsley House—been there for several years."

"They must like it," I said.

"Their family didn't want to care for them at home."

"They seem quite independent," I said. "What was the problem?"

"She has Alzheimer's—still in the early stage," Alex said.

"You wouldn't know," I said.

"I hear the aides speaking to her, saying things like, 'Come on, honey, eat your toast,' as if they're speaking with a four-year-old. She is still capable of so much more." We spoke about aging and competence, Alex's classes at Beardsley, and as the discussion wound down, Alex said: "I want to read something to you. It won't take long."

Alex had not done this before although he had discussed several of his poems, sometimes quoting a line or two. He took a sheet of paper from his pocket. Simone came out from behind the counter and sat next to Claire and Alex began to read:

The Painter from Acumbaro

Before the flight from the steps of the ladder,
He spoke of Nelida, his daughter beloved,
Nelida of Acumbaro, his reason for painting.
One day, he assured me, she'll make salt water fresh.

He loved her completely and told me of Acumbaro,
His home and his family two thousand miles south.
He showed me the pictures, Nelida, the college,
Soon she would prosper, when all fees were paid.

Mine was his twelfth house, his last house, tuition.
His hands stained and stroking spread gray yellow white.
Sweat in his eyes before morning coffee
Scraping and sanding and filling each crack.

With dusk fell the full can, the white paint, the brushes,
The ladder, the roller, the painter from Acumbaro.
All for the white eaves, the crisp trim and gutters,
Gloss on the mullions and smooth satin boards.

His uncle from La Calera finished the painting,
Collected the money and wired it south.
Brushes and drop-cloth, trays gloss and satin,
Stored now and useless, soon to be trash.

Nelida from Acumbaro came to get her father
And learned the ladder had vanished one night.
Learned that her father could smile but not hold her.
And cared for him gently the rest of his days.

One customer who had stopped to listen clapped. Alex asked if we had questions. "Is it true? Is it about you?" I asked.

"Charlie, that's a very personal question," Claire said.

"It's fine," Alex said. "You're asking if I had my house painted by a man from Acumbaro? Or are you wondering if it's my father who fell from the ladder?"

"It's none of our business," Claire said. "It's a very moving poem."

"It's a sad poem—but beautiful, Alex," Simone said.

Henry nodded, smiled at Simone, and returned to check out a customer.

After a moment, Alex turned to me. "Let me ask you a question—about truth and fiction. For my poem ... does it matter if it's true—or about me?"

I drew a blank and Alex continued. "I presented that question to the group I teach at Beardsley. Here's the problem I posed: Does it matter if there was a Ulysses, Roland, or King Arthur? If, as we assume, Tom Sawyer and Huck Finn never lived, would it matter? And if there is—and there is—a shred of truth in Macbeth, Richard II, Hamlet, and Othello, is that what ensured the lasting brilliance of those works?"

There was an uncharacteristic silence. I don't think anyone expected anything vaguely like this from Alex.

When no one responded, Alex continued. "If the poem you just heard is not a recitation of fact, is it a lie? You asked if it was true—I will tell you. It is not entirely true—it is derivative. I was born in Acumbaro—a village in Mexico, northwest of Mexico City."

"But your name, Alex...."

"What about it?" Before I could explain yet another set of assumptions I had made, this time based on the name Alex, he continued, "Charlie, Alex is a common name in Mexico." Maurice nodded as if he knew that all along but I was fairly sure it was news to him as well.

"We moved to the United States when I was young." Alex explained. "Still, I stay in touch with friends from my hometown. My poem is not about me—but it draws on the experience of many people I have known. So—does that make the poem better? Worse?"

Alex's questions evoked that familiar discomfort I experienced when called on during my first year of law school. I knew there must be good answers to Alex's questions but for some reason, I couldn't think of anything but the comment that Alex was a common name in Mexico and said: "Does that mean you are Catholic?"

Claire rolled her eyes. "Oh my God, Charlie."

Maurice, in a gesture of kindness to me, deflected: "Alex, that's quite a topic for a poem. You discuss that with...." His voice trailed off.

"Old folks? People who have trouble walking, hearing, or remembering the names of their grandchildren?" Maurice was silent. "You bet. We discount the intelligence of our most experienced citizens because, for lack of a better term, they are not quick—not quick on their feet, not quick with a comeback. But ask them whether they enjoy a poem more because it's true, give them time, and then listen to what they have to say, and stand back." He paused. "Being thoughtful and being swift are not the same thing."

As the discussion on the virtue and limits of truth faded, I sat in quiet recognition that I had no idea what compelled Alex to teach poetry and piano, buy lottery tickets, or write so blue a poem. I did not know what memory he longed to expunge, problem he was trying to untangle, impulse that pushed him to overspend on the lottery. One thing was clear—he was far more than my naïve assumptions about his brown uniform suggested.

As the poem went back in his pocket, Maurice deflected a second time: "How's that dog of yours?"

The question, as usual, brought out a series of remarks about Flynn and dogs in general. Alex claimed that while those who deliver the U.S. mail are often the target of an angry dog, a similar fate was unlikely for people in the business of parcel delivery. He explained that this was the result of both the calming color of the uniforms and the size of the packages he delivered. It was a ridiculous theory and shifted the discussion. As was evident from his question about Flynn, that had been Maurice's goal and the tactic made me smile.

It was late February. Claire and I were now a week or so from leaving for the wedding and all restraint had vanished in our group. Some mornings there was talk of little else. Alex asked if we were both bringing gifts, Maurice asked if I wanted to borrow his tuxedo sweater, and Henry instructed the group on the formality of weddings in Nepal. I should note that Henry qualified this by making clear he was not from Nepal. Just why he chose to explain in great detail Nepalese nuptials was not easy to understand.

I assured everyone I had taken care of the gift. I then wondered, sharing the mystery with everyone, just what a tuxedo sweater might look like. Maurice began an extended discussion of how a sweater can serve many purposes and that the shape and colors of a tuxedo, including the bowtie and studs, can be woven into a sweater. Although intrigued, I passed on his offer.

Claire addressed the wedding in Nepal: "Since we are not headed to the Himalayas and this is presumably not a Buddhist wedding, my guess is that the traditions you described are probably not relevant to the wedding we will attend." She hestitated, "But if elephants are involved, I promise I will bring back many pictures."

This comment seemed to surprise Simone who said: "Henry does know a good deal about elephants."

Questions were raised regarding shoes, floral arrangements, the delicate matter of who will walk whom down the aisle, and of course questions about the venue. Where the guests (naturally, that meant us) would stay suddenly seemed an important topic, satisfying Claire's first hope that everyone at the Market would be wondering just what would transpire between her and me. This delicious uncertainty would remain an unknown, a source of speculation and mystery, and that satisfied Claire.

I, on the other hand, found the discussion embarrassing. At this juncture in the planning process, my goal was to survive with Claire as my friend. Anything more than that was unlikely, unexpected, and bordering on the impossible.

The morning ended unexpectedly. The discussion of the ceremony, good weddings and bad, and other gatherings where ritual mattered, led Alex to a statement none of us expected: "Weddings," he began, "are full of the unknown—always emotional. They are a great moment of hope, aren't they?"

He stopped and looked over our heads, out to the street. "The rituals associated with weddings matter in the moment, particularly the religious overlay, but at the end of the day or at the end of life—when things go as wrong as we fear they might—ritual and religion don't step up and mend the sick or pay the bills. All that happened at the wedding is past—and what remains is unbridled but fragmented faint hope." It was his exit line and Alex was gone in a matter of moments.

Maurice watched as he left. "By unbridled, did he mean unmarried?"

I was sure the answer was no—he meant unrestrained—but in deference to the sincerity of the question, I told him only that I didn't think so. Claire, rather than interpret Alex, ended the discussion.

"As long as I've known him, Alex never ceases to surprise me," and everyone nodded.

It was getting late. Within a few minutes, chairs squeaked, remaining coffee cups were emptied, coats were put on, and with only a few passing goodbyes, we left.

Chapter 7

Crossing the Susquehanna

A normal morning followed and I savored the simplicity. Even the coffee seemed better. The aroma, born of the familiar combination of milk and the mahogany brew, stayed light but well-defined and led me to hope, with some basis, it would not degrade to that dank, infected essence coffee can generate over time, a universal olfactory signature. After the first few sips I closed my eyes, content with my place at the Market.

Looking around the table, it appeared everyone was comforted by the same pleasant narcotic. After a time, comments from a customer at the counter caught my attention. As I turned, I saw Henry, passively and mechanically, taking in money for flashlight batteries and several bottles of soda.

He looked alone, disinterested in our reverie over his coffee. Something was churning in him, and his effort to sustain neutrality in affect and appearance may have fooled the customers—but I knew. Henry was going through the motions but inside, something was upside-down and out of order.

Perhaps it was as simple as this: not long after we were all assembled, Maurice left the table, walked to the counter, and began to chat quietly with Simone who, within a few moments, muffled a laugh as Maurice walked back to the table. Henry easily could conclude from that interaction that he was the subject of a private joke between these two indiscreet lovers—or he could conclude that Maurice had explained the reasoning behind his sweater, a cardigan masterpiece with multicolored fish diving above and below the waves. If it was the sweater explanation, I wish I'd been included. This garment required justification or, at a minimum, an apology.

Perhaps it was the intoxicating color wheel that was Maurice's sweater that caused me to drift, letting idle conversation flow over me as I sat back and took in the Market, noting incredible variation in colors everywhere I looked. Golden hues and multiple browns, four shades of orange, bright and pale whites, and yellows with a reddish cast were mixed with deep blue and turquoise. The colors were in candy wrappers, soda bottles, magazines, tissue boxes, and battery packets.

The entire canvas was bathed in light that varied from beaming fluorescent blue-white, to gray and pale yellow shadows in coves created by display shelves, to the morning glow that penetrated the spaces in the windows not covered by advertisements for soft drinks or phone cards.

Ordinarily, I am not given to observations of color, and thus the store's palette came at me unexpectedly. It crossed my mind that this was the artwork of hundreds of art majors from liberal arts colleges who, unable to make a living selling paintings to collectors and galleries, found careers designing the candy wrappers and soda bottles for countless producers, later to have their works displayed anonymously in the American Market.

There was detail and an intricacy in what I saw suggesting care and thought, levels of expression in animated characters that had to be the work of talented artists who labored in this field. I had taken for granted not just the artwork around me but the whole of the design of the store, the balance of the rows and counters, the calming intersection of the color of the vinyl on the floor and what could be seen of the walls.

Like the work of a confident abstract painter, at first blush the Market appeared as incoherent splatter, devoid of any organizing principle other than the sale of various goods and the desire to make a small profit. This was an entirely different way to see the Market; it was a magnificent collage of shapes and colors, of bold and unique geometric patterns.

That morning, for the first time, I saw the Market as art, modernist, magical, and more compelling than splotches slung by artists declared popular through the writings of critics and devotees determined to show how much they understood what the rest of us cannot possibly see. The Market was its own art form, unsuspecting and open, on display in this curiously convenient store, and as these thoughts ran through me, I wanted to share them with Claire.

I wanted Claire, whose business world was as gray as mine, to know there was more in the market than met the eye, and played out what I would say and how she might respond. I would gush about the beauty of the candy wrappers and then what? Would Claire agree, admit she never noticed, or would she brush it off as nothing more than a recognition that commercial art is a real profession. I looked at her, more accurately stared, trying to guess whether I would be lauded or mocked, and two things happened.

First, I saw that the pupils of her brown eyes had shades of pale green in the outermost rim and wisps of hair that framed the side of her face and covered her ear were faintly streaked with a lighter shade of brown. Second, I felt an urgency to hear her voice and touch her hand. I looked away, sensing my staring was too obvious, but something was different in me. I knew if I didn't say something to Claire, I would regret it.

The table discussion at the time, which I had followed only nominally, had to do with the style, if it could be called that, of oversized jewelry. When there was a lull, I turned to Claire and quietly, since I did not intend this to be a topic for the table, told her that I was quite taken with the all the colors in the Market.

"What do you mean?" she asked.

"The candy wrappers, the advertisements, the magazines—there is something about the colors and designs I hadn't noticed before."

She leaned toward me until she was inches from my face. "Better late than never," she whispered. "Charlie, let me introduce you to your right brain." She said this with a smile but the comment left me uncertain.

"There's something about today," I said. "I can't explain it, but everything I look at seems to have more to it than it had yesterday." It was a momentary victory that I was able to resist saying, "Even you—your eyes and hair are lovely—and your perfume reminds me of lemons and early spring roses."

She smiled and said: "Enjoy the moment. I hope it doesn't pass before our trip—you will be much more fun if you are open to design and color."

She leaned back and, without missing a beat, commented on the earrings worn by a teenager who had been in the store earlier that morning. They were huge and looked like identification bracelets patients wear in the hospital.

"If that is in vogue," Claire said, "vogue is in trouble," and as she was speaking, I felt her leg press against mine, lightly at first and then fully. My thigh muscle began to heat. I was acutely aware of each breath she took. She held that position for a full minute. When she moved her leg, it was all I could do to stop myself from putting my arms around her.

I waited to see if there would be more leg pressing—there wasn't—and was contemplating refilling my coffee cup when Henry cleared his throat. "I once knew a man who carried a pocketwatch the size of an orange."

Simone smiled and I assumed there was more to the story but all she said was, "I wonder if he made it out."

Henry looked down, a gesture that answered her question and added another piece to our puzzle of their past.

Claire broke the silence that followed, describing overpriced gold and jewel-laden monstrosities that cropped up on the wrists of some of her clients and then said: "These ridiculous watches broadcast ceaselessly, 'Come mug me before someone else does.'"

"Or," Maurice added, "the owners just like the feeling of wearing something that cannot help but catch the attention of everyone around them."

"Like a sweater embroidered with flying fish." It was Henry's first marginally light-hearted comment directed at Maurice in weeks and it broke the potent but unstated tension in the Market.

Alex laughed as if he'd been told the world's funniest joke—and we all knew that had not happened since there was no mention of a bar, horse, priest, rabbi, minister, lawyer, psychiatrist, magician, a limerick involving Nantucket, Saint Peter, any and all private body parts, chickens, camels, or, of course, flatulence. Alex's laughter was contagious and soon I heard the beginning of Claire's multi-toned laugh, first a few breathy inhalations, the hopeless suppression of what was to follow.

I walked to the coffee counter in the rear of the Market trying to assess where things stood. The mood was better but felt like a cover. The laughter, at the expense of Maurice's sweater, melted only part of the discomfort. I wanted to join in and laugh—as if laughter was a conscious choice—but it did not happen.

I am cut from a cloth that does not include a single uninhibited thread. All Pratts can smile. We were taught by professional photographers retained to chronicle our existence. These photo sessions were undertaken with the hope that one day there would be reason to put out campaign flyers (some Pratts have political ambitions because of the financial opportunities elected office would create) or write a biography of someone in the clan who achieved prominence by doing something more than reinvesting assets earned by earlier generations. Thus encumbered by genetics and environment (and I really don't know which matters more), I smiled as warmly as I could, enjoyed the depth of Claire's laughter, and nodded, hoping to convey support and approval of the release laughter permits.

Walking out of the Market that morning, I noticed Councilwoman Celia Bell in a car across the street and Maurice leaning into her window. While I could not hear what they were saying, I assumed it was a continuation of Maurice's attack of the failure of the Jackson Park Council to slow down or block the urbanization of our community. I walked a few paces and, for no particular reason, turned back in the direction of Councilwoman Bell's car and watched as it drove off. I expected to see Maurice on the sidewalk after the car left, but he was gone.

As we drove to the park, I wondered out loud (to Flynn of course) where Maurice had gone. Why would he take a ride with Councilwoman Bell? Could it be that she was taking him to see her opponents on the Council so that they could be brought to see her—and Maurice's—point of view? That seemed unlikely to Flynn and me, and we entertained two other possibilities.

First, she may simply be giving him a ride to work ... if he worked at all. While I was aware of and intrigued by his choice of celibacy without theological compulsion, I did not know what he did after leaving the Market each day. I did know—assuming I believed him—what he did not do.

Flynn and I mulled over a second hypothesis while walking in the park, getting soaked in an icy winter rain. I looked at Flynn and realized that, once again, my car would bear his unavoidable and sharp wet dog essence for days. With the long drive to the wedding now only a couple of days away, the timing could not have been worse.

Recognizing there was nothing I could do about the smell that would take hold in my car, my thoughts moved back to Maurice. Suppose, and this also assumes almost everything, including some rather troubling features of Maurice's character, Maurice's story about abstinence was a complete lie, cooked up to keep me from thinking he was having a sexual affair with Simone (that there was at least an emotional affair of sorts was not a debatable point). Suppose further that not only was Maurice involved with Simone, he also had a romantic relationship with Councilwoman Bell.

Flynn was his regular sagacious and affirming self as these thoughts flitted around in my mind. He listened carefully, pausing only to lick my hand at one point. It was the only deviation from the actively listening, Freudian persona he assumed when I needed to work something through. By the end of the walk, I concluded, and Flynn concurred, I was overthinking this. Overthought or not, though, I could not let go of the mystery of Maurice's disappearance.

The next morning, I arrived early and waited outside in the cold until I saw Maurice. I did not want to bring this discussion into the Market. "I noticed you speaking with Councilwoman Celia Bell after you left the Market yesterday."

"Were you following me?" Maurice asked.

"No. Of course not. Her car was across the street. I saw you speaking with her before the car left."

"And?" Maurice asked.

"And—what happened?"

"She gave me a ride," he said. I wanted to ask where he was going and why he agreed to ride with Councilwoman Bell but thought better of it.

"Why the questions, Charlie?" The true answer was that I wanted to know if he had made up the entire story of his asexuality to avoid or qualify any discussion of his personal life.

"It was odd — that's all. You just seemed to disappear into thin air."

He smiled. "It's nice that you care." He hesitated. "I'm just fine."

Before we were inside the Market, Maurice stopped me. "Speaking of unexplained encounters with the opposite sex, I think that British woman — the one with the donut dog — fancies you."

"That's ridiculous. I've never spoken to her, beyond that day in the Market — and it's not donut, it's Dunker." Maurice smiled. "Have you ever seen a Dunker?" He shook his head. "They're a third the size of Flynn but solid — an impressive breed. The one in the park is businesslike. He walks at the exact pace of his owner, rarely strains on the leash, and appears on constant alert without being aggressive."

The truth is, I remembered more about the dog than his owner, perhaps because in contrast, Flynn is an un-Dunker. He's lazy, overweight, and when motivated — almost always by something he thinks he can eat — strains on the leash to the point of dragging me. I can't imagine the Dunker doing similar things. Then again, I can't imagine the Dunker understanding me at the level Flynn does.

It was not my morning to sit — at least not right away. Claire followed me to the coffee counter and said: "Don't you think it's about time? Isn't the wedding this weekend?" I nodded.

She turned and looked at Henry who was on the other side of the store. "I am looking forward to our drive," she said. "It will be nice to be able to speak to you without everyone listening or guessing what we're saying."

I turned toward the table and she was right — Alex, Maurice, and Simone were all staring at us. "I'll call you tonight. We will need to leave early on Friday morning."

"I assume you are boarding Flynn?"

"He's staying at my vet's — they board dogs."

"You should leave him at my place — Melissa will take care of him."

"I can't risk it," I said. "I don't trust Flynn around teenagers—
or people on bikes, men with beards...."

"I know the list," she said. "Everyone knows the list." She smiled.
"I hope you're looking forward to this, Charlie."

Thursday morning, the day before the journey to Vermont, started
with no mention of the upcoming trip. Perhaps, at least at first, it
was too real, too intimate, too personal to be within the safety zone
of the table. Even Henry stayed away from the topic. It was not until
people started putting on coats and were getting ready to head out
that Maurice said: "Have a safe trip." That prompted a series of nervous good-byes, as if Claire and I were heading to the Himalayas to
climb K-2 without ropes or oxygen. Simone came out from behind
the counter and urged Claire to take pictures. Alex shook my hand
and said: "Have fun." I waited for a knowing wink but there was
none. As we were walking out the door, Henry called out: "Stop by
before you get on the road. I will have fresh coffee waiting."

Shortly after seven that evening, for the second time in my life,
I spoke with Claire on the phone. I was more prepared than when
we had spoken weeks ago.

"I've been looking at maps," she began. "I had no idea how long
a trip this was."

"Burlington is a haul—I think we can make it in under twelve
hours."

"I don't know about you," she said, "but the prospect of driving that distance in one day is unappealing. I don't want to arrive exhausted."

I thought it odd, even under these unusual circumstances, that
Claire would back out at the last minute. I had thought about this trip
so much, considered every aspect of it in detail, played out the options and possibilities, that a change in plans—particularly a change
that involved her bailing on the weekend—left me speechless.

"Are you packed?" she asked.

"I have been packed for several days." I had made lists, laid out
a few last-minute items to minimize wrinkling, and had filled the
car with gas. "I should have told you that this was a long drive. I
grew up in Maine and almost everywhere we went involved long
drives. I'm sorry I didn't ..."

"You haven't done anything wrong." I sat down next to Flynn and waited to see what she would say next. "Let's leave tonight. We can drive three or four hours then stop and get some sleep. That way, the drive tomorrow will be more manageable. Are we invited to anything tomorrow night—a rehearsal dinner? Cocktail hour?"

My mind was racing. The prospect of a third night with Claire— even in different motel rooms—suggested new possibilities. Suddenly I knew why this could not work: Flynn. I had made arrangements to drop him off at the vet's early tomorrow morning. They were expecting me around 6:00 am. In addition, Henry expected us to stop by and pick up coffee before we left. I raised these concerns with Claire and received another unexpected response.

"I love the idea that everyone will be expecting us to stop by tomorrow morning—and we're not there. I can see Henry pacing around and snapping at people." She said this with excitement, as if the prospect of adding mystery to our weekend was something she valued more than I suspected. It passed through my mind that the whole point of the trip, at least for Claire, was to create uncertainty at the table. She continued, "Call your veterinarian and see if anyone is there. If not, you can drop Flynn off at my house and Melissa can take him to the kennel tomorrow."

I called, and to my surprise, one of the assistants was still at the animal hospital and told me he'd be there for some time.

I drove to Claire's house, met Melissa, and were on the road before 9:00 pm. We had gone less than five minutes when Claire turned to me. "You didn't answer my question. Is there anything planned for tomorrow night?"

No doubt there was an insert card in the invitation with instructions and details for the wedding, and supplemental information for Friday night—or not. Unfortunately, despite my obsessive planning for the weekend, I had absolutely no recollection of that one detail.

I am not the type to be invited to weddings, outside of family, and more often than not I come up with an excuse not to go. When I do attend a family wedding, and Pratt family weddings tend to be large, expensive, and completely scripted, family are invited to whatever takes place on Friday night. Sometimes it's a rehearsal dinner, sometimes a "meet and greet," (often an excuse for a second showy reception and dinner), or, as was the case recently with one of my cousins, a martini bar and heavy *hors d'oeuvres*—a riotous event in which almost everyone drank too much, leading to a series of loud arguments and even one shoving match that resulted in torn trousers. In short, Friday nights are often the most interesting, least predictable, most revealing, and least scripted part of such weddings.

The invitation to Jennifer's wedding was safely packed in my bag—and my bag was safely stowed in the trunk of the car. Unable to get to the invitation, I turned to Claire and said: "There was something tomorrow night ... I am not sure about the details." This was not entirely true but I did not want to appear unprepared.

"You don't know whether it's a formal event or a clam bake on the beach?"

It took me a minute to respond. "Burlington doesn't have beaches—although it is on Lake Champlain." I stopped. Maybe there were beaches. I was not sure.

"We'll find out tomorrow. I was just curious." She paused. "These questions—I'm sure you understand I am just as nervous as you. I don't really care about tomorrow night." It had not dawned on me that she was anxious about the weekend. She was probably more aware of the implications of this weekend than I—and realizing she was a bit on edge was endearing.

We drove through suburban streets, weaving between trucks, buses, pedestrians, and bicyclists, and in less than fifteen minutes turned onto an entrance ramp to the Capital Beltway.

Everyone in this region is aware of the Beltway as an important, jam-packed part of the ground transportation network in the city—and everyone here and beyond is equally aware of the Beltway as a political symbol. Smug commentators speak of those "Inside the Beltway" as a most special in-group, some of whom are part of a secretive and byzantine legislative and regulatory process. Thinking about our group at the American Market for a moment, none of us are involved in lobbying and none rely on or seek out government funds. From that perspective, I see our Market as a common place, recognizable in any state, in any city or town. For us,

the Beltway is little more than a highway that, under the right circumstances, can save time—and under the wrong circumstances,
leave you motionless in your car for a very long time.

Claire reached to the dashboard. "Mind if I turn on the radio?
Let's see what kind of traffic we'll hit." I nodded and soon heard
the good news that the evening rush hour was over and we would
have smooth sailing. We left the Beltway and headed north on Interstate 95. While this is also a heavily traveled route, traffic had
thinned and we breezed along toward Baltimore and through the
old tunnel, the Harbor Tunnel, as opposed to the lateral gaping
maw of the newer Fort McHenry Tunnel.

We rode on, chatting about Maurice's sweaters, the weather,
and Flynn. As you might suspect, Flynn's essence was still lingering and Claire noticed it almost immediately. I was a bit unsure
how things would go when her first words after getting in the car
were: "What's that smell?" But we drove with the windows open
and, after a time, I think she acclimated ... or, more likely, was
nasally numbed.

Our main discussion, of course, focused on the wedding. Claire
talked about family weddings and the spate of weddings that followed her graduation from college. "I came to dread the invitations—each one meant time and money ... after the first three or
four, I'd had enough."

I was not burdened with multiple wedding invitations from
friends after college or at any other time. Moreover, as you know,
time and money have not been issues for me in my adult life. "I
can see how that would be draining," I said, hoping that would be
the end of it—and it was.

It was well after ten when we crossed the Susquehanna River on
the simple flat elegance of the Miller E. Tydings Memorial Bridge.
While the Susquehanna does not compare in commercial value to
the Mississippi, Missouri, Ohio, and the great rivers of the West,
it is one of my favorite rivers. It has been overused for commercial
purposes, polluted and then the subject of long and marginally
successful cleanup efforts, not to mention hosting, on Three Mile
Island, the site of the worst disaster at a civilian nuclear power plant
in the history of this country.

Below us, this great river flowed under one of the most heavily traveled stretches of interstate highway in the Western hemisphere. However, almost every time I cross this river, my thoughts drift back to a time when none of the magnificence and horrors man created rested on its shores.

What a sight it must have been for hunters venturing south, predecessors of the Nanticoke and Lenni-Lenape, expanding outward, seeking routes for commerce, to find this miracle flowing through forests, ready and waiting. On occasion, I think of those who followed—ecclesiastically or politically funded explorers in search of new lands to conquer and populations ripe for trade and commerce—or to civilize to the point of extinction.

"You're somewhere else," Claire said. "What's going on up there?"

"The river. Did you see it?" She nodded. "The first time I drove to Washington from Maine, I crossed the Susquehanna and pulled off the road. I knew the Hudson and the Potomac—but the Susquehanna took me by surprise. In later trips, I pulled off at different exits to get closer to the water."

I rambled on about the river, sharing with Claire some of what I just shared with you. She turned in her seat and leaned toward me. "You're full of surprises." After a moment, she continued. "I've lived in Washington most of my life. I know this road well—and, I hope this is not a disappointment Charlie, but I have often driven over the Susquehanna without giving it a second thought."

Before I could continue my riparian monologue, she reclined her seat. "I'm going to close my eyes for a few minutes," she said. "If we decide to split the driving, I'll do better if I sleep a bit beforehand."

I had not considered that we would share driving responsibilities and said nothing. I don't recall ever allowing anyone to drive my car, perhaps because no one ever asked.

Claire crossed her arms, tilted her head to one side, and was asleep in a matter of minutes. I could hear her breathing and every now and then saw her body move slightly. We passed Wilmington, crossed the Delaware Memorial Bridge, and headed up the New Jersey Turnpike.

We were beyond Philadelphia when Claire woke with a start. "Where are we?" she asked.

"About a half-hour south of Trenton."

"It's after midnight," she said. "We should stop."

Stopping meant finding a hotel and confronting the complex question of who sleeps where. We exited the Turnpike and within fifteen minutes were speaking to a tired clerk at the Stansfield Hotel who asked if we wanted a king-sized bed or two double beds. Before I could answer, Claire said, "Two double beds and some extra towels."

"I'm fine with either," I said. I was sure we were talking about two hotel rooms.

The clerk looked exasperated. "Well, which is it—king-sized or double beds—we have both—same price."

Claire was in control. "We want one room, two double beds, extra towels, and a wake-up call at seven thirty."

"There's a coffee maker in the room," the clerk yawned, "and you get our complimentary breakfast buffet."

The room, priced surprisingly high—presumably the captive market generated by the Turnpike allowed for such piracy—was clean but otherwise modest. While no extra towels arrived, there was small hotel refrigerator and a cabinet (along with a form to check off any item consumed) well-stocked with various bourbons, whiskies, vodka, beer, and an assortment of nuts and crackers.

Claire left the room, brought back a bucket of ice, sat down on one of the two beds. "Be a decent host, Charlie. Make me a drink. You said you weren't tired, and I just slept for most of the drive—are you hungry?"

I was neither hungry nor thirsty but decided to join Claire and poured two bourbons over ice, splashed in some spring water—a bottle was available in the room for $6—and sat down next to Claire. "Here's to an interesting trip," she said and lifted her glass.

We heard people talking as they walked down the hall outside our room. "These walls are paper-thin," Claire said. "Find something on the clock radio—there's one on the nightstand. I'm enjoying our privacy."

I began fiddling with the buttons on the radio and was getting nowhere. "Does anyone actually use these?" I asked.

"I do," she said. I handed her the radio and a few moments later heard a soft voice explain that they—Claire quickly concluded it was a public radio station—were celebrating piano concertos tonight and we would be treated to works by Chopin, Schumann, Ries, Brahms, Liszt, Mendelssohn, and others. "Perfect," she said. She set down the radio and turned up the volume slightly.

We discussed our drinking habits briefly. Neither of us, we noted, drank often, but this was a special occasion and a drink or two felt about right. I remember pouring the third drink because it was the end of the little bourbon bottles and the start of a more aggressive rye.

After that third drink, I was well across the border of sobriety and during the fourth, in an impromptu game Claire invented, was unable to spell or pronounce without slurring the word *Susquehanna*.

Somewhere between the final notes of Liszt and the increasingly inviting whisky, Claire got up and turned off the remaining lights in the room.

She came back to the bed in the new near darkness, sat close to me, took the glass from my hand, and placed it on the nightstand. I turned to her and she whispered: "Take off your shoes, Charlie." With that, she put her head down on the pillows and pulled me toward her.

Brahms began, clothing fell to the floor, and there was Claire—soft, strong, passionate, surprising, and complete.

I awoke the following morning, shielding my eyes from light leaking through the curtains. I had a headache, but I have had worse. My dominant sense was physical, a powerful longing for Claire. I called her name and when there was no response, looked around and discovered I was alone. An impressive collection of small, empty liquor bottles stood on the dresser. The other bed in the room had been slept in but was empty.

I took a few shortcuts with my morning ablutions and walked to the lobby. Claire was sitting at a banquette with a cup of coffee and a Danish pastry in front of her. "I wondered how long it would take you to find me," she said. "I tried to be quiet when I left the room." She sipped the coffee, told me it was better than Henry's. "You snored only lightly."

"And you," I asked, "how did you sleep?"

After a long pause, a quiet, "Fine, thanks for asking," was the extent of her response.

Before my first sip of coffee, in the coarse light of the Stansfield Hotel Breakfast Room, I looked carefully at Claire and quickly drew the conclusion that in the interest of letting me sleep, her noiseless exit from the room required her to bypass almost entirely her morning personal routines. I'm not saying she looked askew or disheveled—but I realized there must be things she did every morning, makeup of one sort or another, before coming to the Market. Today, perhaps for the first time, as I saw her closer than I usually do, I knew those rituals had not taken place.

Before you conclude I am even more presumptuous and shallow than this assessment of Claire's appearance suggests—and I recognize my tendency to critique human externalities is not among my better qualities—I hasten to add two things.

First, unadorned by whatever it was Claire did to her hair and face before joining us at the Market each morning, I found her powerfully attractive. Second, and I'm sure you've already made this realization, while I have been intimate with other women in my 42 years, these experiences rarely went beyond one evening. I can count on one hand the number of times they extended to the following morning—and those mornings consisted of rushed goodbyes as either my date or I headed home.

I reached over and with one hand, gently turned Claire's face toward mine and was going to kiss her but she turned away.

That one gesture brought to an end my idea of a happy return to our room to spend more time listening to public radio, a euphemism I'm sure Claire would understand quite well. Instead, the reality of time and what I feared was her unstated doubt prevailed. We packed, checked out, and were back on the road.

Leaving the hotel, I had never been more enamored with Claire nor more uncertain about our relationship. I wanted affirmation. I mulled over different options as we pulled onto the northbound lanes of the New Jersey Turnpike and after a time decided on a direct approach.

If you have been in a similar situation, you know that on the morning after it is next to impossible to discuss usefully your first intimacy—but I was so uncertain, so unsure, and words began to take shape in my mind. I sensed that questions such as, "Well, how was it for you?" or "Did you—you know—really feel satisfied?" were not just idiotic. They were traps, highly unlikely to produce an honest or productive response, and so I opted for the declarative. "That was quite a night."

I hoped Claire would volunteer something, but instead, she seemed transfixed by the car in front of us, a light-green Ford sedan with two occupants and Illinois license plates. "I wonder if they're headed to New York City," Claire said, and then, without moving her head added, "Maybe they're visiting for the first time."

To say she seemed a bit distant does not capture her detachment. After a time she continued. "I remember going to the City with my mother when I was nine. We saw the New York City Ballet perform *The Nutcracker*." Discussion of the Illinois couple was fading to nothingness.

"I've never been to a ballet," I said.

"Maybe I'll take you one day." After another pause she said: "Back then, Balanchine was still...." She stopped, turning away from the touristic Illini and hypnotic green sedan and looked out the side window. "Don't take your eyes off the road but there are deer grazing just off the Turnpike. I see four—no, five."

"I've heard of Balanchine, of course." I stopped, quite sure she was not listening to me. She was looking out the back window at this point, presumably taking in the last glimpse of the deer. "Did you take ballet lessons when you were growing up?" I asked.

"I still do," she said without turning around.

As this startling piece of information floated around for several seconds, it crossed my mind that if I opened the window, even a crack, one by one her words, reduced to gossamer pointillistic letters, would fragment and, dot by dot, fly out and upward, disembodied with the rush of outside air.

I wondered when Claire, who seemed busier than any of us around the table in the Market, found time to take dance lessons. Instead of asking "When do you go—you seem so busy," which seemed fawning and patronizing, I said, "Is it like aerobics—something you do to stay in shape?"

I did not realize my irretrievable response was quite so problematic. "Right, Charlie. I dance because I need the exercise."

I should have seen—but didn't—that this was not headed in a safe direction. "I jog—that's my exercise—I feel better when I can run a few times a week."

"Helps keep your girlish figure?"

I have a fairly normal body for a male of my years but girlish is certainly not a term that seemed even vaguely accurate. Had I known at the time that Claire's question was not meant literally and was somewhere between humor and satire, I might have answered differently.

"Not really girlish," I said, and then: "Is that why you dance?"

Claire took a deep breath, exhaled slowly, and said, "You really have no idea how to speak with women, do you?"

I instantly played back what had just transpired and still did not see where I had made a wrong turn: "We got sidetracked. I was asking about last night." And after more silence added: "I really liked it."

"You liked it?" She stopped. "You liked having sex? Did you expect you wouldn't?"

I was out of answers and shook my head.

"Is that a yes or a no?"

I gave myself a few moments and finally said: "I don't know what we're talking about."

"Let see … dance, sex with me for the first time in our lives, exercise, deer along the side of the road—take your pick."

"Sex with you?"

"Charlie," she said quietly, "are you trying to ask if it was good for me? If I was content—meaning, I guess, if you were a competent lover?"

This time I smiled the most ambiguous smile I could manage, taking a page from Henry's book of non-responses. When I did not answer, she said: "Do you really need to ask me that question?"

I managed another smile.

"Is sex like a contest—you perform and then see if you scored well?"

"No—nothing like that. I just wanted to know if you…."

I thought she would say, "That's none of your business," but instead she said, "It was very pleasant. I thought I was pretty clear about that last night."

I looked ahead, hoping to find the hypnotic green sedan—something on which I could focus before I answered her truthfully. "I don't remember all that was said towards the very end of the evening. I know I was happy, tired, and had too much to drink."

As I look back on that part of the drive, I realize that with those words, I nullified some important aspect of last night. What did she say that I should remember? What did I say? Did we confess our love? Assess the satisfactory nature of our intimacy? Compare our lovemaking with other experiences we've had?

A thought occurred to me as we got our first glimpse of the southernmost contours of Newark and New York City. We had made love on our first date. That almost never happens in my experience. Actually, sorting through my barely sordid past, it never happens—but was that common for Claire?

In sharp contrast with my one and perfectly remembered sexual experience with Jennifer Strong—who, I confess, has been on my mind for weeks—I felt sure we'd made love last night and not just had sex. I awoke feeling we were a couple—no longer single—but now I was unsure.

It dawned on me after a time that I was reading too much into all that had happened from the first bourbon forward. My hope for greater clarity was extinguished when Claire, rather than giving more definition to last night, said: "Let's listen to some music," and began to search the radio for something to blot out, for now, the possibility of further discussion.

The next phase of the drive was a blur of gas stations, restrooms, a diner, and commentary on traffic. Just after Chicopee, I pulled over at a rest stop and asked Claire if she wanted to drive for a while. I did not tell her it was the first time I had ever let anyone drive my car—but it was.

An hour or so later, she breezed through a radar trap on I-91 and was almost immediately pulled over by a Vermont state trooper. After collecting her license and my registration and confirming with me that the car was not stolen—an inquiry requiring the trooper

to take my license as well—he asked Claire: "Were you aware that
you were going 80 miles an hour?"

"I wasn't going that fast," she replied.

"You were clocked on the radar gun at 80 mph."

"There's something wrong with the radar gun—or the speedometer in the car."

Both Claire and the trooper looked at me as if I could confirm
her assertion that the speedometer was off. "It might be off," I said.
"I haven't checked it lately."

"No one checks their speedometer," the trooper said. "And whether
it is accurate or not is irrelevant. Ma'am, you were speeding."

"I wasn't—I was going slower than the flow of traffic and my
speedometer was right at 65.

"Can you step outside of the car please?"

"What? Why?"

He paused. "Because I smell something—it is fairly strong—
and I wonder whether you've been drinking. That's why."

It was downhill from there. While pedestrian hotel bourbon can
leave a not-so-subtle after-taste and aroma, we later concluded that
it was the potent Flynn funk the officer mistook for alcohol. Thus,
when Claire took a breathalyzer, she passed—and then glared at him:
"What did I tell you?" That comment prompted a lengthy roadside
sobriety test that she passed as well. Finally, as she was getting back
into the car, Claire said—and not *sotto voce*, "What a jackass."

I'm sure this did not help the situation. Claire's ticket for speeding and, thrown in undoubtedly on the strength of the jackass comment, for reckless driving, was for $450. When I said to give me
the ticket and I would take care of it, she sighed. "I can pay for my
own ticket—and I have half a mind to come back here and challenge this in court."

"I'll go with you. A lawyer at your side can't hurt."

"Good." By that response you might think she meant "thank
you" but the tone implied unequivocally a quest for vindication
and justice ... and it was not the end of her reaction. I will not
share with you what she said next in reference to the police officer.
It's not the kind of thing she would want me to report. When she
finished her rather colorful diatribe, we returned to the far safer

topic of the beautiful Vermont landscape. We stopped at an over-
look and took pictures and when we were back on the road, finally
began to focus on the wedding.

As it turned out, before I awoke, Claire found the wedding invitation on top of my clothes in my suitcase with the insert card.
Apparently everyone was invited to a rehearsal dinner this evening,
though it did not seem to Claire that anything was going to be rehearsed. "It said this would be a relaxing evening before the festiv-
ities on Saturday. Does that mean informal?"

"I have no idea. This group is not given to informality." My comment convinced Claire that this evening called for something more
than business casual but less than dressed-to-the-nines.

Satisfied with the matter of attire, Claire transitioned. "Since I
won't get to see your hometown on this trip, tell me a little about
Brampton."

Anxious to find something positive, I read into her question the
possibility of another trip. However, a junket to Brampton would
not be my choice, assuming I had an option on destination, and I
gave her a straightforward answer disconnected from the matter of
future travel. "Brampton has a small town center—I guess one
would call it quaint. It's smaller than Jackson Park—but the broad
legal entity, Brampton Township, covers more than two-hundred
square miles, about half state parkland and the remainder divided
into residential tracts where the minimum lot per single-family
home (the only type allowed in Brampton) is 25 acres."

Claire took this in slowly and after time said, "I've never heard
of anything like that."

"If you want a community consisting exclusively of the very
wealthy, the minimum acreage requirement is all you need." Claire
needed no further explanation of exclusionary zoning in Brampton and the shifted gears. She seemed intent on building in her
mind a picture of my childhood surroundings and asked about the
house in which I grew up. I told her only that it was very large—
and that the only part of the property in which I had any interest
was the guest house I inherited when my mother passed away.

Her interest in our real estate faded after a time, and the discussion moved to the more immediate topic of the brides, Saman-

tha and Jennifer. This led to a thumbnail sketch of Samantha's family, the Eckingtons, and Jennifer's, the Strongs, and that, somehow, led to a more detailed discussion of my relationship with Jennifer. I may have given more information than necessary because, when we were just south of Mount Ascutney State Park, Claire stopped me. "I think I get the picture," and then almost as an afterthought, "I can't wait to meet this woman."

We turned onto Interstate 89, passed the exit to the state capital, and were in Burlington at sunset. We found the New Marlow Inn, changed clothes, and in short order made our way to Plackingham Farm, the setting for the rehearsal dinner and tomorrow, the wedding and reception.

Chapter 8

The Wedding
March 2013

The rehearsal dinner was set in one of several massive barns on the Plackingham Farm property. As we approached the barn, we saw a corral with a number of saddled horses, each attended to by a groomsman. When I mentioned that I thought it odd for there to be groomsmen for each horse, Claire turned to me. "Do you think they're groomsmen—or groomsmen?"

"What?"

"Think about it."

From where we stood, I could see the interior of the barn and groups of guests—painfully familiar faces from Brampton and beyond—and my mind went blank.

"Charlie?" When I did not reply, she said: "The word—groomsmen—is a wedding term—you know, ushers—and is also the word used to describe people who care for horses."

I hope you see the wit in this—Claire did—but I barely heard her.

We walked inside. Toward the rear of the barn were thirty or so large tables set up with white linen table cloths, elegant china and silver, twelve place settings per table.

Guests were assembling on the right side of the barn that was connected by an enormous open archway to another building where waitstaff in formal dress were serving appetizers and drinks. Although there were at least a hundred guests by the time we arrived, I saw my father and his wife, Priscilla Coughlin—I cannot stomach calling her my stepmother at this point—almost immediately. As we walked toward them, my father saw me and said, "Charlie—I wondered if you were going to show up."

"It never crossed my mind that you would be here," I said. I had been holding Claire's hand and she gave me a healthy squeeze. I turned and looked at her and realized I had failed to introduce her. "Dad, this is my friend, Claire." My father introduced his wife whom I had met only a few times before.

Priscilla Coughlin was at least twenty years his junior and had been a reporter for the *Entertainment, Life, and Leisure* section of one of the large newspapers in Boston. She met my father doing a story on the remnants of the Maine aristocracy. It was not long after the death of my mother and, while this may seem callous, she saw an opportunity and seized it. My father is nobody's fool—I believe he knew exactly what he was doing and the implications for the rest of us in the family. That made his decision to marry her even more unpalatable.

After a round of insincere but firm Prattian handshakes, near-miss kisses and non-contact hugs, there were awkward exchanges about Brampton, the house, and a few inconsequential relatives. Out of the blue, my father said: "Well, Charlie, I guess this is the end of hope for you and Jennifer."

My father had been part of the conspiracy to marry me off to Jennifer and presumably this was his idea of a joke. The Strongs owned a massive, publically traded, enormously profitable lumber company founded by their ancestors before the Civil War, and I'm sure a union between the Strongs and the Pratts had made great financial sense to the elders in both families.

"You know that was an act to keep her parents from prying into her life," I said.

"Maybe on her part," my father said, "but I think this whole lesbian thing caught you off-guard." He turned to Claire. "Charlie was sweet on the bride—or do we call her a bride? And what will they declare tomorrow—'I now pronounce you wife and wife'?" He laughed as if he had stumbled on a matter of great and theretofore undiscovered humor. I was dumbfounded.

Claire opened her mouth to reply but before she could form a response either to the comment about my relationship with Jennifer or my father's ill-mannered humor, Priscilla Coughlin stepped in. "It's a wedding, dear," she said, "between two people." She paused. "Back when I was with the newspaper, I would have covered this from stem to stern." She looked around. "History is being made, dear."

I couldn't decide whether her reference to my father as 'dear' or her use of a nautical term was more offensive to me.

Claire smiled. "I like the idea of being a witness to history."

"History—hell—there's nothing here that merits inclusion in the history books my grandchildren will read." My father's eyes narrowed as he scanned the room. "What a show," was all he could manage.

Claire had had enough. "It was such a pleasure to meet you," she said. "Charlie, let's get a drink."

There is a statutory minimum for such exchanges and in my view it's five minutes. Certain it was the conclusion of the fifth minute (you would be happy to know I did not check my watch—I could just tell), I said, "Sounds great. Excuse us."

"My friend, Claire?" Claire asked as we walked away.

"What do you mean?"

"You introduced me as your friend." She stopped. "At least I could have been your good friend."

"You are my good friend," I said.

"Oh, Charlie. What are we doing?"

"Trying to enjoy this weekend?" I was at a loss. It was as if, in the presence of my blue-blooded father and the assembled self-designated aristocracy of my childhood, someone had taken hold of the last twenty years of my life and packed them carefully in a steamer trunk.

"And Jennifer? Is he right?" Claire asked.

I almost said, "About what?" but recovered enough to provide the non-answer: "My father is an ass, Claire."

We ended up at a bar at the far corner of the barn. Claire and I had vodka martinis and thusly marginally numbed, walked past waitstaff offering appetizer platters mounded with three different types of caviar, assorted meat and herb stuffed pastries, fresh sliced tropical fruits (flown in this morning, we were told), sections of duck breast, bacon-wrapped diver scallops, and walked out into the evening air to regroup.

Jennifer and Samantha had taken an extraordinary risk. It was early March in Vermont and it could have been minus 10 degrees, but the weather had cooperated. It wasn't warm but it wasn't intolerably cold either.

Above were the remarkably clear stars I knew well more than a quarter of a century ago. Here, a few miles outside the limited lights of Burlington, all the common constellations were evident as was the gauzy belt of the Milky Way. We were freed momentarily of my father, Priscilla Coughlin, and the select of Brampton, Bar Harbor, Cape Elizabeth, and beyond. Those who graced this event with their barely cloaked superiority were the members of the generational aristocracy I knew as a child.

I kept to myself my assessment of this sea of arrogance and turned to Claire. I'm sure she saw something very different. After all, this was her first exposure to this group. Most were in good shape, courtesy of personal trainers and plastic surgeons, and most, but not all, wore beautifully tailored outfits.

I watched as she glanced inside the barn, looking from couple to couple, probably wondering how such seemingly staid and conservative guests found themselves at one of the first—if not the first—Vermont high society gay weddings. As I watched Claire scan the room, taking in details, I was certain I was in love with her. I was about to say just that and then, for some reason, stopped. I found myself staring at Samantha's parents, Isaiah and Faye Eckington.

I pointed them out to Claire. "I didn't think they would show up," I said. "I look at them, think about my parents and the people with whom I grew up, and wonder if there are any happy marriages left in New England."

Claire took a step back. "Of course there are," she said. "We are about to see one celebrated. This barn is full of people who are married—why assume they're all unhappy?"

"It's not an assumption. I know this group. I am one of them. These are people of incredible wealth—and they are, when you peel away the surface, a bitter group. It's the reason I left Maine."

"Are you telling me you think it is not possible to have a happy relationship?"

"No—I am not that pessimistic."

"Let's go back inside, Charlie. I want to meet Jennifer and Samantha."

It took twenty minutes of circling before we had our audience with the brides. Jennifer shook her head slowly as we approached. "Oh my—Charlie Pratt." She hugged me and said quietly: "I knew you'd come—oh, my dear Charlie … I'm so happy to see you." She kissed my cheek and then, as we separated, said: "Look at you. I can hardly believe you're here."

The words and embrace traveled two decades. It was impossible not to recall acutely and sense intimately the contours of her body, the familiar and natural perfumes of her hair, the irresistible tone of her voice.

There was a brief and regrettable silence before my common sense reengaged and I said: "This is my guest—my very special friend, Claire Beaumont."

Handshakes were followed by sequential hugs with Samantha and Jennifer. Before anyone could say another word, a woman Henry would have characterized as handsome (who we later learned was part of the wedding planning collective) put her hand on Jennifer's shoulder and delivered an undecipherable whisper. Jennifer's visible disappointment almost made unnecessary her explanation. "I'm sorry, Claire. I'd love to chat but apparently we have to run— let's make sure to talk either later tonight or tomorrow." With that, Jennifer and Samantha were rushed away to join several photographers who had assembled what appeared to be one contingent of the wedding party.

"She's beautiful," Claire said as they walked away. "I can understand your infatuation."

"Yes … well … a long time since.…" I was sputtering and then stopped as a long and straight line of grim-faced waitstaff passed directly in front of us, walking in step much like members of a marching band. They came from the rear of the barn and carried precariously balanced and impossibly large trays, each with twelve salad plates. There was ceremony and inexplicable pomposity in their entrance, and it was my good fortune that it struck Claire as absurd.

She covered her mouth to keep from bursting out laughing and said between gasps: "This is what you New Englanders consider an informal dinner? State dinners at the White House are less formal."

"I've never been to one."

"Neither have I," she said. "But it's a fair guess."

It was also a seamless way to glide from any further discussion about Jennifer who, as you might have guessed from Claire's comment, was beyond description. Her long, light-brown hair was braided and pulled into an intricate knot atop her head (which Claire later called 'wedding hair'), giving emphasis to her wide-set gray-blue eyes and smile. Hers was that rare and unforgettable visage that welcomed and comforted, acknowledging your decency, your contribution to the social order, your fundamental goodness.

All thirty tables would have their salads delivered simultaneously. The salads would sit, warming and wilting, for as long as it took to get the crowd seated. Huge heater fans blew warm air through the barn, staving off any chill and ensuring the sad fate of the salads.

A few minutes later, we saw my father, Priscilla Coughlin (who I assume is now Priscilla Coughlin Pratt, though I am as yet to receive written confirmation of that horrifying fact), and Samantha's parents in the corner of the vast barn.

Isaiah Eckington was casually dressed—gray slacks, a blue oxford shirt opened at the collar, and a dark blazer. I found it reprehensible that, as father of Samantha, he couldn't bring himself to put on a tie. Even a club tie would have been better—and God knows, Isaiah Eckington probably had two dozen club ties.

Faye Eckington looked like she had just walked off the tennis court—or, from a distance, could have been mistaken for a tourist who had happily and accidentally arrived at this astonishing wedding. All she needed was a camera around her neck to complete the picture. She wore a polo shirt, white Capri pants, and athletic shoes. I assume she had the shred of decency needed to remove the green sun visor that usually goes along with the attire she selected for her daughter's rehearsal dinner.

As you know, for too much of my life, I used clothing as a measure of those around me. I know this is stunningly superficial—

but assuming one owns more than the clothes on their back, consciously or not, clothing is a choice. True, we wear what we wear to keep warm, stay consistent with the purpose of an activity or the attire of those around us, and maybe, in some small way, introduce a hint of color. But still, we make choices.

Historically, I thought my clothing said nothing about me but I was wrong. The bland attire I chose was, and it pains me to be so blunt, me. I recall that on the morning I first saw the colors in the candy wrappers, designs and images in the soda, I became quite self-conscious and envious of the rainbow palette that was the wardrobe of Maurice.

From a distance, Claire and I speculated on the meaning of Faye Eckington's attire. "There's really only one interpretation: Faye Eckington thinks this marriage is ungodly—a heathen encounter she just *had* to witness for herself."

Claire disagreed. "The invitation for this dinner implied a casual evening—her mother dressed to make comfortable those who actually dressed down for this event."

"You're wrong, Claire. You don't know this group. Faye Eckington is, by self-declaration, a High Episcopal—as are my parents—which I suppose means more Latin in services, more gin in the early afternoon, and more exclusivity—all divinely ordained. Using her clothing as a means of indirectly condemning this union between Jennifer and Samantha as unnatural fits right in with her acidic theology."

"What's going on, Charlie? You've actually changed—and in a matter of minutes. Every comment you make is a condemnation based on nothing but the most negative assumptions about these people." Claire looked around. "Here is the one assumption I'm willing to make: most of these families are not exactly on the cutting edge of liberal left-leaning politics. It's not surprising that some of them are taken aback by a gay wedding. The idea that this is an obvious or easy transition for these people is heartless on your part."

Claire turned to walk back into the crowded barn but I took her arm. "Hang on a second. Condemnation? I've heard Faye Eckington—she is quite capable of using religion—or any other discipline—to condemn anyone including her daughter. This group uses faith—or any other belief system—like a hammer. It's all about justification of their limitless superiority."

"Faith? What are you talking about?"

"Misquotes, decontextualized readings of Leviticus, strained readings of Romans and First Corinthians to support angry views of anything and anyone unlike her are par for the course. These people revel in condemnation."

Claire shook her head. "How can you possibly know that? Faye Eckington hasn't said a word to you."

"It's her party—she's not going to make a scene tonight—and even if she did, that would not be the ultimate insult."

Claire turned to me. "You're doing exactly what you criticize in this group—being completely presumptuous." She stopped. "The ultimate insult?"

"That title goes to the Strongs, Jennifer's parents, who decided to boycott the wedding entirely and stay in Brampton, stewing in their patrician juices." I described Jennifer's parents—Murielle (known to her friends as Mu Mu and of the Putnam family, with roots and wealth traceable to the early eighteenth century) and flint gray Thomas Strong. "Under the circumstances, it was actually surprising the Eckingtons or my father and his gold-digger wife, came at all. These are intolerant people, reliant on fixed modalities for almost everything and that includes family and relationships—and certainly not same-sex marriage."

"Enough, Charlie. Stop it."

~

Initially, the rehearsal dinner was indistinguishable from any other event of a similar nature. We were seated at a table with people from all around the state, from Brampton and Bar Harbor, Mount Desert Island and Cape Elizabeth, Falmouth and Bangor. They were tightly connected by their money and had known each other since childhood and—I'm obligated to tell you—were people I knew well.

At first they talked little about the upcoming wedding and more about the Champagnes offered (Grand Cru) and the incredible Shiraz from Australia or, if one preferred, a Chilean Peumo Carmenère, that accompanied a dinner of lamb chops, salmon, or pumpkin ravioli—or all three if one was so inclined.

It felt cold and familiar. The discussion at our table was arid and insular, a retelling of ancient boozy disasters culminating in someone else's embarrassing moments. This changed instantly when the focus shifted to my relationship with Jennifer.

Claire was seated next to Carter Strong, the black sheep of the Strong clan. It made sense to seat us with Carter. As you may recall, Carter and I were friends, after a fashion, when we were growing up. He was the fourth in our tennis matches, usually teamed up with Samantha while Jennifer and I co-habited our side of the court. Carter's career as the family alcoholic farce did not begin until we were in college. Carter, who probably promised his sister he would behave and stay sober, was thoroughly and visibly intoxicated.

Carter stumbled through a few tennis memories in which I played a role, and various minor car accidents, one I recall vividly since his car ended up on my parents' front lawn a good 50 feet from the road.

Recollections concluded, Carter paused, struggled to sit erect, and said: "I really thought you were in love with my sister. I remember you used to hold hands and everyone...." Carter somehow required six syllables for the word *everyone* and it wore him out just saying it. He regained his focus and continued. "Ev-er-y-one thought you were in love." It was only four syllables this time but the impact was nonetheless direct.

Claire, who had been holding my hand under the table, gave me an eye-bulging hand-squeeze. I have found that some women from whom you would not think it—and I would not have thought it of Claire—are capable of a vice-like grip as a means of making a not-so-subtle point. Her hand relaxed and my eyes returned to their normal position. She turned in Carter's direction, primed to follow closely his sloshy recollection.

"That was a long time ago," I said.

"What made you think Charlie was in love? He's not so easy to read," Claire said.

"Ob-ser-ne-va-tion-ne," Carter slurred. "They were always whispering—I assumed, and I wasn't alone in this—that they would

get married one day." Several people at the table with serious ex-
pressions nodded affirmingly as if my failure to marry Jennifer was
central to a sexual identity they found discomforting.

Lest you think this was just my imagination, Phinney Whitman, who inherited and was now sole owner of Whitman Brothers, a private financial advisory group that handles hundreds of
millions of dollars in assets for many in this barn, followed Carter's
remark with, "She was the fish you couldn't reel in, Charlie-boy.
Too bad—Carter's right—you would have been a good couple.
One of us."

"And now, Carter?" Claire asked Carter, thankfully ignoring
Phinney. "What do you see?"

Carter paused, trying unsuccessfully to process the import of
the question. Everyone sat, waiting for this 40-year-old man-child
to pronounce my fate. "Charlie is probably still a great tennis player."
He looked at me and then at Claire and, even in his current state,
seemed to realize what he had done. "Charlie looks like his old
self—except this time not in love with my sister."

Phinney cleared his throat but before he could say anything,
Claire asked me: "Were you in love with Jennifer?"

"We were good friends—that's all."

Claire turned to me. "Friends? Like me? Your special friend?"

I should have realized I'd tapped the limits of the otherwise innocuous term *friend*. It was, as you know, how I introduced Claire
to my father. However, I don't think that is why the term sounded
an alarm for Claire.

As I mentioned, in a burst of openness on our drive earlier
today, I told Claire, in far too much detail, about the night on
Cape Cod. I ended that discussion by saying, now regrettably, that
we were thereafter just friends—that was the extent of it. Claire
leaned close to me and whispered. "I'm worried, Charlie. Are we
just friends—the way you and Jennifer were just friends after your
night on Cape Cod?

"That's ridiculous." It was not much of a protest.

"I'm not sure," she said. "I've been your friend for many years.
I will always be." She put her hand on my shoulder and continued.
"But you need to be honest with me."

"If this is about my feelings for Jennifer, my friendship with her, then fine. She was my friend—and only that." It was a safe statement—but it was not entirely true. I looked away from our group to the head table. There was Jennifer, exquisite, resplendent, the woman of the hour, the woman I once knew fully and loved deeply.

When I learned she would never experience more than simple affection for me or any other man, at some arguably unhealthy level, she became more interesting, and—you may find this unsettling—more loved. I cannot explain why this was but it's a fair guess, at least in part, that the potency of my feelings were in direct proportion to the improbability of rejection. That my conscious mind knew the boundaries of our relationship did not matter. In some stratum of my well-concealed interior, she became the idealized and impossible measure of all other women—until Claire.

I would not take issue if you're thinking these thoughts and emotions approach or cross the border of pathology. I will say only that some people—perhaps many—harbor longings they know perfectly well can never be realized. I have shared with you mine and should add quickly that after our night on Cape Cod, I never considered seriously the possibility of an intimate relationship with Jennifer. However, after that night, there was no doubt: she was within me.

"Charlie?" Claire asked, but I was not fully there. I was in Wellfleet in a hotel room and I was here, at this spectacular wedding. "Charlie—talk to me."

I looked at Carter and realized that at some point Jennifer must have told him enough detail to answer a brother, younger and naïve, whether his sister was sure about her sexuality. I can see her saying to Carter: "I've always known—but I experimented once—with Charlie—and it was completely wrong." It would be a way to make him understand this was her true identity, not a choice or preference—it was who she was, her innate and preordained orientation—and, importantly, who she wasn't.

Before I could respond to Claire, out of the blue, Phinney attacked. "You've never known what you wanted." He cleared his throat and continued: "You blew it, young Pratt—and the result? Our Jennifer, the best of us, ends up marrying another woman! Those are the facts … and so here we are."

I was done with Phinney. "This is completely insane. Jennifer is who she is—and has always been—and that has nothing to do with me. Shame on you. I came here because Jennifer was and is my good friend. She invited me to celebrate her marriage. That's why I'm here. I sure as hell hope that is why you're here, Phinney."

Quite suddenly, the confusion, bile, pent-up bias, prejudgment, fear, and hostility at our table regarding gay marriage spilled wildly, viciously, and unrestrained. Everyone was talking at once. Gay marriage was defended aggressively, criticized, politicized, praised, characterized as courageous and long-overdue, questioned, mocked, toasted (by Carter), supported, and misunderstood.

In the din, Claire leaned over again and whispered to me: "I'm not sure you know exactly why you're here." When I looked at her questioningly, she continued. "Maybe you wanted to see for yourself—to be sure about Jennifer." She stopped, took a breath. "Maybe that's why you brought me. Who wants to be alone when they confirm the loss of their first love?"

"That's just not so," I said—and then entertained the possibility that she might be right. There had been sex since Jennifer—but not love. Not once. Not until Claire.

The arguments at the table increased in volume and ranged from supportive and empathic to vile, degenerating into the foul, familiar nastiness I knew from my life in Brampton. The debate was a plague, spreading to other tables, bringing out the best and the worst. Some were standing, shouting, pointing fingers, and then, over and within the din of deafening arguments, Mavis Shields, a purple-haired octogenarian and distant relative of two presidents, rose to her feet, balanced on her bejeweled rollater, and declared, clear as a bell, "I love these women." She looked at Jennifer and Samantha. "Such is beauty," she exclaimed. In the quiet that followed, she continued: "All my life I've loved both men and women."

This staggering piece of news silenced the room until Phinney, after issuing a porcine snort, said, "No man would want you, Mavis."

From the other side of the room, Penelope Fitzgerald yelled, "Shut up, Phinney, you old prune." And so it went.

Without a doubt, things would have continued in a terrible direction but, thankfully, during a brief pause, Pru Whitman, Phinney's ghostly thin wife, shifted the discussion. "I rather like the barn," she said. "There's something about being in the home of hay and farm animals—it's rather fitting, don't you think?" I'm absolutely sure this was not meant as a compliment. Still, when others commented on the steps taken to make this cavernous space elegant and memorable, I joined in, happy to have the focus shifted away from gay marriage, Jennifer, and me. Gradually, while pockets of conflicts rumbled on, most seemed content in the belief that they had said their piece and vestiges of civility resurfaced.

The volume of the music increased as dessert was served. The songs selected had that identifiable syncopation that prompted those inclined to dance. The music got louder as all plates were cleared and Claire stood. "Let's dance, Charlie." I was still trying to process all that had been said and barely heard her. "Are you even uncertain about whether you want to dance with me?"

I looked up at her. "I'm not a very good dancer."

Notwithstanding endless lessons that began when I was in elementary school, I have never been good at nor enjoyed dancing. I am familiar with the fact that on special occasions, excluding funerals, people are expected to dance. It always struck me as odd that people dressed formally, wearing garments worth a fortune, would then somehow change all of the rules for the evening, occasionally taking off shoes and loosening ties, sweating until their shirts were soaked and makeup ran, moving and touching in ways that many of those in this room would never do elsewhere—including the bedroom.

I must have missed that part of the college class in anthropology or abnormal psychology that explained why it was *de rigeur* to go through exertion limited normally to compliance with the directives of some sadistic personal trainer simply because one was at a wedding or anniversary party.

As I contemplated far too long the baffling necessity of dancing, Claire gave up, grabbed Carter, and was already out on the floor. I waited for the song to end with the hope that Claire would return to the table but when she did not and simply continued dancing with Carter, I decided to act. On the dance floor I tapped Carter on the shoulder. "My turn."

Carter, lost in a haze of alcohol, loud music, and whatever narcotic cocktail he ingested before coming to the event, turned away
from Claire and kept dancing, looking like a drunken racehorse
moving sideways on the track.

Just so there is no misunderstanding, I've never seen a drunken
racehorse. I doubt they drink, when it comes right down to it.

I did my best to appear to enjoy dancing but after a couple of minutes, Claire said: "Sit down, Charlie. You're not required to dance
with me." I knew if I left the dance floor, Carter, like a spinning
top, would make his way back to her and decided to stay, making
an effort to smile.

The volume of the music made speech difficult and with each attempt to repair the damage, I somehow reinforced Claire's hesi-
tancy and fears—and she seemed to back away further and further.
By the time we sat down, I was covered in sweat, distrusting every
thought that came to mind.

As a waiter refilled our wine glasses, Claire said the three words
I most dreaded: "What a mistake."

I realize in retrospect that this was one of those moments where
telling someone you loved them is vitally important. Claire needed
to hear it—and I didn't say it—or anything else. "Think back,
Charlie. When you got this invitation—when you asked me to join
you—what were you hoping for?"

"I wanted to be here for Jennifer—not because I am still in love
with her but because I know these people. When I sent back the
RSVP, that's what I was thinking. And when I asked you, I wasn't
thinking about Jennifer. I was thinking about being with you."

We were among the first to leave that evening and drove back
to the Inn in relative quiet. As I was parking the car, Claire said:
"Thank you for getting a separate room for me, Charlie. I need
some privacy." She gave me an unexpected hug. "And Thursday
night ... I know that was quite real for both of us."

That embrace and those words stayed with me for months.

We had breakfast in the Inn and, after reading a few brochures
we found in a display rack next to the cash register, decided to go
on a hike. The Inn made us a boxed lunch and, at the recommendation of the desk clerk, we drove to a state park southeast of

Burlington and found a trailhead that wound through dense woods and then up into the foothills of the White Mountains.

For those of you who know well this part of the state, you might be thinking we had to be in the Green Mountains. That was my assumption as well, but the clerk designated them White. Regardless of the color, this was no modest stroll through a mature Vermont forest. What we thought would be an hour or two walk turned out to be a loop of almost ten miles. Our discussion throughout was about almost nothing but the trail and the views.

There were long stretches of heavy breathing—though in this instance, that was the result of rough terrain and, I'm sorry to say, nothing else. The White Mountains may be old and worn, but in places the footing is perilous and the trail steep and poorly marked.

It was late afternoon when we returned, sore, sweaty, and exhausted. After showering and putting on my dark gray suit, I waited for Claire in the lobby. She walked in an hour later wearing a white and black dress with silver side-buttons and a pearl necklace.

"Stop staring, Charlie."

"It's the ultimate compliment."

"Telling me I look nice might be a more understandable alternative. A blank stare does not exactly convey your feelings."

"Point taken." I smiled at her. "It's beautiful, Claire—and so are you."

"Better," she said, and then: "Before we head out, I wanted to say something about yesterday. You can't change or help your origins any more than I can alter mine. I was brought up by working class parents in College Park, Maryland. Regardless of what they wanted me to know, their lives, their challenges and successes, their values, fears, and goals are deep within me. I can't change them—any more than you can undo yours."

"I don't know how else to say this but I am not like my parents. I've spent twenty years living a life that is my own."

"And I appreciate that, Charlie. I don't want to argue about this. I simply want you to know what I've observed not just yesterday but for years. You are a product of your home in Brampton, your parents, the friends they had, and the friends you knew. Coming here has helped me understand that world a bit better."

I repeated my denial. "I am not like them—I don't fit in here anymore."

"I can see why you wouldn't want to but your past came out in the Market in ways you may not see or expect. There was that initial standoffishness—or shyness ... I was never sure which, your judgments about people, your approach to work and money, your relationships with other women—and now, as I watched you last night, I can see both what you hate about this entire group of people ... and what you are, within this group."

There was another long pause and finally Claire said: "You are one-of-a-kind—and also one of them, Charlie. You will always be one of them. You are different in many ways—and I love those ways that you have redefined yourself."

"I feel a 'but' or 'however' coming."

"You are part of something foreign to me. My life, my parents' life, revolved around work, paychecks, painful but important savings every month. A job was everything to them and is vitally important to me. I am a working woman, Charlie. Work was a meaningful part of who my parents were and who I am. It's normal—even common—but it is not the world from which you came—and not the world that defines you."

"My job is important to me."

"You're a lawyer first and Charles Emerson Pratt second? Hardly. You are who you are—and it would help me if you simply accepted that and then let me figure out what all this might mean down the road."

I started to respond but stopped, focusing on the hope that there might be a 'down the road' for Claire and me. That was a far better prospect than 'the end of the road,' 'dead end,' 'hit the road,' or any other paved or unpaved thoroughfare-based analogy.

I held out my arm and Claire took it, letting me escort her to the car—which, I regret to report, still had a powerful aroma. Five hundred miles of driving with open windows had not yet cleared the air, so to speak. As we got in the car, I entertained the possibility that Claire would sense the potent Flynn funk as evidence of my independent life, freed of my cool, distant, scrubbed-by-servants, buffed-by-butlers Brampton roots.

The barn was transformed with towering monuments to the flowering arts. What seemed like acres of white lace sails bellowed from every rafter continuing into the side building, now a chapel with rows of chairs facing a spectacular nondenominational altar.

Following tradition, we were escorted to seats (on Jennifer's side of the assemblage). Everyone stood as the large wedding procession began with a substantial contingent of ushers and bridesmaids, one fantastically cute child bearing rings and another clutching the wedding bouquet, and finally, there they were, the main actors in this wedding of weddings.

Carter Strong, sedate, standing straight and seemingly sober, walked Jennifer down the aisle.

Isaiah Eckington, now in white tie and tails, escorted Samantha.

Faye Eckington was decked out in a golden silk dress with shimmering emerald and citrine accents suitable for the event — in fact, suitable for a coronation. She entered just before the brides, looking fully the role of regal mother, sporting a diamond necklace that was easily worth three times the value of my house in Jackson Park.

I suppose Faye and Isaiah concluded it was time to show their finest to northern New England — or perhaps decided they'd made their point last night. Claire was unimpressed with Faye and whispered to me: "She must have spent all day getting her hair and make-up done. If she smiles she'll crack her cheeks."

"I'm sure she spent the day with Pru and their friends attended to by a battalion of beauticians and stylists of one type or another," I added. "It's a ritual — except normally the bride participates ... and it's a fair guess Jennifer and Samantha got ready on their own."

"She is beautiful," Claire said slowly.

"Faye?"

"Right. Faye. No, don't be ridiculous — Jennifer."

You might think I had a clever response, or at least a denial on the tip of my tongue, but I was consumed by unwanted honesty and agreed. "That she is," I said.

Claire's eyes crinkled as she whispered, "You are remarkable, Charlie — a miracle of anatomy and physics — it's amazing that someone can be so thoroughly dense and fully transparent at the same time."

As I nodded (and a nod was at the high end of things I might have said or done—I'm sure you can conjure up the less fruitful options by this point), I had a sudden, out-of-context, powerful and fully understandable sensation: I missed Flynn. I missed my constantly forgiving and unrelentingly loving Flynn. Flynn does not parse sentences and dissect reactions. He does not probe and assess responses, gauging sincerity.

Moreover, Flynn would love this barn—both with and without the wedding. I imagined him at my side, wearing a black-tie collar (he has one for special events purchased some time ago—it's really quite fetching) looking around, taking in the spectacle, and then plopping down at my feet, content to wait for the food soon to follow, signature aromas already—and easily—identified.

A string quartet and three vocalists performed so magnificently during the processional that they generated a sustained standing ovation.

Once all were in place, the ceremony began, officiated by Congressman Hugh Seymore, with whom Jennifer had worked—and to whom she had given generously. Far too many members of Congress can be rightly criticized for failures of intellect, character, or judgment, but even so, in the right setting most can give one hell of a speech—and Hugh Seymore did just that. He began the event with a welcome followed by remarks lasting under five minutes and in that short time chronicled the lovers' journey, their courage and commitment, and then spoke of law, family and obligation, political struggle, and the triumph of this moment.

The vows came next, and to the surprise of most, Jennifer and Samantha sang their statements of love and commitment. Each had written vows and then worked with the musicians who accompanied them. It was risky and romantic and none of us had ever seen anything like it.

With vows and rings exchanged and the congregation promising to support the couple, it was time for the finale, as if one was needed—and a finale it was. The two huge doors in the rear of the building opened and the herd of saddled horses we saw yesterday trotted in, each guided by a tuxedoed groomsman.

The entire wedding party saddled up, with Jennifer and Samatha atop two of the larger horses, sitting side-saddle, wasting no time trotting in tandem up the aisle. Next was Carter (who was a talented rider when we were young but today bounced along and barely stayed mounted), the Eckingtons (both sitting quite erect in the saddle), followed by all those who stood with the couple during the ceremony. Some members of the wedding party rode skillfully, while others were guided like children clutching a pony during their first ride at a birthday party.

The musicians played an Aaron Copeland medley (which you may judge as trite but it worked beautifully) as the horses trotted down the aisle. We stood by our seats, cheering and clapping, as more tuxedoed groomsmen ran down the aisle with shovels and sacks, picking up droppings from the herd. When they were done, guests were led out, row by row, by more groomsmen.

As was the case last night, waitstaff were ready with appetizer platters—and tonight was all about lobsters and oysters. For those who could not or would not have shellfish, there were trays of more traditional fare including cubed beef filet with dipping sauce, cheeses of all kinds, and massive fruit and vegetable platters set out on tables twenty-five feet long.

Dozens of trays sailed by at fingertips, piled high with the most tender lobster meat I've ever eaten, carefully skewered for easy consumption. There were iced tables in every corner and in the center of the great barn, set up noiselessly during the ceremony, covered with plump, shucked Connecticut, Maine, and Nova Scotia oysters. Cocktail sauces of every conceivable variety awaited guests at multiple serving stations. Chilled martinis and endless flutes of champagne were everywhere I turned.

"Is this how it's done in Maine?" Claire asked as we walked through the main hall of the barn.

"Not really. Usually wedding dinners are more formal."

"You mean there aren't horses at every wedding?" she asked. "This must have cost hundreds of thousands of dollars."

"Easily. This is what wealth can do. The Eckingtons decided to throw a party. I think the wedding was simply an excuse to...."

Before I could finish, we heard a series of explosions and rushed outside with the rest of the guests. The fireworks had begun. The pyrotechnics were pathologically excessive. However, like the rest of the wedding, they, and everything else, made sense, even the horses, though this only seemed sane after an articulate Swiss woman, one of Samantha's former nannies, explained to us that Jennifer and Samantha were devoted to the cause of wild horses. They supported programs that cared for or rescued island horses on the east coast and the remaining herds of wild horses in the west. They owned a horse farm in Vermont and another in Kentucky and sponsored a world-famous clinic outside of Boston that relied on highly-trained horses as part of a system of therapy for people with brain, neck, and spinal injuries.

When the fireworks ended, we walked back into the barn, ate more lobster and oysters, listened to music, and watched as a half-dozen professional photographers and videographers circled, determined to memorialize the event.

Before the wedding dinner was served, Claire and I managed to have a few minutes with the brides. Jennifer, as always, was gracious and decent, asked a few questions about our lives in Jackson Park, and then took a step back and said to Claire: "That is one of the most beautiful dresses I've ever seen."

Though her words were over the top, they came with a smile that rendered insincerity an impossibility. Claire thanked her and, in a seamless gesture befitting an experienced diplomat, took Jennifer's arm and walked a few steps away from Samantha and me. They spoke for a time and returned.

As we were walking away, before I could ask what that was about, Claire said: "Don't ask, Charlie. Let's sit down," but I thought I knew and wanted to confirm my suspicion.

"You asked her if she thought I had gotten over her."

Claire grabbed my arm and whispered, "How can such a bright man, a decent lawyer, at least according to Henry, be such a complete ass. Of course I didn't ask her that. She's not thinking about you this evening. You shouldn't be thinking about you either."

"Well, no, of course not...."

Whatever Claire and Jennifer discussed remained private that night and thereafter. While I was smart enough not to bring it up again, I remain sure that Claire wanted to learn what she could about the only other woman I'd ever loved.

Dinner provided more choices—a variant on Beef Wellington, dense and succulent monkfish filets in a buttery phyllo shell, and a baked eggplant and Portobello creation set in a perfectly cooked, hollowed, and splayed artichoke.

As simple as it sounds, and it was by appearance and ingredients just that, dessert was traditional wedding cake. It was about as good as cake can get.

Champagne and toasts brought the dinner to an end and, having learned my lesson from the prior night, I danced with Claire as soon as dancing was suggested.

The weekend had drained many of the guests, including Claire and me. People left fairly early for an event of this magnitude. If there was an after-party, happily we were not invited. Claire told me her feet ached and I confessed that the hike had done me in and I was looking forward to getting back to the Inn.

We began our exit by saying goodbye to Samantha and Jennifer, who were mobbed by the first round of those seeking to leave. When we finally had our moment, Claire focused on Samantha. "I can't imagine how difficult it's been for both of you to hide such powerful feelings for so many years."

Samantha deflected the question and responded quietly. "You must be a very special person—Jennifer certainly has high regard for Charlie."

"I'm sure the feeling is mutual," Claire said.

Even I knew this was a bad direction for a simple farewell and interceded. "Claire and I would love to show you and Jennifer around Washington—please let us know if you ever come our way."

Clumsy and disconnected as this exchange was, it worked. Final hugs were short and we were one step closer to being out the barn door.

The next round of farewells was with my father and Priscilla. The most notable thing about this parting was Priscilla's comment: "I'd like to get to know you, Claire. You seem to bring out the best in Charlie." Just what was the worst that had been brought out pre-Claire was a mystery to me.

Next was Carter. After the damage done on Friday night, I was quite ready to leave without saying anything to Carter ever again but Claire was not willing to leave without saying goodbye to Carter—and I understood why.

At one point about an hour ago, Carter had wrested the microphone from Phinney Whitman (who was in the process of toasting, "The wealth and prosperity of the great families in this—what shall I call it—agricultural complex …"). In the grand tradition of songs of the inebriati, Carter slur-sang, "For She's a Jolly Good Lady," to the familiar tune.

The musicians matched the key and Carter led the assemblage in a second rousing verse (which is, as you know, is exactly the same as the first). Midway through the third verse, there was considerable swaying on Carter's part during the last "which nobody can-ne deny-ye," a prelude to the inevitable. Responding to the calls to shut up—and worse (I heard Isaiah Eckington say, quite clearly, "Sit down Carter—you're a damn drunk") from every corner of the barn, Carter finished his memorable performance with a deep bow that went poorly, particularly from the nervous perspective of the percussionist on whose snare Carter nearly toppled.

His fall left him kneeling next to the drummer. With his mouth close to the microphone, Carter had more to say. "There is, dear-rr friends, one ve-er-re-y last thing." There were more calls for Carter to stand down but he was having none of it. "I may be dr-rrrunnnnk, well … I am just that … but I'm not deaf. I heard you last night—I hope Saman-an-na-tha and you," he looked at his sister, "ignore the ignorr-am-ouses — the people who can't accept your marriage."

Quite suddenly, alcohol driven or not, tears ran down Carter's face and the entire room had his attention. "I love both of you—and this is the best marriage, the best wedd-ded-ing—any of us have ever seen." Then he turned to Phinney. "Don't like it, Whitman? You suuuure liked the food—and the wine—when you send your thank-you note, add an appolllllllogy to my sister and Sam-mmanthaaa. They're in love. An I love them. And I hope everyone loves them, too." He found a glass on the edge of the stage. "To my sister and her wife," and now fighting back more tears, "like this empty glass, you begin your life a-ah-new—fill it with love and happppiinesssssss."

His toast complete, chants of "here, here" resonating, Carter sat and sobbed. Moments later, Jennifer and Samantha were with him. Carter, for all his faults, ended up all right.

By the time we got to him on our way out, he was barely conscious. His farewell, a handshake and a simple but ironical, "Drive carefully," left Claire speechless.

We thanked Faye and Isaiah Eckington, snubbed Phinney and Pru, and walked into the black night where stars lit the spiny crescent canopy of a leafless New England forest.

Chapter 9

Return to Jackson Park

I spent the second night alone in my room at the New Marlow Inn. When we met for breakfast on Sunday morning, Claire was packed and ready to go.

We took a different route home relying on local roads that ran due south and, at the base of Lake Champlain, headed west to the New York State Thruway. We talked at length and without any particular purpose about the guests at the wedding and despite my claim that I knew almost all the attendees, I failed more often than not when Claire asked me to connect names with outfits.

"Remember that woman with blue-white hair, white frilly dress, and the remarkable sapphire necklace—she was with that mousy fellow—gray hair, navy pinstripe suit, black bowtie...."

I considered the description and drew a blank. After the third or fourth failure on my part, Claire smiled for the first time that day. It had become a game and she was in her element.

It ended with: "There were two women who arrived at the rehearsal dinner just after we did without escorts, one with long, braided auburn hair and one wearing a large floppy hat and smoking a cigar."

I was as flummoxed by this question as any of the others and stumbled along, suggesting names and then backing away. "Maybe that was Lucile Decker and her cousin—no, wait, not Lucile...."

Claire laughed—finally. "I made up that one." She paused. "Come on, Charlie—it was a joke."

And on and on it went.

When Claire tired of the game, we turned to a rambling discourse on the Market. Somewhere around the Tappan Zee Bridge, we speculated at length on Alex's life as a poet and Henry's political and personal history.

We were still north of the exit to the Stansfield Hotel when Claire said: "I've been thinking about what you said yesterday while we were in the lobby of the Inn before leaving for the wedding."

"And?" I hoped for a beginning of what we would have 'down the road' — but that was not to be.

"Tell me if I'm wrong — but I have a sense that your work is almost like a hobby — from what I can tell, you actually don't need your job. You could go back to Brampton, live in your guest house, survive comfortably on your trust fund, and never give me another thought."

"I don't want that life," I said. "You saw these people at their best. Some may have come to terms with a gay marriage, giving the appearance of warmth and affection, love and support. At the wedding service, when we were asked whether we support this couple, a common question at every wedding — when the whole congregation said 'we will,' most were lying. Jennifer and Samantha are on their own."

Claire shook her head. "Except that they too can fall back on family wealth, on their own trust funds, and never miss a mortgage payment. They will never extend a credit card to its limit and if they have children, never have to say no when their son or daughter asks about going to camp, buying a musical instrument, the cost of tuition, or any of the thousand other needs children have that stretch families to their economic limit.

"You know nothing about that, Charlie. For you, if you have a child, saying no would be a moral or educational choice, something based on your view of the needs of your child or of the value of the experience. You would never have to say 'no' because you could not afford something from which your child would benefit."

"I live off the money I make at work — and while I'm comfortable, I don't think of myself as wealthy."

"Think again. That is exactly what you are. It's not what attracted me to you — but it's something I knew about you. I simply didn't know what it would mean in terms of other aspects of your life."

I protested more, assuring Claire that the modesty of my existence was a well-documented fact, that my love of the Market was evidence of a set of choices that led me to my bologna and cheese sandwich on white bread wrapped in wax paper, to my great and cherished comfort with Alex, Maurice, Henry, Simone, and her. I meant this as a defense, a protestation, but instead it evoked this response: "I know you think that." With that, Claire closed her eyes.

I felt certain she was not asleep. "I am the person you thought I was when I picked you up on Thursday night. I am not the person you are describing." When she did not respond, I continued: "You think I don't appreciate how hard you work, how much you sacrifice, how decent a person you are. I don't think you understand the depth of my feelings for you."

When she did not respond, I said it. "I love you, Claire. You must know that."

Without opening her eyes, Claire said, "And I love you, Charlie—I never would have slept with you were that not the case … but that's not what we are discussing. I am past that point in life where I have the energy to invest in a relationship that is doomed."

"Doomed? We are just starting."

She opened her eyes and looked at me. "Starting what? You're enamored with an image of me based on what you've seen in the Market. Now you know more. I am more than that woman who can go toe-to-toe with you and Henry and the others. Maybe it was the fact that you didn't have much information about the other parts of my life that made me so interesting. I was aware of your feelings a long time ago, and I had and have similar feelings for you.

"You are a nice and attractive man, Charlie Pratt. You need to think long and hard about where you're headed, how you want to conduct your life, and of course with whom. You have many choices. Very few people can even imagine the options you have at your fingertips. This weekend you wanted to be with me—and many years ago you thought you wanted to be with Jennifer—I'm not sure you know what you want." There was a long silence and then she sat up, turned to me and said: "You know I've been married—and divorced…."

"You told me that when we met."

"My husband was an electrician. Not long after Melissa was born, his company sent him to San Jose, California, to work on a commercial installation. He was supposed to be gone for a few weeks—

but he fell in love with California." She stopped and smiled. "He was seduced by an entire state. Who can compete with a state?"

I was not about to answer and waited for her to continue. "I couldn't go to California, if that's what you're thinking. My parents were still alive and I was their primary caregiver. We were divorced a year later. Within six months of the divorce, he was killed in an accident at the work site—it's the kind of thing that happens from time to time in big projects. Because we were already divorced, I was no longer the beneficiary of his life insurance, not the recipient of any widow's benefits, and certainly not likely to receive any further alimony payments. He was gone and I was on my own. I have been that way ever since."

My response to this was sincere: "He was a fool." Based on her facial expression (a silent, 'What the heck?'), I surmised it was the wrong response and so I followed with: "May he rest in peace."

When the 'What the heck?' look transformed into a simple, 'What?' achieved with a quick shaking of the head, I said: "I mean he was a fool for leaving you. I never would have...."

Claire cut me off: "You've never been married—and obviously never been divorced. This is too simplistic but it will have to do for now. Sometimes, divorce is essential, clears the air, liberates both people to begin again. Other times, it is wrenching, humiliating, debilitating, and devastating. My divorce was the second type." She stopped and I wondered if there was more to come. "I thought I knew him. I didn't. And he, as it turned out, really didn't know me. That's a mistake I will never repeat."

"I'm so sorry."

"Obviously, it's not your fault," she said. Before I could say I was sorry for saying I was sorry, she continued. "I figured out how to live as a single mother—and now grandmother—and it's taken years, but I like my life. I like my job and am fairly well paid. I'm not rich, however, and I certainly don't have a trust fund. There is an economic margin in my life—there's an economic margin in the lives of most people.

"If I lost my job, I could probably go eight or nine months or so but after that, unless I had another position, we would be in trouble. That is our margin. About nine months. Your margin is very different. You could lose your job and from what I've observed, it wouldn't matter at all. That's your margin — wide and almost endless."

I knew denial was out of the question. "To an extent, I suppose you're right. The Pratt family has wealth … and I am a Pratt. I decided that my life would be different than the rest of my family. I live entirely off my salary and if I lost my job would do exactly what you would do: work hard to find a new job."

Claire made a sound I can best describe as *pfff* and said: "Tell me that if you got into serious trouble — owed a lot of money, found yourself in critical need of expensive health care your insurance did not cover, tell me your family's assets would not be there for you. Tell me that in an emergency, you would turn away from those resources."

"If I was lucky enough to be with you, would you want me to turn away from those resources? If I was with you and something happened to Melissa that required more money than we had on hand — and all I had to do was pick up the phone and call the family accountant and the crisis would be resolved — tell me you wouldn't want that."

Claire pfff'ed me again and said: "Cheap shot, Charlie. This isn't about Melissa."

"You're pushing me away solely because of my heritage." I was angry at this point. "And that's not a cheap shot — it's a fair question — essentially, the same question you just asked me. And stop pfff'ing me." She issued a final pfff, closed her eyes, and we drove on in silence.

It was dusk when we crossed the Susquehanna. Apparently Claire was not deeply asleep because she turned to me and said quietly: "One day you can tell me more about the river, Charlie. Not tonight." It was the most hopeful thing she'd said all afternoon.

Neither of us said a word for more than an hour. Finally, we were back on — and then off — the Capital Beltway. As we headed down the exit ramp Claire said: "I'm not asking you to renounce who you are — and if we were together and facing a problem, yes, I would want to use any resource available if it meant the well-being of my family.

"The assumption that makes your hypothetical difficult isn't money—it's the idea of being together. I would be bound to you by marriage, Charlie, and you would be bound to me. The last time I did that, it ended poorly. While I do love you—there are so many parts I don't know—and I assure you, there are parts of me you have not met and maybe won't like. You've been on your own for almost 20 years. You don't know what it means to be together.

"Together means together with Melissa, my son, his wife and my grandson—together means with my brother and sister, aunts and uncles, cousins, many nieces and nephews, and friends, none of whom have what you have, Charlie. Together might mean relatives who think that being with you is like winning the lottery. People would ask for money, for loans, for help, because they need it. Are you prepared for that?" She stopped. "Some mornings—and this has been true for many years—I watch one or two of my nieces and nephews until their sitter arrives." She allowed the smallest of smiles. "They throw more food than they eat ... and I get spattered." As I told you at the outset of this tale, I'd noticed those stains on her clothing but decided not to mention that fact. "The real world is messy, Charlie. Your world isn't."

"Isn't real or isn't messy?"

Claire ignored my question. "Let's agree on this: tomorrow morning, we will return to the Market. We will be that mystery that everyone wants to solve—and let's have some fun in keeping it that way."

"Agreed," I said.

I carried her suitcase to her door and as she was unlocking it I put my hand on her shoulder. "I want to work on this, Claire."

She turned to me, kissed me on the cheek, and said, "We'll see. We both need time."

I drove slowly from Claire's house, examining sidewalks and street trees, brick houses with small front porches, taking it all in. I nearly ran a traffic light at the end of her street as I crawled along, imagining her daily drive to the Market.

It was too late to pick up Flynn, yet the drive from Vermont left me wide awake. I cruised through the municipal center of Jackson Park (such as it was) looking at the remainder of the old town. I passed the post office, a limestone tribute to urban architecture of the 1920s.

A granite Depression-era statue of a pioneer mother and child standing beside a plow and a mid-sized breedless dog stood in front of the post office. Flynn and I have walked by that statue many times and almost invariably Flynn (and most other dogs I have observed) find the granite dog irresistible, possessed of the same allure as the trunks of select trees and certain fire hydrants. I can understand why a passerby might conclude that Flynn's selection of this stone canine magnet is a desecration of sorts. However, while my guilt is easily accessed, Flynn's use of the statue does not faze me.

Next to the post office was the Jackson Park Trust building and beyond that a few ancient one-story restaurants and stores. Surrounding and in some instances overshadowing these older structures are recently constructed office and apartment buildings, a health club with floor-to-ceiling tinted windows and black and silver exercise machines, and the newly renovated and expanded Beardsley House where, for some reason, Alex, our parcel deliveryman, taught piano and inspired creativity on a regular basis.

Main Street, the heart of Jackson Park, has a wide median with trees, park benches, and enough room for art shows and the annual Jackson Park food festival. This celebrated civic event provides an opportunity for the few remaining local farms to sell vegetables, fruits, and pies, for select vendors to sell everything from funnelcakes to falafel, and for many of the area restaurants to offer small tastings to attract future customers.

During the food festival, Main Street closes at both ends and cars park everywhere. Several years ago, I made the mistake of bringing Flynn to the festival. I noticed other people with dogs and it just seemed a nice thing to do. In that afternoon alone, several items were added to Flynn's list, including people on motorized skateboards and clowns on stilts — but, really, on whose list are they not?

Flynn moved through the festival in what can only be described as a crab-walk. Somehow, he spread his front feet and scuttled along, trying to pick up food thrown or dropped on the ground. Between bites of discarded haute cuisine, Flynn toppled a stilt-mounted clown (who swore at both Flynn and me) and growled menacingly at a pastry chef. I think it was the hat, a towering *toque blanche*, that got him. I spent the entire time pulling at his leash, apologizing to mothers, a bearded rabbi, clowns and chefs, trying desperately to avoid various other indignities and finally, with some effort, dragged him back to the car.

I know he was disappointed but as anyone who has had a dog knows, among their most wonderful characteristics is a short memory for human failures (in all honesty, the food festival debacle was the result of my poor judgment, not Flynn's) and a capacity for forgiveness that should serve as a model for all species. As soon as I said to Flynn: "Let's go to the park—here's your ball," his tail wagged noisily against the seat and we were on our way.

I made a U-turn on Main, looked across the center of my town, and found myself staring at the front windows of the Market. After hundreds of miles of driving and sadly clear memories of my family in Brampton, of Jennifer and Carter, of all things Pratt and Strong, I was seized with one of the few undeniable and absolute truths in my life: Behind the windows, in the familiarity of each shape in the Market, in my new and sensational knowledge of Claire, in my longing to see Maurice and Alex, Henry and Simone, in my anticipation of being at our table, in the foreseeable taste of that simply tuned coffee, somewhere in all of this was my home, my real home.

Before I went to college, there was no question about home and hometown. It was the Pratt estate on the outskirts of Brampton, close to the harsh and magnificent North Atlantic seacoast, a domain of titanic white houses with pale blue trim, monumental lawns and front porches with a dozen rocking chairs, heated swimming pools, and police who understood their job was private security and the burial of embarrassing misconduct. My home was, but is no more, the residence of my father and Priscilla. (I have dropped the Coughlin for now—I can't promise it won't return.)

For some, the transition from one's home of origin to a new home, when examined honestly, can be difficult. The change can be natural, though my observation is that it is more often forced. It descends on us through death or disaster, family upheaval or collapse, financial calamity—or perhaps a slowly evolving and contentious concession that home is too much, too hard, too many things to do that can't be done, and suddenly it's time to go.

Old home, once gone, can leave one adrift, haunted by the fear
that in truly bad moments, when the bottom falls out, there will be
nowhere to go, no safe haven, no familiar chairs and couches, no
wooden-handled tools in the garage, no smell of roast chicken, that
loving and longed for sustenance of a bygone unconditional welcome. It's all gone—and we must start over.

A friend at my law firm lost her mother and within a year her father, served as executor of their estate, and orchestrated the sale of
her family home. For several years thereafter, she complained regularly that she never should have sold that house—her home, her
parents' house—because it was the only real home she knew.

That complaint might sound odd since she lived in a nice part
of Jackson Park and had an attractive house, a spouse, and two
children. She told me her husband and children had no difficulty
calling their house in Jackson Park home … but she did not feel
that way, at least not immediately. Home had been where she lived
as a child. She lived there no more and it was no more. Thus, in
addition to mourning her parents, she mourned the loss of that
fragile notion of home.

I am different—and I know that Claire is not sure of that difference. My ancestral home exists, and barring a financial catastrophe I cannot begin to imagine, will exist for generations to
come and yet, I now realize it is simply not my home.

I've changed. This is my hometown, Jackson Park, not Brampton, and as I looked at the Market and up and down the streets, it
seemed full of promise, controversy, the hope it would forever stay
small and manageable—and the hope it could become something
grand and important. Whatever it was and however it ended up, it
was now my home, my hometown, and I belong here.

As to my current house, there's little to say beyond the important fact that it is comfortable and suits Flynn and me. I pay a
monthly mortgage, and while I could ask for the trust to pay off
the principal at any time, it is the last thing I will do.

My favorite part of the house is an extraordinarily wide deck—
though I am more comfortable with the term porch—running the
length of the back of the house, elevated above the yard by a full
story, and happily under-furnished. I leave outside year-round a

few comfortable beach chairs, three Adirondack rockers (an homage of sorts to the front porch of my family's home in Brampton), and a thick-planked teak outdoor table large enough for dinner with friends. Each year, I buy a few terra cotta pots—one for the center of the table and the others randomly placed on the porch— planted with Impatiens and globe amaranth, Mexican sunflower and rose moss, vinca and zinnias, and then fight an uphill battle to keep them alive through the insect-infused external oven that is Washington's summer.

There is one other item on the porch: a wicker settee with cushions so airy that after a downpour they will dry in under an hour. The settee fits Flynn perfectly and, in addition to food and his tennis ball, the settee is high on the list of Flynn's enchanted and beloved items.

My home, a modest center hall colonial, is one of hundreds in Jackson Park. It is about seventy-five years old and, unlike almost all the properties in my family (originally and continuously owned and occupied by Pratts and their descendants), I am the fifth owner from the fifth unrelated family to live here.

I have been here twenty years, yet there are parts of the house I barely know. After all, it's just Flynn and me and so, for example, I can't remember anyone ever using the guest room and can count on one hand the number of times I've been in the basement. Still, I have no interest in living anywhere else.

While my neighbors discuss the price of housing at the drop of a hat, for obvious reasons, I don't need to think of my house as an investment—it is where I live. Whether it is my true home is another matter. True home, that place of comfort and acceptance, could not be the unoccupied, elegant, sprawling guest house I inherited on my mother's demise nor the family house in Brampton, occupied by Priscilla Coughlin (as an army occupies), ruled over by my father.

I considered the concept of *home*, rolling over the variants on the term. Home as an abstract notion, home seemingly solid for life, suddenly fragile, and then gone in a heartbeat. I drove from the town center and was in my driveway a few minutes later. Looking at my front door and considering the ease of my finances, I was nervously aware that Claire—and you as well—easily could see me as an ingrate. Given the resources seemingly at my disposal, that would be a logical conclusion.

It would be fair to assume that I could and should engage in charitable acts that make a difference in the world, fund research and development leading to a cure of life's most dreaded diseases. It would be normal to wonder why I don't support inner-city schools, protect the environment, support politicians who seem likely to advance just causes, engage in all things eleemosynary and benevolent.

It is time to make clear that I can do no such thing. My trust, while substantial, has strict limiting terms. I can access money only for clearly defined and predictable needs in terms of my health, education, and wellbeing—and wellbeing is defined narrowly. The trustees of this fund, a group of bankers and lawyers (all of the Family Pratt) oversee a number of these trusts, and the notion that they would permit money to be used broadly for charitable purposes, unless they were connected with some family business venture or agreed-upon goal, is unthinkable.

It's not that the Pratts don't give to decent causes. Giving, however, is orchestrated and always done with a specific purpose. The Pratts have given to symphony orchestras and hospitals over the generations because our name appears on the donor list of every program and every plaque the recipients produce—a calculated venture designed to advertise the financial strength of all things Pratt.

Four or five generations ago, Franklin Hughes Pratt generously endowed professorial chairs at several different Ivy League schools, a charitable act designed to ensure that all Pratts would be on legacy lists, instrumental in getting each one of us admitted to one of those schools—and we all were.

I'm not saying the Pratts are bad people. There is, however, a familial *sangfroid* central to our genetic makeup. As people marry in, they bring new interests and impulses into the family but, thus far, intermarriage has not produced a spate of charitable giving—and somehow, I doubt Priscilla Coughlin will inspire such a change.

Once inside my house, I found I had several messages on my home phone. All but one could wait. It was from Maurice, instructing me to call him no matter how late I got in. When he answered, somewhat breathlessly, I thought he would ask about the weekend but, after a quick greeting he said: "Do you have any idea what happened at the Market on Friday?"

"No." I was unwilling to disclose that we had left Thursday night. I thought he was fishing for information about my trip with Claire but I was wrong.

"I got there at five after 6:00," Maurice began. "Henry had a thermos of coffee, sandwiches and cupcakes wrapped up, ready for you. He was standing in the doorway when I arrived and asked if I'd seen you and Claire. When I told him I hadn't seen anybody, he said, 'You wouldn't tell me anyway, would you?' I told him that most certainly I would have said if I'd seen you but I hadn't and what's more, I was getting pretty damn tired of the way he was treating me. He was quiet for a moment and then said: 'What's been going on between you and my wife?'

"At that moment Alex walked in. Henry looked at him, unfazed that someone would witness the confrontation, and said, 'You think I don't see? For a long time, you treated Simone like your girlfriend. That's over.' He took a step closer to me.

"I said: 'Simone is my friend. That's what's going on—and that's all that's going on.'

"I turned around and there was Simone. At first I thought she'd been in the storeroom, but she must have been close by. She walked up to him, said his name, and when he turned to her, she slapped him across the face, turning his head ninety degrees. He shook his head, turned back to her—and she slapped him again! This time, it left a clear handprint on his cheek. She said something loudly—not in English—and walked away.

"I expected Henry to run after her, but instead he rubbed his cheek and turned back to the Market. Walking inside he said, over his shoulder, 'So—why are you waiting—get your coffee. Sit down. I think we both know your time with Simone is over. There is no reason why you can't keep coming to the Market.'

"I sat next to Alex and for five minutes neither of us said a word. Finally, Alex said, 'Are you worried he will hurt Simone?' Of course I was concerned but something about the way Simone walked away from the store suggested she would not be returning to her home or to the Market any time soon.

"When I got home that night, I found a note from Simone under my door. She wrote that she was going to stay in the area with some relatives for a short time and asked me not to worry.

"What if I broke up their marriage, Charlie? I told you—and please believe me—I never had an intimate or sexual relationship with Simone. There were times when she wanted to talk, outside of the Market, and we would meet for lunch. I don't think anyone saw us, but even if they did, all we were doing was talking."

Of course I told Maurice this was not his fault. At present, however, fault was not the issue. Whatever would transpire between Simone and Henry would be up to them, not Maurice. "Now what?" I asked.

There was a long delay and finally Maurice said: "There's nothing I can do—and nothing to do, right? I guess we all go to the Market tomorrow and learn about your trip." He paused. "So, how was it?"

"It was quite a weekend," I replied, relieved I'd found a phrase that answered him without revealing a thing. "I just got back, Maurice. I'm exhausted."

"Of course," he said. "See you in the morning."

There was nothing normal about Monday. With some effort, Maurice and I remained silent when, after our coffee was poured, Henry said: "Simone had a bad fall this weekend. She broke her hip. I think she will be fine but, of course, she won't be back to the Market for a long time."

I could tell from his expression that Maurice wasn't buying it but he was smart enough to avoid a direct accusation. "What a shame," he said, "I think we should send flowers, as a group."

"That's a great idea," Claire added—and then, as if she had been coached by Maurice, said: "What's the address, Henry?"

Maurice was on the edge of his seat. I'm sure he thought the broken hip story was a lie. The trap was baited. In the silence that followed, Maurice must have used considerable energy to keep quiet.

Rather than respond, Henry checked out two customers, one of whom had purchased a hotdog. Under normal circumstances this acquisition would have prompted a discussion at our table. Like many convenience stores, hotdogs and half-smokes roasted throughout the day at the rear of the Market on heated metal rollers. In the years we had gone to the Market, no one in our group had the courage to try this chemically infused meat, certain that cooking for hours—and possibly days—rendered these iconic delights not just inedible but overtly dangerous.

Given my interest in all things American Market, you might think I'd given serious thought to the rolling metal heater and its shriveling occupants but for some reason, up until today, the hotdog cooker was simply part of the backdrop. Yet there stood a purchaser, anxious to consume this most American and potentially least healthy object—for breakfast, no less.

For a moment, it crossed my mind that Henry had a duty to warn the customer: "This hotdog, despite its appealing smell and familiar shape, has been turning on those bars for days," but Henry said no such thing.

Once the transaction was concluded, the customer walked outside, sat on a bench, and in five or six bites consumed his purchase. We watched, waiting for him to keel over, but he stayed upright and seemed content.

Henry finished with a second customer who bought coffee, two cans of soup, and a newspaper, and then, almost as an afterthought, said to us: "Johns Hopkins."

Johns Hopkins University has a series of hospitals and clinics located throughout the region. Not long ago, it purchased a neighborhood hospital a few miles from downtown Jackson Park. There are Johns Hopkins medical centers in the District of Columbia, Northern Virginia, and throughout Maryland, including the outlying suburbs and beyond.

"Which Johns Hopkins?" Claire asked.

Heightening the suspicion I was certain Maurice possessed, Henry said, "I'm not sure. She was taken by ambulance yesterday and made clear that she wanted to be left alone, at least initially. I have respected that. I will hear from her soon."

At first blush, it seemed unlikely that Henry would not to know where his wife had been taken. Yet, given the harrowing episode

Maurice described, it was not so far-fetched. If Simone fell at the home of a relative, given the events of Friday morning, it seemed logical that she would instruct the relative not to tell Henry where she was.

Claire, unaware that Simone had slapped Henry and stalked off, continued: "I'll call around," she said, "and make sure flowers are sent."

Not missing a beat, Henry said: "That is so kind of you. Let me contribute." He reached in his wallet, not in the cash register, and took out seven twenty dollar bills, walked from behind the counter and carefully placed them in front of Claire.

"That's too much," Claire said.

"She is my wife—even if she wants some privacy. Please let me pay. Write on the card that the flowers are from all of you."

Henry returned to his station behind the counter, apologizing, anxious to check out customers who had lined up with newspapers, soda, coffee, and also in line, to my amazement, was the hot-dog purchaser who had left only moments ago, alive, queued up, a second hotdog in hand.

Once the flower purchase plan ended, discussion regarding Simone was limited to recovery from hip injuries. Everyone seemed to know someone whose friend or parent had broken a hip. Even Henry volunteered a brief tale about an uncle "back home" (and we were still not sure what he meant prompting Maurice to mutter rather audibly, "Wherever the hell that is,") who had been hit by a car, broken his hip, and recovered without surgery ... and without a limp.

I followed Maurice to the coffee pot to give him a chance quietly to unload and he did just that. "God knows what he's done to her," he whispered urgently, "I wouldn't put anything past him."

"He would never hurt her."

"Maybe he's fooled you—but I know what I saw." Rather than argue further, I simply nodded and waited while Maurice walked back to the table.

When it came right down to it, Henry and Simone, often at odds with each other, had now moved to that stage where anger could have a physical manifestation. And yet ... Henry and Simone have been through horrors that, somehow, held them together. Perhaps Maurice knew more; in their lunches, it's possible she disclosed more about their relationship and her fears, but Maurice had not shared any of those details with me.

I admit I can be very wrong about people—but I am certain about this: at his core, Henry lived for Simone.

I was finishing my second cup of coffee when Alex said to Claire: "You haven't said anything about the wedding. How did it go?"

"It was a wonderful wedding—inspiring—something I am not likely to forget."

Claire went on at length about the food, flowers, barn, horses, the changing landscape of gay marriage, and ended with a discussion of the dresses worn by Jennifer and Samantha. Her comments were relevant to the question Alex asked but naturally not what Alex was hoping to hear. Alex listened politely and then tried to cut to the chase. "How was the drive up to Burlington?"

"Very nice," Claire said. "What one would hope for."

For some reason, Alex lost his nerve—Claire can do that to people—and dropped his line of questioning. I'm sure Claire hoped someone else would try.

The best Maurice could muster was: "I'm sure that's a beautiful ride in the fall or late spring when everything begins to bloom— of course this time of year, things are still brown and gray...."

"Quite the contrary," Claire said. "There were lovely views along the way." I waited to see if Claire would discuss my wonder with the Susquehanna River or her traffic ticket but she said nothing further.

~

When I returned to the car, Flynn looked up from the backseat, eyes wide, and put his head down. We drove to the park and when I opened the back door, Flynn stood but did not make his way out of the car. After some coaxing, we took a short walk and it was audibly, olfactorily, and visibly obvious after a few stops on our normal route that Flynn was not feeling well. We headed to the animal hospital where Flynn was seen by Dr. Eli Bingham.

Once on the examining table (a maneuver requiring two of Dr. Bingham's assistants) his temperature was taken (normal), Dr. Bingham listened to his heart and lungs (all fine), and began to push at his abdomen. "He's eaten something that's upset his stomach — that's my guess. It's not bloat."

Whatever bloat was, I was relieved it wasn't. Dr. Bingham went on to explain in graphic and nauseating detail what awful things happen when a dog gets bloat. He gave Flynn something to aid digestion and gave me a bottle of pills to be administered to Flynn twice a day. The visit — costing a mere $110 — was worth every penny. I went home, called work and explained that I had to care for a sick friend ("Fine, Charlie — that's so nice of you" — naturally, no questions asked) and curled up on the couch with Flynn.

By evening, Flynn was more himself and by morning of the next day, we left home ready to begin a perfectly normal day. I parked the car in a sunny spot close to the Market and Flynn spread out on the back seat and I'm sure drifted off to sleep before I reached the Market.

There was a cursory discussion about artificial lemonade — so cursory in fact I do not recall a word that was said — after which I told the group about Flynn. Within minutes, everyone was talking about Flynn, bloat, twisted stomachs, dogs who lived more than twenty years, hallucinating dogs (focused on a dog who, after his monthly flea and tick treatment, saw things and periodically jumped sideways to avoid unseen hazards), dogs who ran away and returned five years later without so much as an apology, dogs with three legs, and dogs trained to find land mines, drugs, and people trapped in rubble. It was an energized and happy discussion — and everyone had a story.

Chapter 10

Revelation

Throughout the week, Claire glided unscathed through a few more half-hearted attempts to uncover details of our time in Vermont. On Friday, just before that undefined moment when people began to reach for coats initiating the daily exodus, a discussion broke out about scallops. Alex had an issue he was determined to air: Could a store or restaurant cheat customers and, using a circular cookie cutter, "make scallops" from shark or skate meat.

"I don't think they use skate—they are an endangered species." While I am not inclined to give a legal opinion, I was fairly sure about this. It had come up in a case I worked on not long ago when a utility we represented needed a place to discharge heated water it used to cool a portion of its generating system. The idea was to have the warm water flow slowly and, we argued, innocuously, into the wide and deeper lower portions of Chesapeake Bay.

An environmental group opposed the issuance of the discharge permit on the grounds, among other things, that warm water would disrupt bio-homeostasis, increasing algae and other plant growth, jeopardizing what was left of the skate population in that area. The environmentalists and the skates, more commonly called stingrays, were victorious and our client had to build cooling pools.

Undaunted, Alex continued: "Sharks are not endangered—at least not all of them—and one shark could produce hundreds of so-called scallops. Think about it. It is just impossible for there to be so many scallops given the effort required for them to grow to mature size." He described the shells of larger scallops, noting they take years to develop.

Maurice joined in opposition to the premise, claiming there were regulations that made it impossible to perpetrate such a heinous fraud and what's more, if the taste was pleasing and the thickness and density of the meat seemed right, what difference did it make?

Claire, who seemed completely disinterested, pfff'ed Maurice and Alex several times, and left early muttering something about an appointment. Her departure did not end this discussion. Maurice wondered why a stingray would be called a skate. "Is it the same word, the same spelling, as ice skate?" he asked no one in particular.

"While words matter," Alex answered, "the order and use of words is everything. Take the words 'death and sadness.'"

Maurice shook his head. "Can't we go with something a little more upbeat?"

Alex plowed on. "If a line in a poem includes the phrase 'the sadness of death' you know something bleak lies ahead. If instead it reads, 'the death of sadness,' something entirely different is suggested—and it is likely to be upbeat. Sadness has ended—hard to see it any other way."

Henry was straining on this and asked Alex to say it again. Alex repeated the phrasing, flipping death and sadness and, when Henry still seemed uncertain, said: "Try it with death and silence—I'll use same words but note the difference between: 'the silence of his death' and 'the death of his silence.' The first is terminal and dark, the second is liberating—the person, whoever he is—is free at last to speak his mind."

Henry nodded, but I think the lesson was lost on him. What entered my mind was simple: it's no wonder Alex teaches poetry. You only get a few words in a poem.

Maurice was quiet for a moment and then said: "That's true with dumplings. The dumplings in chicken-and-dumplings are like noodles and bear absolutely no relationship or resemblance to the dumplings served in Thai and Japanese restaurants—and those are wildly different than apple dumplings and other dessert dumplings."

Henry weighed in on this one, noting that in his country—whatever it was—the dumpling was common and looked quite different than other dumplings he could recall. "I used to have *mont lone gyi* between meals. Sometimes different ones were served as breakfast."

"Maybe you should offer those in the Market," Alex added and then said to Maurice, "You know we are talking about two distinctly different phenomena, right?"

Maurice tilted his head as if to say, "Don't insult me by even suggesting I was unaware"—and then announced: "I'd love to stay but duty calls."

I had no idea what duty was calling and was disinclined to ask. Once outside, I joined Maurice on the sidewalk. "What's the big secret with Henry's homeland?" Maurice followed me as I walked toward my car. "Where do you think he's from?" he asked.

"I assumed India or Pakistan. Does it matter?" I replied.

"I find it odd—dishonest—that he would tell us about his imprisonment and journey to the States and not tell us where he lived." Maurice was speaking loudly. "I'm at a point where I don't believe a word he says." Maurice peeled off to the right down Washington Boulevard and was gone before I could tell him I disagreed.

I was stunned to see Claire waiting at my car when I arrived. She had left the Market some time earlier for an appointment—yet here she was. "I wanted to talk to you alone."

"Of course," I said.

"This won't take long," she said. "I know you were sincere in all that you said while we were driving home from the wedding on Sunday. I also know that I am more complicated than you may have guessed. I'm not sure you have really thought about what it would mean to be with me." She paused and put her hand on my arm. "We might work out, Charlie. For now, however, I think we should keep our relationship alive just at the Market."

"I'm not giving up that easily, Claire. I've waited a long time, alone, with the hope that I would meet someone like you."

"Then you can wait a little longer. Let's take a breather and see how we feel." She paused. "I need time. Don't rush me, Charlie."

That night, I made a conscious effort to put in context the situation with Claire. I left Brampton more than two decades ago and am two years past forty. I considered the males over forty I knew as a child—some potbellied fathers of families, others graying, balding, complaining about their teenage children. I like to think I am nothing like those men.

I know this: I have been in love just twice in my life, once with a woman of great beauty who, as it turned out, was and always had been a lesbian, and now with a lovely, compelling woman who is independent, smart, sensuous—and a grandmother. None of those 40-year-olds I knew in Brampton could say that.

~

Mornings came and went and we passed the Ides of March, a time in Washington when there can either be wet and unwanted snow that hobbles the city or seventy-five-degree days that cause the cherry blossoms to bloom prematurely. On one of those warm March evenings, Flynn and I had dinner outside on the porch, waiting for the darkening dusk and lights to come on in the neighborhood. We inhaled the first strands of spring, a simple blessing before the insect world descends.

It begins with gnats, then mosquitos and flies, and by mid-July, they are joined by moths (some large as a nectarine), bees, wasps, Japanese beetles, cicadas (who appear more often than their seventeen-year hibernal cycle suggests), and spiders of every shape and size. They are everywhere, suggesting caution in all actions, including breathing with one's mouth open. It is a more varied infestation than the summer plague of black flies of Brampton that swarmed over my adolescence. This night, however, there was nothing but the nutrients of night air and beginning of starlight.

Normally on such a night, Flynn and I take one last walk in the park, but tonight we decided that benign fates limited us to the confines of the yard. At one point, Flynn slid off his beloved settee and trotted off into the bushes that camouflage the ancient rusted wire fence, that fragile but sufficient barrier separating my backyard from my neighbors. Flynn took care of his affairs, and then rummaged in leaves I should have collected in the fall. A few minutes later he returned, rubbed up against my leg like a giant cat and then, as he is inclined to do, flopped to the floor covering my feet and pushing against my ankle. His head rested between his front paws and moments later, I heard his soft snore.

Who among us has not yearned for the wondrous simplicity of a dog like Flynn? He was not, at least as far as I could tell, the slightest bit lonely. He had me. And while I had and loved him, Flynn was not enough.

A week later, the warmth of mid-March reversed, giving way to the last lingering, vindictive, gray sinew of winter. It flexed one evening as Flynn and I were lounging, watching the basketball play-offs on TV, both half asleep. I glanced outside and saw rain suspended in the arched lumen of the street light. An hour later, Flynn and I heard the unmistakable tac-tac-tac-tac as ice pellets hit the roof, bounced on the sidewalk and street, clung to utility wires, and gave notice that the morning rush hour would, in all likelihood, be a debacle.

Of all of the meteorological phenomena that manifest in colder weather, Washingtonians know the worst: the ice storm. Utility lines weighed down by the ice snap rendering neighborhoods dark and chilled. Crystal-laden tree branches fall on newly hazardous roads, and sometime in the middle of the night all the area schools close. However, it was late in the year for such a storm and the falling ice turned to rain just before sunrise. The schools were already closed, the streets empty, and as I drove to the Market, to my great relief, the roads were just slushy.

Henry was behind the counter, and Maurice and Alex were at the table reading the paper. Things were quiet until Claire arrived almost an hour later. Alex looked up: "You've been late more in the last month than in the prior six years. You're going to get detention. That's the third tardy arrival this week."

Claire glared at him. "Are you keeping tabs on me, Alex?"

"I was kidding," Alex said.

Claire softened only slightly.

About a week later, I arrived at the Market determined to stay just a short time. I had a meeting at work later in the day and needed time to prepare. After drinking half a cup of coffee and feeling a little bit sorry for myself, I filled my thermos, chatted briefly with Maurice — the topic was the curious popularity of olive oil — and walked toward the door.

When it became clear to Henry that I was leaving, he called my name and when I did not stop, came out from behind the counter and ran after me. There were two people in line in front of the counter waiting to be checked out, but apparently whatever Henry needed to tell me was more important than his commercial obligations. He grabbed my elbow as I was leaving. My momentum pulled him through the door and onto the sidewalk.

"You wanted to know—I heard the talk." His eyes were fixed on mine. "I am from Burma. Now the government calls it Myanmar, a name I will never use. To me it means nothing but sadness." He was breathing heavily as if stopping me had required considerable exertion.

"Burma was a poor country, and below the surface there was fire. The worst in people can surface without warning." He looked beyond me. "That Simone and I got out together was a miracle."

I stood silently, trying to make sense of the situation.

"I want you to see this," he said.

"What?"

Henry did not reply. Instead, on a relatively busy sidewalk in front of the American Market, Henry took off his shirt and turned his back to me.

Long gray, pink, and white scars crossed the upper shoulders and center of the back. There were crude stitch lines where wounds were sewn hastily in a manner that made obvious the lack of medical expertise. Just above his waist was a large clustered brown scar raised a quarter-inch above the surface of his skin.

He lowered his shirt and, risking the charge of indecent exposure, Henry DuChamp pulled down his pants.

His boxer shorts hung like a kilt on his thin body. I squatted, examining the backs of his legs. More scars, more stitching that would have been more appropriate on a rag doll than a human being.

He said nothing for a minute and when I stood, he pulled his pants up and turned to me. He reached in his pocket and pulled out a passport thick with visa stamps. I looked through them quickly, matched up his picture with his face, saw his real name—he was correct, we never would have been able to pronounce it.

The sidewalk scene did not go unnoticed. Alex, Maurice, and Claire stood in the doorway. Behind them were now four customers in line at the counter, all looking through the windows wondering why it was that the proprietor of the American Market had pulled down his pants on the sidewalk in the middle of downtown Jackson Park.

"There is more," Henry said looking at me. "I am not a perfect man." He inched closer to me and said quietly: "You think I do not love Simone because we are not always nice to each other. Some of her back looks like mine. I know, sometimes I say things that hurt her. Sometimes she says things that hurt me. Sometimes she does things that hurt me. This may be hard for you to understand, Charlie, but that is not abnormal. Relationships are never perfect. Anyone who claims a perfect marriage is a liar or incapable of self-observation."

"Where is Simone?" I asked.

"Simone fell and was taken to a hospital."

"Claire looked—there are many institutions in this city affiliated with Johns Hopkins—and she called all of them. No Simone DuChamp. What happened, Henry?"

He took a step back and then nodded several times. "Other than for purposes of immigration in the final phase of the asylum process, Simone never uses the name DuChamp. She uses her family name, Vredeesha. Tell Claire, and I am sure she will find Simone."

He stopped for a moment, caught his breath, and said: "At first, I was told she would not walk again. Now I am told she may be able to walk—but maybe won't be able to come home."

"Maurice told me what happened the Friday Claire and I drove to Vermont. He said Simone slapped you and left."

"She did. Twice. You would be surprised how hard Simone can slap. She has done it many times before. I have never touched her, however, and never will."

"So now what?" I asked.

"I have told you these things for two reasons. First, I asked if you would be my lawyer. It is not too much to ask. It is not because Simone and I will get divorced, if that's what you think. That will never happen. It is because some people in Simone's family will try to take the Market from us and we want to fight them. I think with your help we can win."

He paused. "I have documents, including a title to the property and a series of contracts that I need you to review. Simone and I signed them without realizing the limits on our ownership."

"Henry, I am not the best person for this. It's not the kind of legal work that I do."

"You are the only person for this, Charlie. Of that I am sure." I was anxious to leave and process all that had happened but Henry was not done. "You understand now that although Simone and I have difficulties, say angry words—a slap in my face in front of others—I still love her and, while you may think otherwise, she loves me. Were she here at this moment, she might say something like, 'I should not love you because you are selfish, but I do.'"

"I'll speak with some of my colleagues at the firm. Maybe we can be of some help."

"There is a second thing, Charlie, and it may not be my place— it may never have been my place. Sometimes it is helpful to know that two people can be right for each other, love each other, share a life together, and also, from time to time, seem completely unsuited.

"There is a fable in Burma about a beautiful princess who cannot find true love until one day in the palace garden she sees a flower in full bloom and decides to pick it and place it in her bedroom. As she is pulling on the stem, the flower begins to grow and change. There is intoxicating dust on the blossoms and as she breathes it in, she becomes drowsy and falls asleep. When she awakens, the flower before her is her prince, the man of her dreams.

"This is a story for children. It tells of magical love and perfect affection. It does not tell how a prince could be formed from the stalk of a flower nor does it tell anything about the life of this couple. The idea of happily ever after is the greatest delusion fairytales can produce. Life will have some happiness, some sadness, some anger, disappointment and even betrayal, and still there can be love and a lifetime together. Don't give up, Charlie Pratt."

Henry returned to the Market, seemingly anxious to serve what had become a long line of customers who had been staring at the scene on the street. I stood on the street and processed only one thought: I had been wrong about Henry.

~

The weather changed quickly and any vestige of the ice storm was gone. All of a sudden, it was the second spring, the real spring, pregnant with new opportunities for Flynn. Grasses reawaken and take on an exciting and tasty essence, no longer subdued to January's brown dormancy. As we walked through the park, had I not known better, I'd swear Flynn pranced.

In the days that followed, I told and retold the stories and observations Henry provided on the sidewalk, explaining why he had pulled down his pants, sharing my renewed faith that he was the person we hoped he would be.

On Friday of that week, Claire returned to the Market, sat down at the table and said: "I had no difficulty finding Simone using the name Vredeesha." She turned to Henry, expecting to learn why he waited so long to provide this critical fact but when he returned a hollow smile, she turned away and continued. "The flowers have been sent. The hospital is quite a distance from here." She hesitated. "I have the phone number and called Simone. She asked me to tell you that while she would love to return to the Market, she is not sure she will ever come back."

"What? Why?" I asked.

"There are other complications."

From behind the counter, Henry stood, startled, and said with quiet sincerity: "What complications?"

Claire looked at Henry and shook her head. "I wasn't given permission to speak with you about her, Henry. I'm afraid you'll have to do that yourself."

"I spoke with her by phone and will see her this weekend." Henry said no more and busied himself at the counter.

It was not until Wednesday of the following week that Henry reported on his visit with Simone. On Monday and Tuesday, he met every question with a smile, a nod of his head and then a deflection or affirmation, usually, "Okay, everything is okay," or, "Yes, I did get to see Simone." The vacancy of these responses only fired Maurice's belief that nothing Henry said was true.

To hear Henry discuss Simone that Wednesday, one would have thought she was a child recovering happily from a tonsillectomy, watching movies on the TV in the hospital room, sipping slowly small spoonfuls of slushy sherbet.

On Wednesday afternoon I decided to see if I could penetrate the mystery of Simone's wellbeing and, armed with the phone number Claire had provided, called the hospital. When asked my name, I said, quietly and dishonestly, "Pratt—Dr. Charlie Pratt." For all I knew, there was a Dr. Charlie Pratt on the staff of the hospital because my call was put through. In a small voice, Simone picked up the phone and, rather than a standard hello, said: "Good afternoon. How may I help you?"

The phrasing, eerily familiar from the thousands of encounters between Simone and customers at the Market, shook me. "It's Charlie, Simone. I wanted to see how you were doing."

"Oh, Charlie, thank you so much for the lovely flowers. Henry told me that you and the others ask about me every day."

"We were told we cannot visit or I would have been there right away as would the others. Henry has been quite cautious," and then, genuinely unsure of the situation I added, "protecting your privacy."

"Henry can be so horrible and so caring. He is loving, jealous, and suspicious but does what I ask." She hesitated. "In the end, he is always the one who knows what to do."

"I won't keep you, Simone. I just wanted to see how you were— see if there is anything I can do to help. Do you have an idea when you'll be able to go home?"

"I know Henry told you I had a fall. That is true. I also have some other matters that will keep me here." She did not elaborate but I assumed that whatever illness affected her earlier in the year, rendering her unconscious in the Market at one point, keeping her from work at other points, was the subject of her comment. Then, in a slightly stronger voice, she said: "I cannot come back to the Market because it will be embarrassing." I heard someone at her bedside ask a question and, before I could say anything more, she said goodbye and hung up.

The following day, I related this to Claire as we were walking to the Market together. It was one of those April mornings in which the leaves on the trees in Jackson Park take on a luminescent light green hue, as if backlit. This happens once a year before summer's fierce heat and moisture brings out the deeper colors.

I asked Claire what she made of Simone's comment regarding her embarrassment. She stopped on the sidewalk and said quietly: "Do you have a theory—why would she be embarrassed?"

"I assume that there are marks on her body or something has happened to otherwise affect her appearance."

"Think, Charlie. This has nothing to do with scarring. She is suffering from an illness—I really don't know what it is. But sometimes, when one is very sick, they lose control of certain bodily functions."

I'm not sure why Claire decided I couldn't handle the term 'incontinence,' but simply nodded.

It was twenty after six when Claire and I sat down at the table. Alex had already spent over a hundred dollars on the lottery and had a stack of tickets next to his cup of coffee. As we sat down, Maurice said to him: "I don't think this is your day."

Alex gave him a dark look and said: "It's not your precious money. Back off."

Maurice was too stunned to respond. Over the years, we've joked with one another and, in sincere moments, been brutally frank but not nasty or insulting, and not, as was the case with Alex's comment, rude and dismissive.

Moments later, Alex walked to the counter and spent another forty dollars, this time on High-Stakes Keno and Insta-Match tickets. The win he sought evaded him. When the last ticket produced nothing, Alex took the entire stack of tickets, neatly squared it, and tossed it in a trashcan on the way to the door.

Before reaching the exit, Claire got up from the table. "Alex?"

"I'm late—I'll talk to you tomorrow."

"Alex, this is important."

He turned and faced Claire. "Why, Claire? Do you think I am unaware of the money I just lost?" Claire said nothing and Alex continued. "Do you think I enjoy this?"

No one said a word. "You think this is just a whim, a hope and a prayer for me?" Alex took a step toward Claire. "I have few options at this point. You want to know what that feels like?" Claire shook her head but Alex pressed on. "Try shame. Frustration. Disappointment. Anger. You'll get to personal failure quickly."

Everything stopped in the market. "Did you think I was unaware of what I was doing? How much I was losing?" His voice was starting to crack. "Believe me—I know."

"Then why? ..." Claire's question trailed off as she saw Maurice shake his head.

Alex walked toward the door and with his back to us said: "Stop worrying. I'll be fine." As he walked out he called, "Maurice?"

Maurice joined Alex on the sidewalk in front of the Market. They spoke at some length before Alex left and Maurice came back inside.

"I didn't mean to upset him," Claire said.

"I don't think you're the reason he's upset," Maurice said.

"Obviously I touched a nerve." Claire looked at me. "Charlie, has he said anything to you about this?"

"Not that I recall—certainly nothing along the lines of what just happened." In fact, I was hard-pressed to remember speaking with Alex outside the Market at any point but kept that to myself.

"Where does he get this much cash?" Claire's question hung in the air for a few minutes and then vaporized.

"Have you ever sold a ticket that won a lot?" I asked Henry.

"To Alex?"

"To anyone."

Henry looked around as if the answer was hidden somewhere in shelves packed with overpriced deodorant and shampoos, jumper cables and canned meats, nail clippers and hand cream. "What do you mean by *a lot*?"

"A hundred-thousand or more." I considered saying "at least a million" but, as you know, I was at a point with Claire where mention of a million dollars as a threshold amount seemed ill-advised.

Henry continued scanning the aisles, assessing, as if for the first time, tooth brushes and suntan lotion, paper clips and chemically infused dried fruit marked deceptively 'real fruit,' hand sanitizers and mayonnaise. "No—I don't think so," he said finally looking away from the shelves.

"Wouldn't you know?" I asked. "Don't you get a bonus if you sell a ticket that wins that much money?"

"In theory, yes. A ticket of that size can only be cashed with the State Lottery Commission. The computer at the State Commission should show where the ticket was purchased once it's cashed."

"So you'd find out."

"In theory, Charlie. I've never had it happen … and never known another store owner who had it happen."

That Henry had not sold a winning ticket of great magnitude was not as interesting as his comment revealing that he knew owners of other convenience stores. Did they meet regularly to talk shop? Have a union? Have annual picnics where softball was played and hotdogs and beer were consumed — hopefully not the hotdogs that rolled into shriveled intestinal nightmares in the Market.

Alex's losses stayed with all of us throughout the morning. I paid careful attention to lottery customers and tried to see how much was spent and how much was paid out. Not counting Alex, Henry took in around five hundred dollars in under an hour and paid out under half that amount.

Before we left that morning, Claire turned to Henry. "Why don't you just stop selling Alex tickets?"

"He will buy them somewhere else," Henry responded. "I know this because it happened to me, much earlier in my life. I know this sickness. Gambling is a powerful addiction — it's not so obvious, like drugs or alcohol, but it's very strong, very difficult to stop and, the more it is driven by real needs, not just the hope of winning simply because it might make you feel good, the more powerful and less rational it becomes."

"A few lottery tickets are hardly compulsive gambling," I said.

"This time, Charlie, you are wrong." Henry was not smiling. "You are a wise man and a good attorney but you don't know everything."

"I never said I did."

Henry paused before continuing. "Many people — in fact most people — will buy a ticket every now and then. That is not gambling. Some people buy them every day with hope of winning a jackpot. It's a small amount of money for hope, for the dream of financial independence. But some people not only buy them every day, they buy lots of them — and they can't stop themselves even when common sense tells them they've spent too much. They are addicts—there is no other word for it."

When I decided to share with you the story of the American Market, I did not expect to tell you how it was that this—or any—convenience store had characteristics of a basic casino, a place of almost entirely unmet hopes, where the possibility of great wealth tempts those who can least afford it. You may be wondering how that could come to pass—and whether it was true for the convenience stores you know. I cannot tell you it is true for all such stores but I can assure you it was true for the Market.

"Speaking of tickets," Claire said calmly, "are you going to fight mine?"

"Your what?"

"Speeding ticket."

"I told you I'd pay the fine," I said.

"I don't need that—and that's not what I asked." She paused. "Charlie, are you willing to fight for me?"

"Absolutely," I said and added, "it's possible to fight a speeding ticket—but not easy." Claire was attentive. "We could try to show the radar gun wasn't accurate, hadn't been calibrated in a timely way—or that it was not reasonably likely the reading on the gun applied to our car."

That I called the car 'ours' tumbled out easily—but once out, it made the entire table take notice. Rather than elaborate on the implications of calling it ours, I continued: "We could question the officer about the number of tickets he'd given that day before yours, ask why he never showed us the readout, try to show he was not able to pick you out from the rest of the traffic."

"And would that be enough?"

"I really don't know. We'd probably lose, but we could put up a good fight, maybe get the points removed from your license. On the reckless driving piece, we could argue the only reason the charge was tacked on was the officer's misuse of power, an emotional overreaction to being called—and you know I agree with your characterization—a jackass."

"You've thought a lot about this," Claire said.

I nodded.

"I'm impressed," she said and smiled. "Thank you," adding after a moment, "So you don't worry, I sent in payment last week — along with a rather pointed letter."

I watched as Claire walked to the coffee counter. She'd tested me — and it only bothered me slightly.

"Next time I get a ticket, you can represent me," Maurice said.

"I told you," Henry said to no one in particular. "Charlie is a great lawyer."

"I'm not taking any traffic cases — and I am not a great lawyer." What I did not say was that rattling off a strategy for Claire moments earlier was more satisfying than I would have guessed.

The morning drew to a close with no more mention of lottery and speeding tickets and I left the Market with but one question: What did Henry mean when he said that at some point in his life, "this happened to me"? I could see no other interpretation than a confession that once, at some undefined point, he was a gambler. I imagined Henry in a smoky room somewhere in Burma, a young man rolling dice, squandering his father's resources, playing complex games in a foreign tongue. Of course, I could be entirely wrong — yet, the image seemed to fit.

Chapter 11

Springtime at the Market

We were approaching the middle of April. The cherry blossoms had come and gone but the tourists remained—and kept coming. They came from Kansas and Kinshasa, Tennessee and Thailand, Peoria and Paris, from the fifty states and beyond. While they clogged the Metro and the roadways, it is a small price for Washingtonians to pay. This is an open city, showing off the great symbols of our government and our history.

They come to take in magnificent monuments to presidents and political giants, wars and warriors, and the greatest of our ideals. They come to shuffle through the Smithsonian and marvel—at no charge—at impressionistic genius and renaissance masterpieces in the National Gallery and the lunar lander across the Mall.

I believe (and here you might take issue) some come to catch a glimpse of—and confirm their suspicions or be inspired by—our federal government. If they take the time to look carefully, they'll learn that cartoon-like visions of national political figures pumped out by the press are just that—fictional contrivances.

The majority of those who work in the bureaucracy with whom I have contact are bright, objective, and hard-working. I deal with several different federal agencies that play a role in energy regulation and those I've come to know are, to the person, dedicated and committed public servants.

As to the tourists, if they look closely, they would discover that the federal government is not a tourist destination and, importantly, not a visible singularity. It is instead hundreds of decision-making centers, some functioning independently, some secretively (the dark, powerful, and mysterious Office of Information and

Regulatory Affairs comes to mind), and some very much in the open. It is an amazing enterprise.

I share this with you in part because I do not want you to think we ignore the world around us. The fact is, all of us at the table, at one point or another, have expressed a commitment to and a love for greater Washington. In a broad sense, like Jackson Park, it is part of our home.

A discussion about April tourists and traffic came to an abrupt halt one morning when Alex looked around the table and said: "Listen, I know you're concerned about the amount of money I spend on the lottery. I appreciate that. I'm sorry I snapped at you the other day." He started to say something, stopped, stood up, looked directly at Maurice, and said: "They need to know." Maurice nodded. "I'm going to take a walk around the block. It will be easier if you tell them—all of it."

"Don't you think it would be better coming from you?" Maurice seemed resigned.

"I know my limits—at least in this regard." Alex put on his uniform jacket and walked out.

Despite the fact that there were a few people wandering around the Market, Henry walked from behind the counter and stood next to Claire.

"Here's what I know about Alex, about why he spends so much on something as improbable as the lottery." Maurice was speaking just above a whisper and we leaned in. "After his stint in the Navy, Alex perfected a tiny electronic component—for a time it was built into the hard drive of most computers—that did something that increased system security. He and a partner formed a start-up, got a patent, and within a few months sold their company for several million dollars. Alex took his share, traveled—saw the world—and ended up in Mexico where he fell in love and got married. He and his wife came back to the States, bought a pricey rowhouse not far from here, and had a daughter, Liliana."

Maurice took a sip of coffee. "A few years later, Alex's wife was in a car accident. The car hit a patch of black ice and spun off the road. Liliana bore the brunt of the crash—she had head and spinal injuries. For some time it seemed she would not survive.

"Alex made sure she had every possible medical treatment, every therapy, both conventional and unconventional. The costs quickly exceeded the policy limits on his health insurance. When the insurance stopped paying, Alex paid the medical bills and ended up spending most of the money he made selling his technology company.

"The bills kept coming and Alex hired a lawyer to help him and learned two things: first, he had too much property to declare bankruptcy—and second, he had no one to sue. The accident, the lawyer explained, was just that—an accident. No one had been negligent—no one was at fault—and that meant the medical bills were 100 percent his responsibility.

"He kept spending and ultimately did what anyone would do if they had good credit: he borrowed. He took out a second mortgage, borrowed to the limit on his credit cards, and took out personal loans. It took more than a year but Liliana, who at one point could neither walk nor speak, emerged with remarkably few permanent effects."

Maurice looked at each of us. "Alex said her recovery is the one and only unquestionable miracle in his life."

"Why didn't he tell us?" Claire asked.

"This is not an easy story to tell." Maurice hesitated and continued. "And even if you'd known, then what?"

"I don't know," Claire said. "Try to help I guess."

"How? He'll never borrow any money again—he's made that clear to me."

"What's his plan?"

"It's not really a plan—it's a gamble. There's the lottery. With every ticket he buys, for just one liberating moment, Alex has a chance to pay off all of his obligations. It's a faint hope, not a financial plan and Alex knows that. He takes that risk with the thought that one morning he will win—and all this will finally be behind him."

"How much does he owe?" I asked.

"I don't know exactly—at least half a million," Maurice said.

Henry issued an involuntary whistle, shook his head, returned to his station behind the register, and began checking out the customers who had been waiting in line.

I turned to Maurice. "What about family? Can't he borrow the money and pay it back slowly? There must be some way to handle this."

The words were barely out of my mouth when Claire said: "Alex is not a Pratt, Charlie. He doesn't have a trust fund. I would guess his family can't bail him out."

"He won't take a loan from you, Charlie, or anyone else." Maurice rubbed his eyes. "There are a couple more pieces to the puzzle. Horrible injuries produce extraordinary stresses in families. Alex's marriage was not strong enough to weather the storm. A year after Liliana was back on her feet, Alex and his wife divorced. She now lives in Mexico City, her family home."

Claire sat back in her chair. "What's he going to do? This is awful."

Maurice smiled slightly. "Alex is an inveterate opportunist."

"I don't understand," Claire said.

"At some point after he started the delivery route, he walked in the front door of the Beardsley House — a destination for a number of the packages he'd been delivering for a few years — and offered his services for free. He was welcomed with open arms." He paused. "Alex had made a fundamental and obvious observation at the Beardsley House."

Maurice hesitated knowing the implications of what he was about to say. "Alex knows his students — the residents at Beardsley are old — more than old — at death's door. His plan is to be a positive force in their lives, awaken them to ideas and interests they had when they were young. If they like him — and they do — and they are at the tail end of life, at the tipping point on the actuarial tables...."

Maurice rushed through the rest of the story but we could figure it out without any further explanation. Alex was gambling at Beardsley House that one of the residents would leave a portion of their estate to their beloved poetry and piano teacher. In the grand scheme of insanely bad bets, this one was powerfully distasteful — but had a better probability than purchasing a winning lottery ticket.

The following morning, April 15th, tax day throughout the country, holds a special significance: it is the National Day of Moaning. Almost everyone in the Market was fully engaged in moans of greater or lesser volumes. The talk was about tax rates, misuse of tax dollars, the complexity of the Internal Revenue Code, and the value of certified public accountants.

No one laid claim to a great knowledge of the tax laws — and when Henry asked me, as a lawyer, to clarify a question he had about depreciation of equipment in the Market, I could not repress a small laugh. "Of the many things I am not, Henry, a tax lawyer is high on the list."

The tax chatter petered out with a few more sorry moans. No one said a word to Alex about his daughter, his divorce, the lottery, or his decision to curry favor with the soon-to-die but he was predictably anxious. He knew what Maurice had said and it played on him. He walked around the Market, picking up and putting down a newspaper, a packet of Marcucci's macaroni, and reading a label on a box of cereal. He downed the last of his coffee while examining a bottle of aspirin and, with a quick, "See you tomorrow," was first to leave.

The moment he was safely down the sidewalk, Claire said: "Did you notice? Alex didn't buy any lottery tickets today. Maybe he's turned the corner."

"If he thinks you will attack him when he buys tickets here," Henry said slowly, "he will get them somewhere else. They are everywhere. Every supermarket, gas station, and of course, in almost every convenience store. In a way, I would rather have him buy them from me so that we can help if he seems to be stretching beyond his limit."

"Really?" asked Maurice. "Buying from you means you make a small amount of money on each sale — I think we all understand that."

There had been something of a *détente* between Henry and Maurice for the last few weeks. It ended in that moment. "I make almost nothing from the sale of those tickets — almost nothing," Henry said, his tone only marginally civil. "You should have told me long ago that Alex had the kind of debts you described. I could have helped him. I could have told him to slow down. Like everything else with you, it's all secretive, a series of lies and misleading statements."

I thought Henry was going to tell Maurice he was no longer welcome in the Market but that did not happen. Instead, Maurice fired back: "Any time you want to talk to me about any of this, I would be happy to do so. Perhaps it would best be done outside or after hours."

"For god's sake," Claire said. "Are you two in high school? Are you going to go out in the alley and have a fist fight? I don't need this. If you can't behave in a more civil way, I won't spend my time here. Like all of you, I face tough things every day, occasionally dealing with angry people—but I do it for a living. I am not going to waste my time in the Market doing the same thing."

She picked up her coffee cup, grabbed her valise, and was out the door.

When she was gone, Maurice said to no one in particular: "We all need a break from this."

Before I learned from what we needed a break, Henry said to Maurice in a flat but commanding tone: "Don't do that—I don't know when Simone will be well enough to come back but I do know that she talks about spending time at the table, hearing all of your interesting stories, being part of this group."

"That's fine with me," Maurice said, "but I need an apology from you, Henry. You owe me that."

"Would you let it go," I said. "Henry thinks, for good reason, that you had an affair with his wife. That he is wrong is enough, isn't it, Maurice?"

"Go to hell, Charlie," Maurice said and left.

So there we were, much as it had started, just Henry and me in the American Market. I waited longer than I had in a long time, watching people come and go. We did not discuss Alex, Maurice, Simone, or Claire and instead talked about the marketability of auto supplies in convenience stores—a topic Simone had raised repeatedly—and the upcoming Jackson Park food festival, always a good source of walk-in traffic in the Market.

I found it hard to leave that morning but finally it was time. I left Henry alone, behind the cash register, smiling at—nothing.

Chapter 12

Liberation

Neither Maurice nor Claire returned to the Market that week. Councilwoman Celia Bell, however, was there every morning. I suspected she might be there as Maurice's spy, snooping around to see what was taking place at our table. On Thursday I decided to make contact and asked if she was doing a little morning campaigning or just taking the pulse of her humble constituency. She raised her eyebrows. "So you're that Pratt fellow."

"Indeed I am."

"Do you have an interest in Jackson Park politics — or are you just nosy?" she asked.

"A little of both." I took a risk. "You must know my friend, Maurice — he's usually here. Have you seen him lately?"

"Oh, my," the Councilwoman replied, "you are more than a little nosy, aren't you?" She stopped. "Is there something you want to tell me?"

"If you see Maurice, tell him I said hello."

Out of nowhere, Alex said: "Have a seat, Celia. You're making me nervous."

I turned to Alex, who seemed quite pleased with himself.

"That's rather cheeky," she said.

Councilwoman Bell assumed what was undoubtedly a stock campaign plastic smile. "Nosy and Cheeky — good names for you two."

As she headed for the door, Henry threw in: "Thank you. Have a nice day. See you soon." After she was gone, he said, "She seems quite fond of Maurice but doesn't seem to like you, Charlie."

Alex smiled. "At one time or another, most of us don't like Charlie." This struck Henry as far funnier than it was — and I am sure it was not that funny.

Alex had been in every morning and still had not purchased any lottery tickets. I spoke with him regularly, asking how he was doing. His responses were thin and uninformative. He was disinclined to discuss his debts, his daughter, or the lottery. He was inclined, however, to try out different topics he planned to raise with his poetry class at Beardsley House.

One Friday morning, Alex was waiting at the door when Henry arrived. I was a few steps behind Henry and the moment I walked in Alex brushed off my questions about his well-being and got down to business.

"Do you remember the poem I read to you a couple of months ago, *The Painter from Acumbaro*?"

I think all of us remembered the poem. I was haunted by the image of the painter falling from the ladder. I imagined him working in a suburb like Jackson Park, charging less than the local contractors, saving money for his family back in Mexico, and of course the loving act of his daughter caring for him until he died. "I remember asking if it was about you and your family."

"You wanted to know if it was true." I nodded. "It's not a matter of whether the things we produce are true—facts are an illusion. Accurate pieces of information can be coupled with a suggestion or an assumption and become the basis for a conclusion about something entirely different. Everyone has their own truth."

If this is what Alex wanted to discuss, I was in. "Extrapolating grand conclusions from limited information is the mark of a small mind."

"Nice," Alex said. "What's it from?"

"It's one of the few valuable things my father said to me when I was growing up."

Alex had some sense of the difficult relationship I have with my father and said: "Cynicism and realism are close companions—and there is no absolute truth."

Henry, who had been leaning so far over the counter trying to hear us that he ran the risk of falling head over heels into the Market, joined in. "Life and death, good and evil—those are absolutes."

"Evil is relative," Alex said, though not in a combative tone.

"Then you haven't seen evil," Henry said. "A person kills another for no reason and without so much as a second thought goes home to have dinner his family. Evil lives, Alex."

A customer waiting to be checked out set down a can of soda and a newspaper on the counter and looked at Henry, then at our table, and back to Henry. "You do this every day?" he asked.

"Only when there's a full moon," Alex said as he walked toward the rear of the store to pour himself another cup of coffee.

I lost the flow of the discourse as I watched Alex and flashed back to Maurice's recitation of the situation with Alex. I tried to imagine being the lawyer who had to give Alex the awful news that despite the unthinkable thing that happened to his daughter, he was without legal recourse. That lawyer was with him when Alex first understood the future he faced. I wondered how I would have handled that counseling moment.

I thought about Alex and his invention. It must have felt like magic when he realized it into a form that, over time, generated more money than he could have dreamed—and then, by an accident no one anticipated, the money vanished. I cannot envision the transition from sudden wealth to the crush of unmet obligations—but I can see how, thereafter, spending considerable sums of money on the lottery regretfully and unhappily could follow.

Having dispensed with the necessity of absolute truth, Alex shifted the discussion. "What do you think—when one sets out to tell a story, should they only write about things they know?"

"Why would you write something you know nothing about?" Henry asked.

Henry's question was all Alex needed. He held forth on the necessity of imagination, of fantasy, the need for invention and creativity. I hope by now you understand that this colloquy was not abnormal in the American Market. Everything was, quite literally, on the table.

In retrospect, I think Alex wanted to give that speech for a long time. It was connected with his life, coping with the numbing repetitive nature of his job, and his belief—expressed in his lottery purchases—that illogical, unexpected, great, dark, benign, improbable things can happen, including those of beauty and burdensome life-altering consequences.

Alex held tight the possibility of transitioning improbable fantasy into form, pressed that possibility to his interior, re-played and re-prayed it in his universe of grace-laden potential, never separated from the possible, and expressed it in his poems so that it would not fade to the nothingness of an unrecoverable dream.

He slid a sheet of paper across the table. "Would you read it, Charlie? I'd very much appreciate hearing it in another voice." I nodded. The customer with the soda can and newspaper took off his jacket, sat at our table, and waited.

"We don't do this every day," I said to him. I cleared my throat and began.

It was a longer poem than his first. When I was finished, the customer with the newspaper and soda looked at Alex. "Did you write that?"

Alex nodded.

"It's remarkable," he said. "Can I have a copy?"

Alex promised to get him a copy.

(I hope you are curious about this poem as well—I included Alex's poem, *Write What You Know*, at the end of this tale.)

"I'll walk out with you," the customer said.

"Fine, but you need to hurry. I don't want to be late. The president is expecting me." Alex straightened his parcel delivery uniform, saluted Henry, and was gone, customer in tow. It was a grand exit.

After he left, Henry walked to the table and asked if I had any weekend plans. When I said I didn't, he stepped closer. "I'm bringing Simone home from the hospital this weekend. Would you accompany me?"

I was charmed by the simplicity of the request. I assumed there might be a need to help with a wheelchair, stairs, or transitioning into a car, and agreed immediately.

On a warm Saturday toward the end of April, I met Henry just before noon at the Market. He closed out his account on the cash register and reminded Wallace, the afternoon clerk, to get in the order for donuts for Sunday, then led me to his car, an aging station wagon with Delaware plates.

"No sales tax," he said. "Simone has relatives in Dover. Everyone in our family uses their Delaware address when buying cars. It is a little fraud."

"Your secret is safe with me," I said.

The drive to the hospital was longer than I expected. We headed northwest on Interstate 70, past Frederick, Maryland, and came to the point where the highway opens up, with the foothills of the Blue Ridge to the far west and the Catoctin Mountains to the east, and sports one of the most interesting road signs in the region.

We were 60 miles from the center of Washington when we came to our exit off the Interstate that, in addition to routing us to the hospital, also bears a sign reading: "Washington Monument, This Exit." As you might know (or could have guessed), the sign is not—nor could it be—referring to the great obelisk in the center of the National Mall bearing the same name. Instead, it directs travelers to the original Washington Monument.

Quite coincidentally, I had been here once before while walking with Flynn on a short hike along the Appalachian Trail. It was some years and about 15 pounds ago for Flynn. In any case, the monument passes only a few yards from the trail. So you have a point of reference, it is shaped like a 30-foot-tall milk bottle, was built decades before the Civil War, and is not far from the Antietam Battlefield.

We drove along the back roads leading away from the Interstate and the monument until Henry announced: "The hospital—we're almost there."

"Why is Simone all the way out here?"

"This hospital was recommended by her doctor—they specialize in highly complex situations like Simone's." He stopped. "It's peaceful out here. You almost always see deer in the woods, just beyond the edge of the parking lot. I have to be careful driving home in the evening. The deer are everywhere."

We headed down a winding two-lane road. A dozen deer grazed close to the road just past the sign directing us to the hospital. The proximity of the Catoctin Mountains, the idea of saving Simone, the deer, the very fact that I was alone in the car with Henry, was more than I could ignore. I don't know what to say about an event that coincides inexplicably with the dream I had months ago. I can neither explain nor be at peace with it. I could not tell Henry I had seen before images of this drive. He was properly focused on Simone, and I was not about to regale him with cloudy tales of my late-night interior.

I even hesitate to repeat for you the images from that dream since they may seem sacrilegious, childish, or preposterous. You may judge it to be all those things—but perhaps not. You may find value in contemplating, as Henry put it, that all things come from and go back to the orchestrated dust of the cosmos—and the cosmos is held together, embraced, by an All of Alls, a god-like presence. I again recognize that even a passing reference to any of this presents a hazard. Yet it was part of my experience with Henry, both in my dream and as I looked at the hills beyond the hospital.

The comparisons with the dream faded as we pulled into the parking lot of a hospital with the words *Johns Hopkins* on a new sign over the main entrance. It was clear from the moment we entered her room that Simone was desperate to go home. It was equally clear from everything said in the first five minutes that her doctors were disinclined, adamantly, to release her.

Simone was frighteningly light, pale, and, as Claire had predicted, in need of disposable garments to deal with her apparent inability to control releases from her body. We wheeled her to the nursing station in the center of the wing. With great effort Simone said to the charge nurse at the station: "I will be going home today."

"That is not possible, dear," the nurse responded. "We don't have the releases from your doctors. I'm sorry. It will be some time before they let you go home."

"I don't think you understand," Henry said in measured tones. "My wife wants to go home. She no longer wants to stay here."

"I understood perfectly, Mr. Vredeesha. We cannot release her until her doctors approve. I spoke with them this morning after they saw your wife. They expect her to stay in the hospital at least another month and probably more."

"Maybe what you should do," Henry said with remarkable calmness, "is call your billing office. We will take care of any charges the insurance company does not cover—but we will be taking her home today."

"Mr. Vredeesha, it is not possible to release your wife."

"You should address her directly," Henry said. "She is right here— in front of you. Her name is Simone."

The nurse turned to Simone and said, in that awful way some healthcare workers speak to the elderly, that insulting, marginalizing, cloying, infantile speech, "Simone, dear, going home today is a no-no. You cannot leave."

Henry turned to me. "I want to take her home."

Simone had tears in her eyes. "Charlie, please. I can't stay here. I belong at home."

In the silence that followed, I realized I would need to say something I had avoided saying for years: "Ms. Shipley," the name printed on the nurse's name tag, "I am Simone Vredeesha's lawyer."

The nurse turned to me and, without missing a beat, said: "Good for you. She can't go home."

"You can't keep her without her consent. Even if you believe, even if her doctors believe, even if the whole of the medical world believes that it is in her best health interest to stay, unless you have a court order or its equivalent, she must be allowed to leave. Naturally, she will sign all of the waivers of liability required. As Mr. DuChamp— to whom you refer as Mr. Vredeesha— told you, all of her billing will be covered in full."

"You're serious?" Ms. Shipley replied. "She can't leave. She is recovering from a broken hip and has other serious complications." She stopped, probably not sure whether she could disclose Simone's medical condition.

"My clients understand that. Still, we will be leaving with her as soon as her things are packed."

"I'm calling security," Ms. Shipley said.

"Good," I replied. "I suggest you also call the hospital's lawyers. Ask them to tell you about the civil tort of false imprisonment. Tell your lawyer you have a mentally competent and alert patient who has revoked her consent to stay and who has a safe means to leave. Tell your lawyers that you want to keep Ms. Vredeesha against her will, depriving her of a fundamental and dignitary civil right. It will be a helpful call for both of us."

"Have a seat," said Ms. Shipley and quite literally turned her back on us.

Ms. Shipley called security, security called the lawyers, hospital administrators were summoned, first one and then several, and, for the first time in many, many years, I engaged in the kind of lawyering I had avoided my entire career.

I was fortunate that the issue presented was straightforward: people cannot be detained without consent unless (and there are many other exceptions not relevant here) there is a legal order to do so or they are a danger to themselves or others.

By the mid-afternoon, the struggle came to an end. Documents were produced, a notary appeared, doctors and lawyers were contacted on golf courses and at their homes. Lawyers argued with each other and with me—but in the end, Simone's belongings were packed. We wheeled her from the conference room (where most of this drama took place) to an elevator, down to the main exit and out into the afternoon sun.

Simone was weak as we left, asleep by the time we got on the road, and barely conscious when we pulled into Simone and Henry's driveway. Henry had hired a private nurse who was waiting outside along with their family doctor when we arrived. Once inside, Simone revived slightly, looked around, and said to me: "I knew you were the one, Charlie. If I go, and one day we all do, I want it to be from here and not from a hospital bed."

After we carried Simone to a seat in the living room, I started to look around at the collection of framed pictures on the walls and shelves and on the piano. Henry joined me, pointing out portraits of their two adult children and seven grandchildren—all of whom, Henry explained, live in England. "If things get worse, Simone will decide if she wants them to come home, here, to Rockville. For now, as is her wish, I've told them to stay where they are."

Along with the array of framed photos and portraits of aunts, uncles, brothers, sisters, nieces, nephews, and friends, were a collection of large and small vases and landscapes that, I guessed, depicted scenes in Burma. In one corner of the room were a number of framed documents, some pertaining to family matters while others were diplomas and various certificates of accomplishment. However, what caught my eye was a hand-scrawled receipt for transit on a freighter called *The Jersey Jane* with passage from France to Baltimore along with a cargo invoice listing, among other things, a shipment of men's black socks from China.

Almost immediately, cars arrived at the house packed with friends and relatives with covered platters and bowls, breads wrapped in cloth sacks, trays of appetizers, and bottles of wine, all heading to Henry and Simone's dining room table. Soon the smell of homemade foods began to fill the house.

Henry told and retold the story of Simone's release from the hospital, emphasizing and exaggerating my role. I was congratulated excessively and celebrated to the point of absurdity. At one point, I was introduced by Henry thusly: "And this is the great Charlie Pratt, Simone's barrister, solicitor, and savior."

Being lauded and being at ease with praise are two very different things, and by late afternoon I felt adrift and out of place. As you know, these are familiar sensations for me. I was ready to go and told Henry I would call a cab.

"No! Out of the question. Give me a minute." He regrouped and explained that a cab would be far too expensive since his home was ten miles north of Jackson Park — a twenty-minute drive when there was little or no traffic.

Henry excused himself and went into the kitchen. He returned shortly joined by a young woman he introduced as his niece, Lucy Vredeesha. "Lucy will drive you back to Jackson Park."

I stayed close to Lucy as she worked her way through the crowded house. Before we left, she asked me to give her a few moments alone with her aunt as if her actions were subject to my approval — of course, that was not the case. I waited inside as she wheeled Simone to a screened porch off the living room. In the yard, not far from them, was a small stand of trees and, to the left of that, a stone bench, vine-covered arbor, and a large and carefully maintained herb garden.

Lucy knelt next to her aunt, stroking her hair, speaking too quietly for me to hear, but anyone seeing them would know in an instant there was something special about their relationship. After a time, the whispered discussion became animated, lapsed into momentary silence, continued, stopped completely, re-started, and finally ran its course. Lucy gave Simone a prolonged kiss on the cheek and left her sitting on the porch, taking in the garden in the late-afternoon light.

As we walked out, Lucy turned to me. "When I was a little girl, Aunt Simone and I used to sit on that bench and read." We walked a few more steps and she stopped. "I wanted to make sure she remembered those afternoons."

Once in the car, Lucy explained she was one of the nieces, as if there were armies of them and then asked, "How long have you been part of the morning group at the Market?"

"From the beginning," I said—and then clarified: "I don't mean I set it up. Your uncle…."

"I know," she said. "It always sounded like a nice way to start the day, but I work out here and couldn't make it in the mornings."

"But you've been there?"

"After the table was in place, we all went one Sunday afternoon. My uncle wanted everyone to see what he'd done. We had tea and cookies while sitting around the table."

"I go to the Market almost every day. It's become an important part of my life. Having a comfortable place to sit has made a big difference."

Lucy continued driving and after a time said, "Comfortable? Those chairs are awful."

"I guess it's a matter of perspective," I said.

She looked at me. "How much do you know about my aunt and uncle?"

"I've known them for years." I reconsidered her question. "I know more about your uncle than your aunt."

She glanced at her watch and a moment later said: "Do you have some time?" She pulled into an elementary school parking lot and looked around as if it was important to check for those who might eavesdrop on our discussion. Satisfied we were alone, Lucy sat back in her seat and closed her eyes briefly. "I know my aunt very well—we talk every day—I think I am the only one who knows."

"Knows what?"

"Mr. Pratt," Lucy began, "I know all about you. You have been the topic of many discussions on weekends around our family dinner table."

"I'm flattered."

Lucy turned to me and began a long and detailed story of Simone's life. She was born in a Burmese village some miles outside of Rangoon, now called Yangon. Burma had gone through waves of bloody domestic conflict for nearly three-quarters of a century, costing the lives of hundreds of thousands of people. While Simone was not politically active, she was, Lucy assured me, a strong woman. When I asked if that was why she kept Vredeesha, her birth name, Lucy laughed. "No, no—she used Vredeesha because she thought Simone DuChamp sounded like a cheap perfume."

Lucy smiled, perhaps remembering the moment she learned why Simone refused the invented name DuChamp, and then continued. "She was in her early twenties when she left her family home and went to live and work with her aunt who owned a shop in Rangoon. Not long thereafter, she met and fell in love with Henry, an account administrator in the city government. After a time, they were inseparable and soon married.

"A year after the wedding, they were driving to the beach town of Ngwe Saung and were caught in a crossfire between rival insurgent forces. During a lull in the shooting, they were captured, confined in a small cell and then tortured by one of the more violent and radical anti-government factions."

"Why them? What did they have to do with these groups?"

"I don't know—we were told the rationale for the detention, beyond sadism, was the government ID my uncle carried which, somehow, convinced these animals he was an operative, not an accountant."

"Henry showed me the scars," I said.

"Then you may already know the rest."

"I knew almost nothing until today."

"Quite by coincidence, one of the guards assigned to them was an old acquaintance of my father—Henry's oldest brother. The guard called my father and soon Henry and Simone's families made a plan. They sold property, liquidated investments, and for a large sum of money, they were freed but not safe. The insurgents believed Henry was a central actor in the old guard, a repressive regime...." She paused. "You know, Mr. Pratt, he may have been—but that was decades ago."

"An operative?" The image did not seem to fit—and yet, it was not out of the question. I waited for her to continue.

"Uncle Henry was a rising star in his office. That he played a role behind the scenes, beyond the tasks of a city accountant ... was possible. As far as I know, after they left Burma, he never spoke of it again—certainly not to me or my family—not even to Simone ... and she tells me everything.

"With things falling apart in Burma, the decision was made by both families to fund their emigration. It was the only way to insure they would not be recaptured. They were in France in six weeks and stayed there until they could book passage...."

"On the *The Jersey Jane*. The bill of passage is on the wall in their house."

"Right," Lucy said. "Once in the United States, Simone needed a safe and predicable life. She wanted nothing out of the ordinary. She worked hard, had children, and created a life for their family. The American Market provided the order my aunt craved."

When she was done I thanked her and (as she was starting the car) asked: "Why was it important for me to know all this?"

Lucy said nothing as we drove along increasingly crowded streets in the outer suburbs, past shopping malls and car dealerships. Finally, when we were a few minutes from my house, Lucy said: "Simone wanted you to know what her life has been like. It has been a full and complicated but good life."

We were stopped at a traffic light and she turned to me. "My aunt wants you to know this: She has had enough. I know this is so—and so does my uncle."

"Enough of ... ?"

"Really, Mr. Pratt—I think you know. Her illness. She has suffered and fought bravely, but she has come to the end of her reserves. She should not suffer when there is no hope. Do you understand that?"

"Not exactly."

"You should not have to think very hard. My aunt is not going to recover."

It was the last thing Lucy said to me about Simone on that drive.

~

I arrived at the Market on Monday, wondering just what I could and should say about Simone. Claire and Maurice had returned, apparently deciding to set aside the anger and disgust that prompted their exit early last week. They were at the table chatting quietly when I arrived. Alex was at the counter, speaking with Henry.

I poured my coffee and joined Henry and Alex. Before I could say anything, Henry said: "How was your weekend?"

It was a simple question, but it told me all I needed to know. It meant my trip and Simone's release from the hospital were bound by attorney-client privilege and that Henry was not about to tell anyone at the Market what had happened with Simone.

"Not bad," I said to Henry. "How about you?"

He smiled more broadly than normal and said: "Very, very pleasant."

Alex and I joined the discussion in progress at the table. Maurice was off on a tear about a variance the Jackson Park Town Council granted to permit two of the last residential properties in the downtown area of Jackson Park to be sold, torn down, and replaced with another mixed-use office and high-end residential complex.

Maurice could not understand why the owners of those two charming Victorian homes, blessed with wide wooden front porches and complex gabling, would want to sell property on which they made good rental income. "Those two homes were central to maintaining the residential character of this innocent municipality," Maurice said with sadness and conviction. "They're going to be replaced with impersonal and towering buildings." He stopped and shook his head. "What a grotesque affront to decency and common sense."

He repeatedly invoked Celia Bell and her efforts on the Town Council to block the variance, speaking of her with obvious admiration and, at least to my eyes, fondness.

As was so often the case, the discussion rattled along and had offshoots involving other zoning decisions and good and bad historical preservation cases. Alex told the story of a vacant lot on Connecticut Avenue, not far from the National Zoo, deemed worthy of historic preservation simply because it had been a vacant lot for decades. Maurice questioned whether that was an urban legend and Alex assured us it was true. To this day, I don't know if Alex was correct—but I am sure it does not matter. Truth, as Alex pointed out, like fact, is by no means fixed, certain, or absolute.

Chapter 13

Counsel Is In

I mark the end of April with Simone's return home and one other event that, while not perched on the border of life and death, was destined to change the dynamics at the American Market.

Maurice, with his staggering array of sweaters and ready humor, his quick transition to self-deprecation, was not an unhappy man. He was, however, fixated on the actions of our local government, the Town Council of Jackson Park, and found their decisions almost uniformly at odds with his unshakeable view of the best interests of the community they served.

It was this set of judgments that, from time to time, rendered Maurice an agent of opposition, sworn and determined to fight change—and this included every proposal for a new building, curb cut, variance, or exception from the zoning laws. He drafted petitions to present to the Council and sometimes stood outside the Market, clipboard in hand, trying to get signatures. Only once did he ask Claire, Alex, and me to sign one of his petitions. We each declined—respectfully—Alex saying what Claire and I felt. "I don't want to be lobbied here—I'd lay down in front of a train for you—but petitions? At the table?" No more was said—and no more was needed.

It was that odd combination of ebullience and fear of change that allowed me to begin to understand Maurice's rapidly growing affection for Councilwoman Celia Bell. Celia Bell, who had labeled Alex and me Nosy and Cheeky, was aloof, officious, and self-righteous. She had become a regular in the Market and while these characteristics were grating, over time, they were balanced by her civic dedication and, from time to time, an enviable dry humor.

The Councilwoman's positions on matters of public concern as well as her comments in the Market made clear that she and Maurice were fellow travelers. She was a deep believer in the virtue of the status quo. She was a voice of fear and caution cloaked as civic concern. She opposed all change—and in that regard, her views and those held by Maurice were utterly indistinguishable.

While there was no general agreement on land use issues, Celia, Maurice, and all of us at the Market agreed on the difficulty of unwanted personal change. The world can turn upside down in a moment. It happens with death or separation, loss of a job, divorce, departure of a friend, and the almost infinite series of things that can go wrong with your health or the health of a family member. And yet, while lives come to an end, families shatter, and vital portions of self smolder unexpectedly, life goes forward. We are capable of forgiveness and fresh starts. We put out fires and begin anew. For Maurice and Celia, however, resistance to change was about much more than personal and familial upheaval. It involved the entire municipality of Jackson Park.

Maurice and Celia emerged in my mind as the Last Knights of the Old Jackson Park. They were sworn to a grail, a sacred mission: preservation through resistance to change in Jackson Park. Their quest was to challenge greedy developers and corrupt city planners who were oblivious to the best interests of the municipality that would suffer the fate of their preposterous buildings. The Town Council could be seduced by the prospect of change and could, if not stopped, legalize the destruction of the last vestige of this small town. Celia and Maurice were there to stop the desecration, to fight change of any kind simply because it was change.

On the last Friday in April, Maurice appeared in the Market with a large "Elect Celia Bell" button affixed to his sweater. It was his Declaration of Independence sweater on which was legibly written: "When in the course of human events it becomes necessary for one people to dissolve the political bonds which have connected them." He had a stack of campaign flyers in one hand and a new coffee mug in the other. The mug, as you probably have guessed, was campaign *tchotchke*; on it was a picture of Celia Bell and the words "Bell for Councilwoman."

On a Wednesday in the second week of May, I found Maurice waiting outside the Market. As I approached, he took me aside. "You know I've been helping Celia with her work on the Council." I didn't know that but said I thought that was a fine thing to do. "We started going out last month." He stopped and whispered loudly through a huge smile. "It's incredible. I'm in love with her, Charlie."

The announcement stunned me.

"Say something," he said.

All I could think about was whether his vow of celibacy was now part of his past. Rather than make inquiries regarding those intimate details—though I was sorely tempted—or grabbing him by his sweater and asking how anyone in their right mind could know they were in love after a month, I did the only thing possible. I embraced him, slapped him on the back, shook his hand vigorously, and said, "Congratulations, big guy."

Maurice waited for me to say more—or to explain why I'd called him "big guy"—but instead I put my arm around him and led him through the doors of the American Market. At the coffee machine, I whispered, "Who else knows?"

"In a few minutes, everyone is going to know—but I wanted you to know first, Charlie."

"Are you going to make an announcement?"

"You'll see," he said. "It's better than an announcement."

On cue, Councilwoman Celia Bell entered the Market wearing the most spectacular sweater any of us had seen in years. We knew instantly. Maurice—and only Maurice—could have given it to her.

The central theme of the sweater was fireworks. Embroidered on the upper arms, back, and front of the sweater, were explosions in every color, some illuminated by sequins, and others—and you really had to see this to believe it—illuminated by a tiny battery pack tucked in the seam that caused lights to flicker sequentially.

It was the kind of garment that causes one to stand and marvel—and we did just that. When she had our attention, she pushed a button on the battery pack, the lights began to flash more rapidly, and from tiny speakers on her epaulets, we heard a scratchy but wonderful rendition of *The Stars and Stripes Forever*.

At the time, I could not imagine why a sweater would bring Claire to tears, but it did. Alex began the applause, starting with a slow and certain clap.

With all deference to the great designers of clothing worldwide, few can lay claim to conceptualizing a garment resembling even vaguely the knitted magnificence in which Celia was adorned.

The applause continued until Maurice realized that we would not stop until he embraced Councilwomen Bell—and so he did. For the first time in months, Claire, having recovered from her first viewing of Celia's breathtaking attire, moved behind me and put her hand gently on my back. Everyone was watching Celia and Maurice and Claire's gesture of affection remained private. Importantly for me, her hand remained on my back, warming me throughout.

Before the commotion ended, I said to Claire, in my quietest voice: "Celia and Maurice are so different—and yet, somehow, they seem almost destined for a long future together."

She turned to me, and said, "Patience, Charlie," and walked toward Celia and Maurice. I watched her, for once sure about the unstated meaning of her gesture. To confirm my best hopes, I followed, waiting for her to conclude congratulating Celia and Maurice, and was standing behind her as she turned to get another cup of coffee. "Stop hovering, Charlie."

We walked together. "How about dinner tonight at my house—Flynn and I will make you a steak."

"Who's the better cook?" she asked.

That was a "yes." "Any time after 7:00 is fine." She nodded—and a nod was all I needed.

The remainder of the morning was given to celebration. Maurice was openly content, unequivocally and absolutely at peace. While my record with relationships was not encouraging, lest there be any doubt, I am quite capable of determining who is and is not happy—and Maurice was happy.

Looking at Maurice's unrelenting smile that morning, I was reminded of a story he told us a few years ago. "You have to hear this," Maurice said, though he could barely get through the story. "It's trite to an extent," and he paused on the word "trite" and then again burst into laughter. "It's a short story...," but it took at least half an hour for him to finish. The story centered on his high school English teacher who, quite unexpectedly, brought forth extended flatulence in the middle of a lesson on Willa Cather's lesser works.

The class went silent. The silence was followed by suppressed laughter and then a riotous explosion sufficient to summon an assistant principal. From that point forward, any mention of Willa Cather rendered Maurice immobile.

That morning no mention of Willa Cather was needed. Maurice was pure joy and even engaged in heady talk about the remote possibility (remote at many levels, not the least of which being that they were not engaged) of a spring wedding on the median on Main Street. The plan, if one could call it that, died when Celia said dryly that assuming such a nuptial was in the offing—a fact, she added with a smile, that was not yet in evidence—she might be forced to vote against issuing a street closing permit.

With the exception of the Jackson Park food festival, Celia reminded us that she had voted against every such request on the grounds that once you start, it becomes a slippery slope. She ended with: "Before you know it, Main Street will be closed for birthdays, anniversaries, and yodeling competitions."

I was sitting next to Alex as Celia spoke and let him know I very much liked the idea of a yodeling competition and could imagine all of us, seated in folding chairs, listening to yodelers from the far-flung corners of the empire. I leaned toward Alex. "You certainly wouldn't want the street open for an event of that magnitude."

"Don't underestimate the difficulty of yodeling," he replied.

As we milled around the store that morning, there were periodic small flashes of light. Henry was standing on his stool, taking pictures of Maurice, Celia, Claire, Alex, and me. While there was no need to say so, when he finished, Henry said: "These are for Simone." Whether this was to share the joy of the moment or confirm that Maurice was committed to Celia—and thus not to Simone— I will never know.

My dinner with Claire that night—and Flynn, of course—felt powerfully familiar, as if we'd cooked together for years. We talked about the Market, gave Flynn a few bites of steak, and toasted Maurice and Celia with our water glasses, Claire announcing that she was not drinking wine as part of a diet. After we'd done the dishes and cleaned the kitchen, we sat outside on my back porch. Flynn snoozed on his beloved settee, and I sipped brandy as we watched the stars in the night sky and speculated on the destination of planes flying five miles overhead.

~

One morning not long after Maurice's grand announcement, Alex came into the Market wearing carefully pressed gray slacks, a blue pinstriped dress shirt, and a dark blue tie. He carried a dark sports jacket coat over his shoulder and was cleanly shaved. I add this detail because most days Alex came to the Market in his uniform, unshaved and, from what we could tell, stayed that way until he has completed his route, cleaned up, and headed to Beardsley House to teach music and poetry … and increase the probability of posthumous opportunity.

Claire studied him carefully. "You look like you are going to court."

"No," Alex said. "Not court."

"A funeral?"

"No." Seeing Claire heading toward a game, Alex said: "Have at it."

"Real estate closing?" Claire asked.

"Nope — not even close."

"Something at Beardsley House? They're opening a new wing?"

"More space for people who stand at death's door," Henry said quietly.

"That's a depressing view of assisted living," Claire responded.

"It's not right for me — or Simone. That's all."

Claire shook her head. "You might think differently one day."

"Never. I am quite sure of that."

"Your choice," she replied. "So Alex, not a new wing at Beardsley … wait — I know — you're having your picture taken."

When Alex didn't respond, I said: "Meeting with the higher-ups in the parcel business — maybe a promotion to the front office?"

Still just a smile from Alex but no response. Claire went out of turn. Technically, I suppose Henry, Celia, or Maurice should have been next. Instead, Claire said: "Something to do with your taxes … meeting with an IRS auditor?"

Alex, enjoying the show, remained quiet.

"You're giving a speech somewhere," Maurice said, closing his eyes as if receiving a Jung-o-gram from Alex's subconscious. "Maybe at a high school or," he paused for some time, "no—no—a prison!" Apparently the Jungian reception had improved and the message was clear. "That's it—you're going to talk to inmates about the working world."

"You get the prize for creativity, but no. No speeches in penitentiaries—at least not today."

"I dress that way when I travel. Are you going on a trip, Alex?" Henry asked.

"Not going on a trip."

Claire looked at Alex and slowly her expression changed. "Oh my god, Alex—have you been fired?"

"No, I haven't been fired, I've paid my taxes, it's not the IRS—it's nothing like that."

Henry made a gasping sound and, ignoring the customer standing in front of him who wanted to buy a jar of peanut butter, said: "You won! You won the lottery! You're going to meet with the lottery officials because you won."

Alex smiled at Henry and shook his head. "Unfortunately, no—not yet. However, something good has happened."

Even the peanut butter customer was intrigued. "One morning, some time ago, Charlie read out loud one of my poems. There was a customer in the Market who seemed to enjoy the poem."

"I remember the guy," Claire said. "He walked out with you."

"Right—him. He gave me his card and asked for a number where I could be reached. It turns out his name is Milton Thurber. He's an agent and represents authors and entertainers for a company called Alpine Equinox. I'd never heard of Alpine Equinox and never considered the notion of being represented by an agent. Frankly, I didn't think I did anything agent-worthy."

"Is he trying to sell one of your poems?" Claire asked, still half in the game mode.

"Yes—and not exactly. The more we spoke, the more curious he became about my music and poetry. Not long ago, he came to the Beardsley House and listened to my poetry class and then sat in the music room while I gave a piano lesson. When I finished, he asked me if I had produced any original music. When I told him I had, although they were short pieces mostly designed to help my students learn the piano, he asked if I had considered putting my poetry together with my songs."

Alex's tone was tentative. "We met several more times. I'm on my way to a meeting with him. He wants me to sign an Alpine Equinox agency contract and talk over the possibilities."

After the predictable congratulations, Henry asked: "What possibilities?"

"Tens of thousands of people write songs, lyrics, seek out agents; while they might tell you they just want to get their work out there, the truth is each song is like a lottery ticket. A song with lyrics that becomes a hit, is performed by a top group, is used in a movie, can bring in more money than I will make in the next five years delivering parcels. If one of my songs becomes a theme for a television series, everything in my life will change in just the same way I expect things would change were I to win the lottery, though at a far lesser order of magnitude."

Claire smiled. "Good luck—and it's a lovely tie."

"It's an average tie," Maurice said. "You're an artist—in the entertainment business—lose the tie. These guys walk around in T-shirts and jeans and drink fancy coffee."

The discussion rolled forward and everyone had an opinion on how Alex could maximize his opportunities through his attire.

After Alex left for his meeting, Claire asked: "How likely is it that he'll land a contract and make the kind of income he is hoping for?" She turned to me as if I, as a lawyer, I had such information at my fingertips.

"I have no idea—Alex knows more about this than any of us. He compared this with the lottery so I assume the odds are slim."

Celia suggested the odds might be better than we guessed. "Normally, it's the lyricist or writer who seeks out an agent—and good agents are extremely selective. That an agent came to Alex is unusual. This Thurber fellow must see something in Alex's work."

The moment she said, "This Thurber fellow," I thought back to her reference of me as "that Pratt fellow" and decided that if Maurice, my brother in coffee at the Market, was in love with this difficult person, far be it from me to harbor a negative thought.

Alex was not in the Market the following morning. We hoped he was on a private plane, jetting off to L.A. to sign contracts with a recording studio, staying in a fancy hotel, celebrating at the most expensive restaurant in the city. However, when he returned to the Market the following morning, he was back in his delivery uniform and initially said nothing about his meeting with Milton Thurber.

Claire made it about five minutes and, finding the lack of information intolerable, said to Alex: "Come on, Alex, we're all dying. What happened?"

"To what?" Alex responded.

"Don't do that," Claire said. "With the agent—Thurber—did you sign a contract?"

"We're talking about options." Alex turned to me. Something about the way he looked, a concession in his expression, suggested he did not want to say what he was about to say. "I need a lawyer, Charlie. I really need a lawyer—and I was wondering...."

"Charlie is a great lawyer," Henry said.

I pfff'ed Henry and then turned to Alex. "This is a complicated business, Alex. There are copyright issues I know nothing about. These are specialized contracts that artists, authors, and songwriters need. You would be better off getting an entertainment lawyer, someone who knows the field. I'm sure your agent can help you."

"I am negotiating *with* my agent—that's why I need a lawyer. Hopefully, he will be negotiating on my behalf, assuming this all works out. It was Thurber who recommended I get a lawyer to review the contract he wants me to sign with him—he told me it outlines his fees and the nature of our working relationship."

"I am at best an amateur when it comes to this kind of thing."

A chorus of groans coupled with Claire's, "Oh, for god's sake, help the guy," followed.

Henry busied himself at the counter, Claire picked up a newspaper, but Maurice looked at me and said: "What's the matter with you? Alex isn't looking for a fancy entertainment lawyer—he is looking for a lawyer who is a friend he can trust, someone to go through a basic contract he's been given. I'll bet you he has the contract with him."

"It's in the truck," Alex said.

"No one is going to sue you for malpractice, Charlie. You can look at a contract, can't you?" Maurice narrowed his eyes. "It's time, Charlie."

"There is a small desk and a few chairs in the storeroom — why don't you and Alex go in there. I will make sure no one bothers you." Henry said.

I never contemplated seriously going into practice on my own — and certainly never thought my first office outside the firm would be Henry's storeroom — and yet. . . .

Alex and I spent almost an hour going over a very simple agency agreement in the storeroom at a small gray metal desk. I told him several times that it was possible I was missing something, and he told me each time he was convinced I knew more than he did when it came to contracts and, when I thought about it, he was right.

I work with contracts all the time. True, they are contracts between suppliers and purchasers of bulk electrical power — but they are contracts. Vague and misleading terms need to be changed before anyone signs — and that is as true with a utility as it was with Alex and his agent-to-be.

When we emerged from the storeroom, everyone was still at the table. I think they would have waited all day had it taken that long. I had the strange feeling that I had just completed an athletic event and, win or lose, the spectators appreciated the effort. It passed through my mind that I could put a sign on the storeroom door that said, "Counsel Is In," and take on all comers. Until my battle with the hospital on Simone's behalf and that morning with Alex, I never felt as if I was practicing law. While I wasn't about to leave the firm, as Henry had suggested months ago, I had a different sense of my options as I left the Market that day.

Two weeks later, Alex signed an agreement with Alpine Equinox and, within twenty-four hours, was on his way to New York with Milton Thurber with the hope of landing a deal that, while it would be nothing like winning the lottery, might take a partial bite out of the mountain of debt he faced.

Chapter 14

The Announcement
July 2013

On a beautiful morning in late June, more than two months after her return home, Simone called me at work and asked if I could drive out to their home in Rockville and pay her a visit. "It is very important you come alone," she instructed. "No one is to know you're here."

I left the office providing the unnecessary explanation that I had a personal matter requiring my attention and was on my way. After a few wrong turns, I arrived at the Vredeesha-DuChamp home. Simone had managed to get out of bed and into the wheelchair and was waiting for me in the living room.

I made tea and we talked briefly about Maurice and Celia, Claire, Alex, Henry, and the day-to-day developments at the Market. After a few minutes Simone said: "Have you and Claire finally figured out how to be together?"

"I'm working on it," I said. She smiled faintly and closed her eyes. I was just starting to discuss the possibility of Alex's success with his songs and poems when Simone bent forward, wrapping her arms around her thighs pulling her head to her knees. Her breathing was uneven and released a vinegary essence.

She reached down to a wire basket at the base of her chair and grabbed a small towel already stained brownish yellow, pressed it to her mouth, coughed, and released a small amount of a substance faintly resembling infant meconium. She gasped several times, wiped her mouth and chin, and with effort sat back up.

"What should I do? How can I help?" I could not think clearly.

"I am at a point where each day is like dying. Each day brings pain ... I can't explain."

"I'm sure you have been working with pain specialists—I know some doctors who deal with nothing but...."

"I don't need more doctors," she said. "They've tried. I have half a pharmacy on the nightstand in my bedroom. Trust me, at a certain point you either render yourself unconscious or experience discomfort that is indescribable."

She bent forward and coughed up more dark fluid. It flowed over her lower lip and covered her chin. I took the nearly soaked towel and wiped the area below her mouth.

"Last summer, a doctor discovered polyps in my lower intestine." She was now hoarse and almost inaudible. "There were more tests; I learned that an aggressive cancer that started in my colon had spread throughout my abdomen and beyond. It's everywhere at this point. Of course I got a second and then a third opinion only to have confirmed that there was nothing to be done other than keep me comfortable."

She hesitated. "Henry and I have a view of life—frankly, it's a family perspective. When it's time, it's time." Simone then echoed one of my first discussions with Henry: "Neither he nor I want to live with capacity so diminished that regular functioning is impossible."

"Everyone ages and changes," I said.

"True—but this isn't about gray hair or forgetfulness. It is about grotesque deterioration, the last stage before death." She gasped several times. "Henry and I know life and death. He does not need the details. He knows more is wrong with me than I have said—but he will grant me what is mine." A silence was followed by this declaration: "It is my death."

I wondered if there was a cultural variable leading to the idea that one had ownership and dominion over their demise, but this was not the time to talk comparative anthropology.

"Is there anything you need?"

"I have a continuous sense that my body is in a vice. It tightens to the point where I think I'll explode and then loosens enough to breathe—but the vice is always there."

I shook my head and told her I felt so sorry and so helpless. "Right now, the vice is closing. I need to tell you before it's too much. First, swear to me, Charlie—swear to me you will never disclose to anyone what I am about to say."

I swore.

"I can't sleep. I can't eat. I can hardly speak. This is not life. I can't wait much longer. I do not want to live if I have to be sedated to the point I am a vegetable." She leaned forward and spoke while facing the floor. "I will end it very soon if it does not end on its own." A few short breaths. "Do you know what I am saying?"

"I do—and you can't do that. You never know what might happen."

"I do know—and I can—and I will. You were my lawyer at the hospital. I need you, Charlie." She handed me an envelope that was on the seat of her wheelchair. "Look at it now—please."

I opened the envelope and found her will and her life insurance policy.

"Please—read the will."

It was only two pages, simply written and clear, and as far as I could tell, properly executed. "It seems fine, Simone." I hesitated, realizing she needed my opinion as a lawyer—and I obliged. "In my professional opinion, this is a valid and enforceable will. Beyond the will, I need to advise you that many things are affected when one on their own or with the help of another...."

"You can say it—commits suicide."

"Right. Among other things, when a person takes their own life, it is possible their beneficiaries will not be able to collect on their life insurance."

"Henry and I bought that life insurance policy you're holding many years ago," Simone said. "What does mine say?"

"These are complicated documents and I am not sure this is the whole contract of insurance. I can look later." I was nauseous. The smells in the house, a wretched by-product of her illness, were powerful. "I can't be part of this. If I tell you the policy will pay out, you might be more inclined to act. I can't...."

Simone found a force within her, something derived from her horrifying circumstance, an energy separate from her depleted reserves. She pushed that energy to the surface and issued a hollow, primitive sound. It was a subdued, guttural cry and lasted several seconds. She gasped and then began to breathe more evenly. Her voice was now distorted and different. "Don't walk away, Charlie. Read the policy—now."

It was not hard to find the clause. Though there were a series of variables, the bottom line was that since more than three years had passed, in all likelihood, the policy would be paid even if the insured committed suicide.

"It seems likely—but not certain—that suicide would not prevent payment on your demise," I said, feeling that I would not be able to stay any longer without becoming sick to my stomach.

"Then Henry will have all he needs."

"He needs you, Simone."

"He is not that selfish," she said.

"This is no ordinary matter between a client and lawyer. I'm not sure I can maintain this confidence. I am bound ethically to protect your interests and your confidences, but if you tell me you are about to commit a crime or hurt yourself or someone else, that falls outside the privilege."

"Do you think what I plan to do is a crime?"

"Yes … I'm not sure. I am not a criminal lawyer." I closed my eyes and tried to regain my intestinal composure. "I wish you had not told me."

"You need to know. It is not just something I tell you as our lawyer. I tell you this as my dying wish." She stiffened slightly in her chair, closed her eyes and exhaled several times, an exhalation redolent of decay and bile. "I need you to keep Henry and Maurice apart. Each will think the other played some role in my death. I know them both. You must be the one, Charlie, the one who convinces them that this was my decision."

"If I say that, I will have violated your confidence."

"No. You must be convincing—but you cannot discuss this day, this visit. Imagine Henry or Maurice learning you knew what I was planning—and did not tell them." She stopped, shifting in her chair. "You must never tell anyone you were here."

An idea emerged in my mind so suddenly that I gasped, taking a gulp of air and nearly vomiting. "How are you going to do this?"

Nothing. "Is Henry going to help you?" She was panting lightly, dark and spoiled breaths. "Maurice?"

She closed her eyes, coughed deeply, and then regrouped. "If I cannot, either Maurice or Henry would do what I asked and nothing would be said. But I do not think that will happen. Should I be unable, I know where to get help."

"Simone, I could never...."

"Not you, Charlie. That is not what I need from you. You must help keep the peace."

Simone had thought of everything. She told me to wipe down any place I touched during the visit and then said: "My neighbors keep an eye on the house—but they are out today. It's why I called you."

There was another long silence. "Has my niece, Lucy—you know Lucy?" I nodded, "or Henry ever told you their belief about death?"

"Henry did. Once," I said.

"We believe that on death, we return to the place from which we came. If you think about that, you may understand why I am at peace with this decision."

I wanted to tell her how much I would miss her, how I was sure this would destroy Henry, how Maurice, so happy with his new relationship with Celia, would be saddened beyond measure, how the Market would never be the same, but that was not what she needed.

I considered picking her up and putting her in my car, driving to a hospital, having her on a suicide watch 24 hours a day, but I stayed still.

For a brief moment, she looked up. Her reddened pleading eyes, sunk in the thin grayness of her face, were covered with a milky film, and I wondered how much she could see.

She looked toward the windows in the front of the house, to the lawn and trees, to the garden, to the driveway lined with azaleas that lost their bloom a month ago. I saw tears flowing down her face, dropping on her robe and in that moment, I knew. "You can trust me. I will not disclose what you have told me."

She nodded once and, for just a moment, her face lightened. "Good, Charlie. I was sure I could rely on you."

I stood, steadying myself on the back of a chair and found a few tissues but when I came back to wipe her eyes, she was asleep. I wheeled her into the bedroom and lifted the near nothingness of her onto the bed, pulled up the covers, turned off the lights, and, as instructed, wiped the areas I touched, and left.

I want to take a moment and share with you what drifted through my mind as I drove off. Family money and circumstance have spared me of many difficult tasks others must face. For example, I played no role whatsoever during the last days of my mother's life. She was sick—I believe she had pneumonia, but I'm not sure—and was in the hospital. The times I called she was fully conversant and optimistic she would recover. Then, in one stunning moment, as she was sipping tea and chatting with a nurse, she had a stroke and was gone instantly.

I learned of her death in a phone call from our family lawyer the following day. He wanted me to know the date of her funeral. Almost all of Brampton's elite and about half the family came to my mother's funeral. It was, my father commented in his eulogy, a *very* impressive turnout, smiling as he placed theatrical emphasis on the word "very." In Pratt world, this was considered a humorous comment.

In any case, I was in complete internal chaos as I left Simone. I was not sure what role I was to play—or already had played—in a suicide, assisted or otherwise. Considering her circumstance, a new thought entered my mind: Simone may be right. It is her life. No one should be forced to suffer beyond measure when there is no hope of recovery, facing a future of continuous unthinkable pain. There must be a moment when someone in Simone's situation can say ... enough.

I cannot recall ever contemplating the morality or the legality of assisted suicide and was not even sure what I would do if asked to assist. And yet my visit was not inconsequential. Simone was going to take her life with or without my help. The things I said to her, as a lawyer, played a role in her decision. That fact will haunt me always.

~

Henry was at the Market the following morning. When Claire asked if there was any word on Simone, he said: "She is sick—and so tired. She rests most of the day." He repeated this report each day for the next week. He made clear that aside from her beloved niece, Lucy, Simone refused to see any visitors.

On the seventh day after my visit with Simone, Henry was not at the Market. Wallace, the evening clerk, was in his place. Everyone assumed Simone had taken a turn for the worse. I assumed something more final.

Late in the morning almost two weeks after my visit with Simone, I received a call at my office from Lucy Vredeesha. Simone Vredeesha, wife of Henry DuChamp, had died.

At my request, Lucy came to the Market a few days later. She talked quietly about Henry and other family members and explained a few things about Burmese funeral traditions.

At one point she pulled me aside. "It was peaceful, as it should be."

I thanked her for that information but must admit that I cannot imagine Simone's end was peaceful. Based on my visit with her, there was no peace left in Simone.

On her way out, Lucy invited all of us to a memorial service for Simone at a pavilion in Gaithersburg, Maryland, the following week. Alex responded for the group. "We'll be there," he said, without needing to confirm with any of us his acceptance of her invitation.

~

Only the eulogies at Simone's memorial were presented in English; responsive prayers and guided meditations were almost entirely in Burmese. Lucy made brief tearful remarks capturing the wisdom of her beloved aunt. Henry, rather than extemporize, gratefully accepted and read a poem Alex prepared for him ending with these words:

Liberated, her spirit free,
To soar in bliss, eternity,
Part of one, the Kingdom forever,
She is all that will ever be.

At several points in the service, a small ensemble played music that floated and dissolved like morning fog. There were two flutes, an oboe, and a percussionist with an array of bells and gongs.

Towards the end of the service, at the direction of a bald cleric who conducted most of the event, as the ensemble played a soft repetitive melody, the audience began singing something between a prayer, a hymn, and a chant in what I assumed was Burmese.

People in front of us and on both sides turned and pointed to a folder placed under the chairs. A mark in each folder took us to the lyrics, written out phonetically. There were only three verses, and after a time I found a point in the text that matched the sounds and phrases that echoed through the pavilion.

I have never been one to sing in church. My parents took us to church although my father, who was an Elder of the church and on the Administrative Board (apparently a position of some consequence), stayed silent during the entire service as if it was too great an effort to participate. Maybe he was unsure of his faith and did not want to appear hypocritical. I did not know then and do not know now why he chose to remain mute but as I stood in the back of the pavilion during Simone's service, I decided it was time for me to sing.

I started quietly, joining only when the sounds "Maa" and "Daa" appeared. Once I was confident I was in sync with the masses, I increased my volume and took on more challenging phrases. My pitch was not exact, and my pronunciation was undoubtedly off.

It was my singing that produced the first hint of a laugh, a snorted inhalation from Claire. A second remarkably similar sound issued form Maurice. I kept singing and turned my head and saw Alex's shoulders shaking.

Claire was to my right and Alex and Maurice to my left and as I turned back from Alex, I saw that Claire now had her face in her hands and knew what was about to happen.

I decided that regardless of their reaction, I was going to sing on. I increased the volume, singing in full voice from my diaphragm as I had been taught during my two years in the high school choir.

I now know, since this has been discussed often around the table, that it was that increase in volume that did in Claire. I heard the beginning of that waterfall of a laugh, turned and saw the tears streaming down her cheeks and heard her gasp, "Oh, Charlie, please stop...." Undaunted, I continued and listened with some pleasure as Maurice and Alex likewise came undone.

There we were, the closest of friends at a funeral proclaiming love and respect for Simone and our support for Henry, and three of the four of us had been reduced to shoulder shaking, nose running, uncontrollable laughter. For a time I thought it possible that someone from the temple would tell us to go outside and compose ourselves but no one did. When the music stopped, I looked at Claire and saw that her eyes were red and the small amount of makeup she was wearing had dissolved. There was an openness that went along with her laughter and I guessed that the pain and sadness Simone's death generated in her had been partially released.

We stood outside on the large lawn in front of the pavilion waiting for Henry, Lucy, and the other family members to emerge. There were tables set up at one end of the lawn with drinks and platters of cookies. Gradually, everyone found a place on the lawn, clustering with friends, remembering the past, waiting to express condolences to Henry and his family.

It was a steamy gray day in early July. In the western sky, where clouds were darkest, small darkish gossamer wisps skittered more quickly than the cloud mass above, unkempt forerunners to a storm.

I looked up and saw Henry, Lucy, and a few other relatives working through the crowd, hugging, handshaking, and, by all appearances, consoling those with whom they spoke. At one point I noticed that as Henry lifted his arms during an embrace, he was covered with sweat. His shirt and jacket were soaked. His hair gave the distinct impression that he had just emerged from the shower. I cut through the crowd and brought him a glass of water.

Twenty minutes later, Henry and Lucy—the other relatives had peeled off and were now huddling elsewhere on the lawn—stood in front of us. "It was a beautiful service," Alex said. "I loved the music. I've never heard anything like that before." Alex was now our resident musical expert, under contract with an agent and a recording company (and thus far full of unmet hope), and I could see why the unique sounds intrigued him.

"There is no easy way to say this," said Claire. "I miss Simone. I loved her like a sister." Claire stopped. I believe she knew that if she said more she would begin to cry. Henry and Claire embraced. It was a longer than normal embrace, and I noticed that Claire had closed her eyes and rubbed Henry's back. As the embrace ended, she turned and whispered something—a longer whisper than most—that made him smile. Later, she told me that she had quickly told the story of the final song, the laughter, and my contribution to the vocal assembly.

Henry hugged me next and then pulled back, shook my hand and said: "Don't look but 30 meters behind me are two men, probably watching me right now. These are the relatives of Simone who lent us money years ago. When we paid them back—the exact sum they lent us—there was an unpleasant exchange in which they claimed that they were owed interest on the loan. No interest had ever been discussed. When Simone became ill, I received a note telling me that they had placed a lien on the Market."

"This was the reason you wanted me to represent you initially," I said. "We can handle this—I assume there is no written agreement between you and them regarding this loan?"

"Nothing that either of us signed—maybe they will make something up."

"Henry, I don't want you to worry about it. If they try to make up an agreement, we will tear it apart and have the claim dismissed. Maybe I will even seek sanctions against the lawyers for wasting your money and the time of the court."

"But what if they have …" Henry said.

"Not today, Henry."

A quick embrace and handshake with Alex left only Maurice.

At first, the handshake and a few whispered comments seemed perfectly innocuous. Then Henry dropped Maurice's hand and took a couple of steps back.

The rain started, slowly at first, and then more steadily.

Maurice, obviously angered, jet-whispered, "Poisoned? What are you talking about? She had cancer." He wiped rainwater from his face.

"She was poisoned. You know exactly what happened."

"What are you saying?"

Henry, dehydrated and drained emotionally, had crossed that last barrier. "You knew how sick she was. You knew she was in pain. You saw her at the house — I have neighbors — they saw your car. You got to spend time with her when I had to work."

Maurice leaned forward. The shoulders of his jacket were soaked and his hair matted by rain.

"Someone made Simone a cocktail," Henry said, sputtering as rainwater cascaded down his face. "Sleeping pills, pain killers — mixed it in a blender — and she drank it. That's why she died. You thought you were helping her. You thought she wanted to go. You thought it was her time. In my country, at a different time, I could kill you for what you did."

"Henry, I did not and would not do that." Maurice looked at me as if, somehow, there would be something calm and logical I could say to change the moment, but I was transfixed, and like Alex and Claire, stood staring.

"This is absurd," Maurice continued. "You're right. I knew Simone was in enormous pain. She was my friend and I saw her when I could. You never had the decency to respect that she was my friend. My time with her was important — to Simone, Henry, to your wife — and in your sick way of seeing the world, all you could do was suspect that our relationship was intimate." He stopped, breathing hard. "I hoped Simone would live — and I hoped, miraculously, that her pain would end."

They were now only inches apart. Maurice, who stood six inches taller than Henry, looked down on him and said: "Don't ever say that again. You're accusing me of a crime." He put both hands on Henry's shoulders. "I understand your sadness, Henry. Above all else, I understand that. If Simone did something that caused her life to end, I had nothing to do with it."

Henry bent slightly at the waist, and a moment later his right fist flew, backwards first, and then thrust forward, hitting Maurice in the center of his abdomen, driving upward towards his solar plexus. His left fist followed almost immediately.

He hit with such power that his fists disappeared entirely within Maurice. As he drew back his arms, Maurice gasped and then sank to the wet ground as if someone had pulled away a chair in which he planned to sit.

Henry took a step backwards and put both hands over his mouth. For a moment it seemed that these blows had taken Henry by surprise. Family and relatives surrounded our group. Maurice, gasping for breath, started to get up, his fists balled.

Alex jumped in front of Maurice, pushing him to the ground. As Maurice tried to get up again, I heard Claire scream. "Stop it!" She silenced everyone momentarily.

Maurice tried a second time to get up, seemingly determined to continue the fight. Alex pressed against him. Henry stood, arms at his side, in complete silence. Lucy Vredeesha ran over to us and stood next to Henry. She was soaked to the bone and silent.

Before Maurice could launch a counter-attack, Claire, her hair straight and drenched, again yelled, "Stop it!" Then, in a loud and clear voice said the one thing that no one in our group expected, particularly me: "I'm pregnant."

Maurice sat back in the grass. Henry, as if bumped by a passing cloud, sat down as well, placing his hands behind him to brace his back.

In a quieter voice, Claire turned to me and said, again, "I'm pregnant, Charlie. We're going to have a baby."

~

It was pouring as we walked to the cars. "I'm sure that wasn't the moment you'd picked to tell me. How are you feeling?"

"Pregnant, Charlie. I feel very pregnant."

"I'm the father...." She kept walking and I followed. "I will do anything...." To say words failed me from that point forward does not really capture the moment. "If you wanted ..." was followed by, "So, yes, well ... and naturally ... because I would never," and finally, "What can I do ... since this ... well, I'm not saying...."

Claire slowed only briefly and as she had done the day I met her six years ago, turned to me and said, "What?"

I tried to regroup and with some effort said: "Can we talk?"

"Of course. We will. I promise."

And then, regrettably, "But how ... ?"

"How do you think, Charlie?" She looked down at the wet ground as she walked and said quietly: "We made assumptions about each other that night—I thought you took precautions and, apparently, you thought I had. Well, we were both wrong, weren't we?"

I replayed our night at the Stansfield Hotel, the bourbon and abandon. Had I said or just surmised that, at 42, pregnancy was not an issue for Claire? The more I thought about it, the more I had the feeling—and it was just that, not a recollection—I had said nothing about birth control. Was it possible that two seemingly intelligent adults had no better control or judgment than a couple of teenagers on prom night after consuming far too much beer? Apparently, it was.

I helped Claire into my car in the thick of the downpour and, with greater care than I had taken before, made sure she was belted in. I stood back after closing her door, watched her blot away the water on her face, and had the strong, warm sense—and I mean this in the most traditional sense of the word—of being blessed. Claire Beaumont, the woman I loved, was pregnant with our child.

It was the single most important piece of news in my life. I knew our lives would never be the same—and it thrilled me.

Chapter 15

Investigation

I spoke with Claire almost every day thereafter. Before I learned we would be parents, we had been going to dinner occasionally. It happened slowly, casually, and, for the most part, uneventfully. It started in late April and was truly innocuous. One Friday, Claire first suggested we grab a bite after work and see a movie. "Let's not make a big deal about it," she'd said. I needed no explanation — she did not want to make this a topic of conversation in the Market, and I quickly agreed.

We were good friends spending a few evenings together — and most of the time that spring it seemed like nothing more than that. However, every now and then, often when I did not expect it, Claire would put her arm around me or hold my hand. Once, in a movie, she rested her head on my shoulder and fell asleep.

We even went to the Kennedy Center — once in May to a musical the critics loved and neither of us liked at all and once in June, as she had suggested on our drive to Jennifer's wedding, she took me to the ballet. We watched the Mariinsky Ballet Company's *The Swan* — which we both loved.

After her stunning announcement in the rain that unforgettable July afternoon, we were together far more often. However, despite my efforts to expand our discussion to include marriage, Claire shut down the discourse: "I have so much to consider, Charlie. Can we leave that issue aside for now?" I nodded. "Please trust that you will always be the father, that you will always be involved, fully and completely from the moment of birth."

She hesitated. "I know you're having a hard time with this — but this is my life. We will love our baby like no other — count on it — and the baby's arrival may mean changes to almost everything

I have worked to balance over the last decade—and that's without getting married. Getting married adds more change and at this moment, I can't devote my energy to that."

And that was that for July.

I waited and watched Claire change. As the second trimester drew to a close, she seemed to be more herself. I realize you could take that to mean there was more of her—and I assure you there was—but that's not what I meant. Claire was not fully comfortable—size ruled out that option—but she was not exactly uncomfortable either physically or in terms of our relationship.

One morning in early August, just before I was about to leave the Market to walk Flynn, Claire said, "Charlie, you have that anxious look."

I was about to say, "Claire—I'm 42, soon to have my first child—of course I'm worried," but I knew that was unwise and instead smiled at her and started for the door.

"Wait." She pulled me aside. "What's going on with Henry?"

"What do you mean?" I asked.

Claire spoke quietly. "Henry called me last night and asked if the police had contacted me. He said they had questions about Simone."

"Have the police contacted you?"

She glared at me. "Don't you think I'd tell you if they'd called?"

For once, I stopped to think before answering. My mind went blank and then, quite remarkably, in my temporarily vacant mind, I saw Flynn. "As much as I love Claire," I thought to imaginary-Flynn, "sometimes her unwillingness to share information bothers me. Even the guessing games she loves to play drive me to distraction."

Imaginary-Flynn looked at me knowingly, and I realized that Claire's tendency to limit information is part of who she is and some type of protective mechanism—and I needed to trust her completely. Just how anyone gets by without a dog like Flynn is a mystery.

"Now what? Where are you?" Claire's tone was not cross but sounded frustrated.

"I'm sorry—of course I trust you."

"We're talking about the police and Henry. Why would Henry and now you ask if the police had contacted me?"

"Right—yes." I hesitated. "That's what I meant—I trust you'd tell me something if it was important."

Claire pfff'ed me briefly—but it was a gentle pfff—closed her eyes, shook her head, and said: "No, no one from the police department contacted me."

I was focused on Claire, unaware that Henry was standing behind me. He startled me when he said, "Charlie knows, Claire. I've told him about the police. Remember, he is my lawyer."

Claire looked at me and while I'm quite sure she understood I could not disclose information about Henry—I was his lawyer—asked: "What's going to happen?"

"I'll work with Henry—try to get things resolved as quickly and quietly as possible."

Claire looked at Henry and then put her hand on my arm. "I'm glad you're handling this, Charlie—very glad." For the first time in the history of the Market, she then leaned forward, pulled me to her, kissed me, and walked out.

I turned to Henry who was smiling broadly. "I knew it," he said. "I knew it years ago." As he walked back to the cash register, without turning, he said, "Everyone knew ... for years—except you."

~

Any death by unnatural causes raises suspicion and the possibility of a criminal investigation. Suicide is a tragedy of immeasurable proportion, leaving in its wake families shattered by grief and an anger that has no ready target. It is a nightmare that can persist, at varying levels, for generations.

Maryland, like almost every state (with the exception of Oregon, Montana, New Mexico, Washington, and, to an extent, Vermont) does not have a statutory framework to deal with assisted suicide. Apart from those states just mentioned, to assist in a suicide is, in the eyes of many, to conspire to commit a homicide.

How a death ends up characterized on a scale from nothing to some lesser manslaughter charge all the way to murder in the first degree varies by state, case to case, and grand jury to grand jury. Prosecutors, referred to in Maryland as State's Attorneys, play a central role in the characterization of the act of assisting in a suicide.

The circumstances surrounding Simone's demise, after review, were nominally suspicious. The State's Attorneys studied medical records provided by the family, the full hospital report, and of course the death certificate.

The medical records made clear that Simone had terminal cancer and was at a level of pain that was untreatable short of complete sedation. Even then, one doctor speculated in a letter to the State's Attorney, there would still be pain. There was some research, the doctor suggested, showing that during periods of sedation, complex intracranial responses have been recorded that are consistent with higher levels of pain. Her death, however, was not caused by cancer.

The State's Attorney's initial determination was that Simone took her own life. That would explain the presence of the deadly chemical combination discovered during the autopsy. Her death certificate read: *"Cause of Death: Toxicity; decedent ingested approximately 900 milligrams of pulverized Zolpidem and approximately 1100 milligrams of pulverized Oxycodone in solution with several ounces of mulberry juice...."*

For Simone, given the havoc in her body caused by cancer, this combination was more than enough to end her life. The drugs had been pulverized, mixed with mulberry juice (her favorite), and consumed. The scenario was predictable at first blush—until one considered her overall condition. Simone was beyond weakness and frailty.

The strength required to collect and measure out the drugs, place them in a blender, add juice, and pour the mixture into a glass was, in the opinion of the medical examiner, beyond her capacity. For that reason, the examiner pushed the State to investigate and determine who, in addition to Simone, participated in ending her life.

After initial interviews with family and friends, a different but wobbly hypothesis emerged, calling into question the medical examiner's findings. Several members of the Vredeesha family said that in her last days, they saw Simone walk a few steps, wheel herself into the kitchen (where the blender sat on the counter) and get a drink of water. In short, it was remotely possible that she acted alone.

However, the death was labeled suspicious requiring the police to conduct a preliminary investigation—and from the outset, Henry was a target of the inquiry, though not formally accused.

I was at Henry's side during the course of each meeting conducted in the storeroom of the Market with Lieutenant William Cavise, the officer in charge of the investigation.

Cavise came to the Market in early August to set the time and place to meet with Henry. I tried to prepare Henry before the first discussion, urging him not to volunteer any information. I told him that Cavise very well might tell him he had information that, in fact, did not exist in order to push Henry and potentially incriminate him. After giving Henry as thorough a warning as I knew how to do—recognizing that in almost two decades, I've never had a criminal case—Henry seemed quite comfortable with what was about to occur.

"I've been through interrogations you cannot imagine," he said.

"This is different," I said. "Just be careful with what you say."

The following afternoon, Cavise, Henry, and I, each with a fresh cup of coffee, went into the storeroom of the Market and sat around the small, gray metal desk.

Cavise opened with a few general questions. He got Henry to talk about how he met Simone—and then Henry, with no prompting whatsoever, did exactly what I asked him not to do: He volunteered information that had not been requested.

He launched into a lengthy discussion, describing how Simone and he had weathered the insanity of insurrection, insurgency, and torture in Burma. Even Cavise tried to divert the discussion back to the present but Henry ignored him. He described in detail how they traveled halfway around the globe and restarted their life here. He ended with: "While no one in their right mind would say we had a perfect marriage, after all that we had endured, assisting her in suicide? Unthinkable."

The interview, if you could call it that, ended, and we agreed to meet the following day. That night I repeated my admonition to

Henry. "Don't volunteer information. Answer with a simple yes or no or tell him you don't know."

Cavise began his questioning the next day by asking Henry to say more about his marriage. Henry was silent. Cavise repeated his question, and I interceded. "You don't need to answer that."

"You don't need to answer any of this," Cavise said. "You're not under arrest. I simply want to have a sense of how things were between you and your wife." He paused. "There was a scene in the Market some months ago. A person walking down the sidewalk called us because they had seen a fight between a couple—they saw a woman slap a man—in the doorway of the Market."

"Who called?" Henry said, before I could stop him.

"A passerby who witnessed what appeared to be an altercation and decided to call the police. As to the name ... I wouldn't tell you—even if I knew." He hesitated for a moment and then shook his head. "You want to know something—I have no secrets from you, Mr. DuChamp."

This seemed a fairly primitive manipulation designed to instill careless openness in Henry and so I cautioned him: "Henry, he knows things he won't tell you—of course he has secrets."

"So?" Henry responded. "Simone is gone—what do I have to lose?"

I shook my head and Cavise looked at me. "Are you done with your counseling, Mr. Pratt?" I nodded, and he turned to Henry. "We sent a community relations officer—a plainclothesman—who stopped by the Market after the call. He spoke with another customer—a man wearing some type of unusual sweater. He confirmed that there was a disagreement between you and your wife."

Henry stiffened but said nothing. Cavise continued. "According to the report, he was a regular—knew you and your wife very well—and said there was nothing to worry about. Apparently he was convincing and nothing further came of it, except, as you might guess, the officer wrote up a report. That report was brought to my attention after the death of your wife."

While there was no way of knowing who called the police, it seemed almost impossible that it was Maurice. After all, Maurice was standing in front of Henry during the incident—and obviously Maurice defused any further investigation. I looked at Henry, hoping he was thinking the same thing.

"We had disagreements," Henry said. "Everyone has disagreements."

"No argument there," Cavise said. "I'm single now—but I've been married—twice...."

Henry nodded. "Only once for me—Simone."

"At the time she passed, were you on good terms?"

"She was sick, Lieutenant. Very sick."

"One does not need to be healthy to be disagreeable."

There was more talk of marital imperfection. It reminded me of discussions we had around the table in the market. It rambled along, Cavise giving details of his marriages as if Henry was an old friend.

Henry, caught up in the moment, told a story about an old friend in Burma who stayed married to a woman with whom he refused to speak for the last fifteen years of their marriage. This struck Cavise and Henry as humorous and seemed like it would go on for hours until I said: "If you're done with your questions, let's bring this to a close."

In the third and last meeting, a week later, Cavise began by asking for a detailed chronology of the week Simone died. Henry's answers were remarkably unrevealing. He went into great detail discussing issues at work—replacement of the coffee machine, a traffic tie-up that delayed his arrival home one evening, and endless commentary about suppliers of Danish pastries. Cavise listened, took almost no notes, and began pushing Henry to discuss Simone and their last day together.

Henry's descriptions of Simone's condition were vivid. I have already told you much the same thing. Life was flowing out of Simone in red-brown rivulets.

Henry recounted awful scenes in the bathroom and difficulties sleeping for both of them. "Simone could not relax. I don't think she slept more than an hour or two without waking up—and each time she was sicker and sicker. She tried to keep from waking me up, but of course, I could not sleep either."

"You cared for her without help?" Cavise asked. "What about your children—your family?"

"Simone did not want anyone there but me. We had many of-fers—but she was insistent. Our niece, Lucy, was the only one al-lowed to visit. She came once a day—but otherwise, it was just me."

Cavise pushed forward. "I thought you had a nurse."

"We did at first, but there was really nothing for her to do. Some-times we'd have her during the day but, in the end, I took care of Simone. She was my wife. I owed her that."

"Was the nurse there Simone's last day?"

"No. The last few days it was just Simone, Lucy, and me."

Another endless line of questions followed, all focused on the final twenty-four hours. Finally, it got down to: "Can you tell me what she ate for lunch on her last day?"

Henry shook his head. "Lunch? I thought I was clear—Simone did not have any solid food in the end."

"What do you mean?"

"Nothing. She could not eat. The last few weeks or longer. The doctors prescribed a liquid formula—the kind you give to an in-fant—to give her basic nourishment … and she would have juice, some tea—but she could not keep anything down."

Cavise pulled out the medical records and asked Henry if he'd seen them. To my surprise, he said he had not. When Cavise asked why, Henry looked at him. "Until the last few weeks, I did not know Simone's illness had gone so far—she did not want me to know—but by then it was obvious."

"So is it fair to say that you did not think she was terminally ill?"

"No—I knew. It was only a matter of time."

"And when she did not die naturally, did you consider helping her out of her misery?"

I stood. "That's it—this has gone on long enough. Henry?" Henry did not get up. "Please—you don't need to continue with this. I'm telling you, as your lawyer, it's time to go."

Instead of leaving, Henry sighed heavily and a sob slipped out. "I did not want her to die. I would rather die than see Simone in pain—but never would I help her take her life."

I tried to pull Henry to his feet but he would not get up.

"Mr. DuChamp," Cavise said quietly, "I need to know what went on in your home the day your wife died."

"I will tell you," Henry said.

"No," I said. "Henry, don't say anything further."

"Why not? I have nothing to hide, Charlie. I want this to be finished." He turned back to Cavise: "It was early in the afternoon. Simone had been very sick and was in bed. I remember asking if I could get her anything. She did not answer so I asked her again. She asked me what time it was—I said it was around two in the afternoon—and she said, 'I would very much like to speak with Sayadaw Oo.' He's our religious leader, the man who conducted her memorial." Henry turned to me as if my affirmation was needed.

"I called our shrine and spoke with him. He does not drive—I don't think he owns a car—but he said that if Simone wanted to speak with him and she could not come to the shrine—and I picked him up—he would visit her at our home. I covered the phone and told Simone.

"She said, 'I'd really like to speak with him,' and so, of course, I agreed. I left her, Lieutenant—that was my fault. She told me to drive carefully—that was the last thing she said to me.

"The shrine is usually a 20-minute drive. With traffic, it took almost an hour to pick up Sayadaw Oo and get back to the house. When we returned, Simone was in bed. He said, 'Don't wake her,' so we sat and talked. Almost an hour passed at which point Sayadaw said he needed to get back to the shrine but wanted to see Simone first. We tried to awaken her—but...."

Henry issued a second small sob and said, "I don't know what else to tell you."

Cavise was silent for some time. Finally he said: "Thank you, Mr. DuChamp. I don't think there's anything more to say."

"What happens now?" Henry asked.

Cavise turned to me. "Your lawyer will explain. The investigation has to run its course."

Cavise looked around the storeroom. "Interesting," he said, turning to me. "I'm told you have a group that meets for coffee in the Market every morning. A number of officers spoke with me about that." He paused. "People don't sit and talk any more—everyone is either in a rush or sending messages electronically. Maybe I'll join you for coffee one morning."

There was another pause as Cavise continued to scan the shelves. "Every day? Even on weekends?"

"Even weekends," Henry said.

Cavise nodded several times and as he was standing said: "Listen. I was skeptical about this from the outset. The glass with the residue of the drugs and juice was on her nightstand. Only your wife's fingerprints were on the glass." A final pause and then: "It sounds to me like your wife took her own life. I am sorry to put you through this, Mr. DuChamp."

I made sure Cavise had my card—and Henry made sure to tell him he was always welcome.

Naturally, I did not mention to Cavise or anyone else that it seemed almost impossible for Simone to have acted alone. She was weak beyond measure when I saw her a month earlier and I'm sure had declined more each day up until her demise.

To his credit, throughout all of the questioning, in fact throughout the entire investigation, Henry did not mention Maurice. There was no doubt he could have told a convincing story about the relationship Maurice had with Simone and how it only made sense that Maurice would have helped. After all, in Henry's view, Maurice would have done anything Simone asked.

Once I knew what appeared to be the story of the last hour of Simone's life, it was not hard to imagine a plan in which Simone assured Maurice that she would find a way to get Henry out of the house at a particular time. Maurice would hide outside, wait for Henry's car to leave, and then go inside and help put together the deadly cocktail that ended her life.

Of course, it was equally possible that Maurice played no role, that Henry provided the help Simone needed before he left for the shrine. And as much as I want to think that neither played any role, I was not at peace.

I wanted to share these theories with Claire—but of course could not. Henry and Simone were my clients and confidentially cloaked all aspects of our relationship.

Had Henry decided to implicate Maurice, my guess is that the State would have convened a grand jury, and had that happened, I might have been under enormous pressure to disclose the information Simone told me in confidence before she died, information that would go a long way to exculpating Maurice.

There is an argument that on death, the attorney-client privilege changes or ends since the privilege belongs to the client, not the lawyer. Also, since Simone's acts created the likelihood of death, there are those who would argue I was not permitted to maintain the confidence and had a duty to report that she was at risk. Thankfully, I never had to face those questions.

~

One excruciatingly hot August morning, as the investigation into Simone's death was drawing to a close, I parked in my regular space a few blocks from the Market and dragged a snoozy Flynn out of the car. While I was in the Market, he would spend the time sleeping on the warm concrete, shaded beneath the Market's awning, periodically lapping water from a bowl of water, graced by a few passing breezes. We had not taken two steps from my car, however, when I saw Lucy Vredeesha sitting on a bench adjacent to the sidewalk. "I've been waiting for you," she said. "Uncle Henry told me this is where you park in the mornings."

We shook hands. "Is something wrong?"

"I hope not," she said. "Are you sure the police inquiry is over regarding the role my uncle played in Aunt Simone's death?"

"I can't really be sure but it seems headed in that direction."

"It would be most unjust if he was punished in any way." She hesitated. "He did nothing...." She stopped and moved closer to me and whispered: "You are the lawyer of my family. Please assure me that this discussion is completely confidential."

"I represented your aunt and uncle, not your family."

"You cannot discuss this with anyone — especially Henry. That is Aunt Simone's wish." She hesitated. "Charlie, please — Aunt Simone assured me we could speak in absolute confidence."

I was disinclined to argue and anxious to find out what she had to say. "Fair enough — I agree."

She was only inches from me at this point. "If this inquisition continues, you and I will need to talk."

She stopped and waited. I thought she would say more — and in the silence that followed I guessed the truth. "It was you. After

Henry left to get Sayadaw Oo—you were there with Simone—at the house."

Her eyes fixed on mine. "I trust you are the fine lawyer my uncle says you are—and hope I will never need your services." With that, she held out her hand, thanked me for helping her family, and walked away.

As things returned to something vaguely resembling normal in the Market, I speculated that in their darker moments, Henry was sickened by the possibility that Maurice had assisted in Simone's suicide—and Maurice considered the possibility Henry had done likewise. Anger and unstated accusations limited their capacity for forgiveness and infected our table.

While I could not help directly, from time to time, following Simone's last wish, I would comment on the power and complexity of Simone's personal decision and emphasize the importance of respecting her choice. Lucy's revelation—the one unutterable thing that would have relieved them of those deadly suspicions—stayed with me.

One evening not long after I got a call from Lieutenant Cavise telling me Simone's file was closed, Claire and I took Henry to dinner. After a modest expression of appreciation and relief, Henry began to talk about leaving Burma. He said nothing to shed light on Lucy's suggestion that he may have been a government operative. Rather than discuss his role in government or their capture, he described their emigration—from a careerist perspective. "My family had contacts in Rangoon, people who could have moved me along." He stopped. "When I was young, I had a recurring dream that I was the Burmese Ambassador to the United Nations." He smiled. "Me. An ambassador."

Once in the United States, having dispensed with diplomatic aspirations, he had to change goals. Financial stability and family supplanted everything, but left unmet his need for a political discourse that the routines of commerce and home-life could not provide. Somehow, what seemed only quaint and endearing at first, our table in the American Market, was Henry's first physical expression of that hope.

In the days following that dinner, my feelings about Henry changed. Perhaps it was the flood of information I had been provided in the last few months that allowed me to see him in an entirely different light—and perhaps it was simply sympathy.

There were times I wanted to join him behind the counter and help with the cash register, telling people who came before him to buy aluminum foil and tomato soup, coffee and soda, that they were dealing with an extraordinary person who was entitled to their respect, a person with a story of consequence, who lived through loss, who had the vision and courage to make something special out of a place so seemingly ordinary.

While I did not jump behind the counter, there was one change in my habits that summer that pleased Henry greatly. From the beginning, I think Henry saw something of himself in me, some set of possibilities that would be realized if I had the energy and nerve—and it involved my more regular use of the odd little office in the storeroom at the rear of the Market.

I wrote and filed a motion in court to dismiss a sinister complaint filed by Simone's relatives who, as Henry predicted, were trying to enforce an invalid lien and take control of the Market. My motion to dismiss was granted (though my request to sanction their lawyers, even though I was convinced their claim was utterly frivolous, was denied).

I rewrote my will to include Claire and our baby. I reviewed more contracts for Alex who reported to me, in confidence, that his royalties were paltry. With some reluctance, he told me he was again spending too much money on the lottery. "Just telling you is helpful," he explained. When I asked why, he said, quite unexpectedly, "I told Maurice—and now you know. It's a small piece of dealing with this addiction." After a time he said. "I'm in a group—we meet weekends—people who face the same challenges." It was the last Alex spoke of the lottery, but not the last legal work I undertook on his behalf.

I was branching out. I revised wills for Alex (who wanted to be sure that Liliana—and only Liliana—would be the beneficiary of his estate), Claire (who wanted to make sure that our soon-to-be-born child was covered in her will), Henry (whose will required a comprehensive rewrite following Simone's death), Maurice, and even Celia. I showed some modest flair, providing testamentary trusts as needed, and for each (including me) a durable power of attorney, living will, and medical directive.

Late that August, I met with the managing partner of my firm and told him that I was taking on a few small clients. I explained they were minor matters, not appropriate for the firm. He urged me to explore the domain of private practice, perhaps even take a few pro bono cases that did not involve personal friends (something that would benefit the professional profile of the firm), and then, standing up for emphasis, told me not to worry for a moment about my job at the firm or my salary. Those would not change. As I explained at the outset of this story, that was a predictable response.

During those late summer months, as my tiny practice began to grow and I contemplated whether I should bill for the work I was providing, Claire began to show more and more. At first it was a slight slope that pushed forward the front of her dress, but by the end of August, the slope was no longer slight.

Each day I came to the Market thinking Claire and I would discuss marriage, bringing up our child, money and parenting—but somehow the marriage part never surfaced. In contrast, Maurice, Alex, Henry, and Celia talked about the upcoming blessed event every day. Advice was given freely and generously. At one point, Henry explained that he had helped with the birth of his children and was prepared to pitch in as needed. Claire shook her head and said: "Will you boil water and find clean towels?"

Henry began to answer, explaining that the coffee machine also produced boiling water—but somewhere through his answer he realized that Claire was kidding him. "Jackson Park is not on the Tibetan frontier," Claire said. "There is a fairly good hospital minutes from the Market. I'm not worried."

Chapter 16

Beginnings

One morning just after Labor Day, I came to the Market determined to take on the obvious. I asked Claire to dinner and told her that it was time we talked about our future together. Claire had been dealing with her pregnancy since February. I had been aware of it for two months.

"And what future is that, Charlie?" she asked.

"We're having a child," I said. "It's time we discussed how we're going to do this."

After all those years of wondering and admiring, of sharing complicated and inane ideas, after the trip to Jennifer's wedding and the craziness of Carter Strong, after all that, there was no doubt in my mind. I bought a ring—a simple platinum band and a blue-white round diamond, just over two carats (half the size of the stone Claire and I saw on Priscilla Coughlin's left hand), and rehearsed the moment with Flynn.

We went to Pauline's, the restaurant where we first met to discuss our trip to Vermont. We had not yet ordered drinks when I walked to the side of her chair, dropped to one knee—and froze.

I was ready—but I could not speak. I looked around the restaurant and saw that my position on one knee in front of my pregnant dinner partner had caught the attention of the other diners. The words I had worked on with Flynn failed me.

Claire guided me back to my chair and kissed me. I sat down and looked at her. She took the box from my hand and set it on the table.

Finally, I was able to speak: "Open it. Please."

She smiled. "I'm sure it's beautiful. Is it an heirloom?"

"No," I said. "Take a look."

She peeked in the box, smiled again, and closed it. "You have good taste," she said. "Let's have dinner. I'm hungry."

"Are you saying no?"

"Charlie, this isn't so simple."

"What are you afraid of? What am I missing?"

"How long a list do you want? Here—I'll start. Delivering a baby at my age, raising another child, keeping my career moving forward, maybe having to give up the only house I've ever owned, having our marriage fail, your family, my family … shall I go on?"

The box sat next to Claire through dinner. At the end of the night she said, "Keep this someplace safe." As I took back the ring, she said: "It's not no. You help me think through the issues I've raised. You're a smart guy. I always listen to what you have to say." She paused. "You know I love you."

"Isn't love all you need?" I asked. She smiled and spared me the "only in songs" response.

The following night, I went to Claire's for dinner. "Melissa went to a friend's house," Claire said. "I wanted time with just you." She paused. "I'm learning more and more about you, Charlie Pratt. Maybe it's time you knew more about me."

"You are my favorite topic," I said.

"Just listen." She took a long sip of water. "You know I was born in College Park, Maryland, and, not surprisingly, went to school at the University of Maryland."

"It's a fine university.…"

"Charlie—no interrupting. My mother owned a travel agency. I grew up running around in her office. Years ago, when every major airline in the world conspired—illegally, I believe—to cut travel agency commissions down to just about nothing, they put thousands of travel agencies out of business, including my mother's.

"After the travel agency closed, she fell ill, my father had a stroke, and within a few years both were gone. At the time, my younger sister, Camille, was already living in France and my brother, Paul, was in the tail end of a work-release program in Pensacola. Paul moved to France when he was finally finished with his legal troubles in Florida. Even so, I was and am by no means the last standing Beaumont in Washington and its environs. I have six uncles and aunts—most married and lots and lots of nieces and nephews."

I passed on the matter of Paul, the errant expatriated brother, and on my staggeringly belated insight that Beaumont was a French name. Despite the many questions that her French connection—or ancestry—raised regarding her notion of a family home, I asked instead: "Were you married at that point?"

"No—that had been over for years." She paused. "With my husband and parents gone, even with a large extended family here and overseas, I was on my own and, strangely enough, found it suited me." She hesitated. "I like being solely responsible for my daughter and for me. My son, the father of my grandson, lives in the same French town as my sister and is, for the most part, on his own. Melissa and I have a good life in Jackson Park—and it's going to change."

"For the better, I hope."

Claire nodded. "I hope so, too."

She told me she always owned her cars outright, refusing to purchase anything—except her house—unless she had sufficient cash. She maintained low balances on her credit cards and had been contributing to a retirement account since her senior year in high school.

Had she not become a regular at the American Market, not met me, not become involved in the lives of Maurice and Alex, Henry and Simone, Celia and the others who found their way to the Market on a regular basis, one could have scripted, with a few variables, the remainder of her days. That ended one night in the Stansfield Hotel just off the New Jersey Turnpike, a half-hour south of Trenton.

When she finished, she sat back. "So, now you know more."

"At some point, I'd love to hear more about your immediate family—particularly those in France—but not tonight." If I had put this together correctly, there was a story to be told about her brother's criminal case in Florida, why he had been in a work release program, why he moved across the Atlantic to France—but this was a time to talk about Claire, not her family.

"You are missing the point, Charlie. I've worked my entire adult life—and I have a home."

"I know."

"I have a 20-year mortgage and it is almost paid off."

"That's a huge accomplishment."

"Charlie, think: I love my home. It is Melissa's home as well. I can't imagine moving." She paused. "What about you?"

"I like where I live — it is important to me." I hesitated. "I really like my back porch." I looked closely at Claire. "Wait a second. Is that what this is about? Where will we live?"

"No, of course not — but it's not a small matter."

"There's always the guest house in Maine," I said. "It sleeps nine fairly comfortably."

"There aren't enough therapists in New England to get you through your first week if we moved there."

"Let me say something." Claire sighed and waited. "My house, which I like, is a place for Flynn and me to live … but my home is Jackson Park. Of that I am certain. My sense of stability, such as it is, does not rise and fall on where I rest my head at night."

After a long pause, Claire shook her head. "Is this about sleeping with me from time to time?"

It was a tricky question. I gave it my best. "Yes — and no. Of course I would like that. But that's not what I meant." In one of those rare moments of absolute clarity, I added: "This is about making a home for our family."

"Oh, Charlie." She smiled. "You finally got one right." There was a long silence. Claire was looking around and, if I didn't know better, seemed to be engaged in a mathematical calculation of some type. At different points, she appeared to agree — and then disagree — with herself. Suppressing every impulse in my being, I sat quietly until she was done. Finally she was ready. "Yes. You're correct. The house is not the issue — and houses can change. Spaces can be modified or added."

A long silence followed — and then it happened:

"Why don't you and Flynn move in with us for now? Let's see how it works." She stopped and again seemed to be calculating. "We'll figure this out."

No preface, no prelude — we were instantly in one of life's very rare moments, and there are very few true rare moments in life. I lost focus and experienced an interior bombardment, infinite queries threatening to emerge from my past, my family, my life. Even within that intra-cranial electrical storm, I realized I could not remain silent. "That would be … yes, of course … as soon as I … well, Flynn…." I closed my eyes, nominally steadied, and uttered a more utilitarian reply: "Give me a day or two to get things organized."

I told her I loved her, she smiled, and we kissed, the sole and fleeting memorial to this astonishing milestone.

And so began, almost by implication, the pinnacle of my best hopes. We would share life's certain and unforeseeable intimacies, the personal and obvious, the bizarre and idiosyncratic, the old ways that would not change, the odd ways that could yield to reason and need, merging longstanding unitary routines, inventing patterns that would become normal. All this would unfold in the urgency of early mornings and as the night went dark, at Sunday breakfasts and in our choice of milk, mayonnaise, paper towels, and bread, and most assuredly on walks with Flynn and trips to College Park and beyond, where bevies of Beaumonts lay in wait.

Just twenty-four hours later, Flynn and I packed carefully and conservatively (after all, we could go back to our house any time we needed something) and moved in with Claire and Melissa. They were more ready for us than we were for them.

"This is where we'll put Flynn's food."

"Your suits can hang here—you do have suits, Charlie, right? Beyond the one you wore to the wedding? …"

"Put the golf clubs in the basement next to the utility sink…."

"Flynn's settee can go on the deck next to the chaise."

"Melissa, take the covers off those pillows and throw them in the wash—have you ever washed those? They're … pungent."

"Flynn! We do not drink out of the toilet. Charlie, get the dog."

"There's room on the bookshelf in the living room for those…."

"Mom! I want to take a shower and Flynn is lying on the floor in the bathroom."

"He likes the cool tiles," I said but moments later Melissa dragged him into the hallway.

"I can't believe you brought your own cereal."

The whole thing took under an hour.

We were home.

~

Claire continued to expand to the point where I wondered if we were having twins. I have never been through a pregnancy (as you might guess) and learned quickly that asking whether it was possible that twins were in the offing was a terrible, terrible idea, particularly when I explained my question based on the size Claire had attained.

In better moments, I cleaned the house, did laundry, attended checkups with her obstetrician, and saw my first sonogram.

While we had not resolved the matter of conventional marriage or a wedding, her actions left no doubt that I would be part of my child's life as well as part of her life and that was all I needed.

Flynn and I fit into Claire and Melissa's routines more easily than I could have hoped. In time, maybe I would sell my house and Claire and I could either build an addition on her home or buy a larger place — and maybe things won't work out — but for the foreseeable future, it did not matter. We were together.

~

Another relationship was evolving before our eyes. Celia and Maurice had become inseparable. They arrived at the Market together and, just walking in, one could sense an intimacy in their casual interactions that left little doubt. Without too many unwarranted assumptions, I was fairly certain Maurice's vow of abstinence was a relic of an earlier time in his life. (In case you're curious, be assured I had enough self-control not to confirm this hypothesis.)

One morning, after a few nervous exchanges about the weather, they stood, in tandem. "We have an announcement," Maurice said. "We're having a party to celebrate ... us."

Celia concluded: "Everyone is invited."

I was not sure Henry would attend, but he rose to the occasion. Putting aside his concerns and suspicions, he asked where and when this event would take place. On the date of the party, he was among the first to arrive.

The party was held in the large and ornate foyer of the Jackson Row Theater. Years ago, this was Jackson Park's one grand movie theater. It boasted one of the largest screens in the region and an auditorium many times the size of modern movie theaters found in suburban malls. The exterior stonework, primarily limestone mined in Indiana, was reminiscent of an early period in urban architecture when quarried stone was common.

On the day of the party, the Jackson Row marquee made clear that the afternoon shows were cancelled. The entire complex was available for the party. Claire and I walked into the foyer and stopped. The high painted ceiling and up-lighting added to the sense that one was removed from the ebb and flow of the outside world. Great rooms of this nature are portals to other worlds, places where unusual, lovely, frightening, touching, and provocative things can happen, the kinds of things that don't happen on Main Street in Jackson Park.

Waitstaff circulated with platters of Japanese dumplings and chicken satay, and finger sandwiches of thin roast beef, egg salad, cucumbers, watercress, and even peanut butter and jelly. I sampled a number of appetizers while Claire munched on the egg salad and cucumber finger sandwiches. After a few minutes, we found Celia and Maurice. "This is a fabulous spot for a party," Claire said. "How did you ever think of this place?"

At first Maurice looked as if he didn't understand the question. He then tilted his head, smiled, and said: "I own this place." Our silence prompted further explanation.

"When my father died, I inherited this wonderful old theater." Almost as an afterthought, he added, "and a number of other parcels of land in downtown Jackson Park." He went on to explain that these assets had been in his family for years. Of all the properties, the theater was closest to his heart. While it had gone through major renovations, his preservationist spirit prevailed to this extent: the stone façade and grand foyer remained. The large auditorium was gone, replaced by nine smaller and undoubtedly more profitable theaters.

So the mystery regarding Maurice's job was finally solved. He was, in the parlance of my family, part of Jackson Park's landed aristocracy. It was a safe assumption that the land he inherited generated more than sufficient income to meet all of his needs.

The party rumbled along happily. After a time, there were a few toasts and speeches and then a short video produced by Maurice and

Celia. They had taken clips of the American Market, Main Street, old buildings in Jackson Park they fought to preserve, a dark montage of the new buildings they opposed, and even a short segment featuring Flynn who, as you might expect, was filmed sleeping happily on the warm sidewalk in front of the Market. When the lights went up, Maurice took the microphone: "We are showing our favorite movies in the theaters behind us. Thank you for coming—and enjoy the show."

Chapter 17

Arrival and Conclusion
December 2013

We had a beautiful fall in Jackson Park. The Washington summer, that vile meteorological constant in June, July, and August, made its exit in mid-September and had the decency not to return. The fall was a miracle of tolerable warm days, cool nights, white corn, and local apples.

Twice in September and once again in October, we drove to the aptly named Delaware Seashore State Park. The Atlantic beaches between Dewey and Bethany are parkland, free (for the most part) of commercial ventures and set aside for surfing, surf-casting, and swimming, and in the fall, they are not just uncrowded—they are often almost empty.

We would drive east on Route 50 early on a Saturday or Sunday morning, cross the Chesapeake Bay Bridge, have breakfast in one of the little restaurants in Dewey Beach, drive a few miles south on Route One, and park in the beach lots run by the state. We'd walk for hours on the wet and firm sand at the edge of the breaking waves and talk about our child, Melissa, our life, and occasionally the institution of marriage.

It was during those walks that I came to understand that Claire was not an unconditional non-believer in marriage. Her initial discussion about her first marriage on the way back from Jennifer's wedding left out critical pieces, including a series of terrible and physical arguments. She said several times that she simply did not know her husband well enough at the outset. It was that fear she carried with her in Pauline's while I was down on one knee a few months earlier. As much as she assured me of her love, somehow I was quite sure she felt there was more to me than had been revealed

thus far. I hoped that living with her—which was going well, I
might add—might give her the answers she needed.

~

The naming debate at the Market began long before our son was
born. That everyone in the Market knew it would be a boy was
Claire's decision. After refusing to disclose the gender for many
months, she tired of the game and revealed that important fact.
Thereafter, we were asked to give consideration to many names including Simon (Celia's touching suggestion, a homage to Simone
of course), Alex, Maurice, Henry, and Jackson. I liked all the names
but none seemed to work when followed by Beaumont-Pratt.

At one point I told Claire that of all my ancestors, my favorite
name was William Mad Mountain Pratt. She processed the name
silently and then, with some effort, said, "That's charming," and
ended any possibility with: "You're not serious?"

As the date of delivery approached, Henry took me into the
storeroom and there, across from the desk in what had become
my satellite law office, were stacks of disposable diapers, baby
wipes, and cotton swabs. "These are from everyone," Henry told
me and then added, "and there is more to come. We wanted you
to have the supplies you need in the Market so that you can bring
the baby here."

Henry was not exaggerating when he told us there was more to
come—it was a baby shower, held at the American Market at 6:00
a.m. one morning about a month before the delivery. Unbeknownst
to any of us, Henry kept lists of customers. When possible, he
would find out a name and address or other contact information.
Henry was also a highly competent researcher and had learned the
names of Claire's and my co-workers and—this was most impressive—found the mailing address for my privacy-conscious father
and Priscilla Coughlin.

While the baby shower was not a surprise party, the commotion at the Market the morning we arrived was a shock. It was
packed. Though a sign on the door read: "Closed for Private Event,"
there was nothing private about that moment. A stack of gifts—including a stroller (from Maurice and Celia), baby carriage (also
from Maurice and Celia), a state-of-the-art infant car seat (from

Alex, as you might expect), and a playpen (from Henry), were in the rear of the store.

Claire and I made the rounds, recognizing most people. I was introduced to those with whom Claire worked, and she met for the first time the lawyers, legal assistants, paralegals, and others from my firm.

The biggest surprise, however, was that my brother Wesley, my father and Priscilla, and Carter Strong were standing by the coffee machine when we arrived. Carter looked better than when I'd last seen him at the wedding—though that's not saying much. I was still ten feet from Carter when he said, "Jennifer couldn't make it—she wanted you to know she was sorry. Something about the horses, I think." He looked around. "You have lots of friends, Charlie." He scanned the group. "Look at all these … different kinds … of people."

"Good of you to come, Carter," I said. "Pass along my regards to Jennifer and Samantha."

"They're doing great," he said. "I really need another cup of coffee." And then: "This is your … place? Like a club?"

"It's definitely my place," I said and wondered if Carter had ever been in a convenience store.

"I'm going to look around." Carter waded into the crowd and disappeared—and that was just fine with me. It was a lovely gesture on his part.

Next there was Wesley. As I mentioned some time ago, I hadn't seen Wesley in years. Shaking hands is as close as we get to human contact. I can't remember ever hugging him. "Dad thought I should fly down and wish you the best."

"You're looking good, Wes." Actually, I thought he'd aged considerably.

"You too, Charlie." He hesitated and continued. "I hope everything works out with the baby." That was it. A moment later, Wesley walked off to find Claire, wished her well, and left. My guess is that Wesley was here to keep the peace, maintain his position as my father's oldest heir, and, having complied with my father's wishes, made his way to the airport to catch the 8:00 shuttle to Logan.

I suspected my father of some similar less-than-caring motive. After all, in the two decades I have been in Washington, he had not visited once—but I was wrong.

I'm not sure I will ever know what is it about a birth, a child, a new generation, that brought out this side of my cool, reserved, distant, difficult, and theretofore unavailable father. He turned to me as if his presence in the Market was an everyday occurrence and said: "Charlie—where is that beautiful woman I met at Jennifer's wedding?"

Priscilla gave me a hug, this time a sincere embrace, and then said: "Time to start over, Charlie."

Claire was at my side a few minutes later. We talked as fathers and sons do, catching up on a few family matters and expressing our unified marvel in the soon-to-be expansion of our family.

It was a big event, full of handshakes and embraces, best wishes from those we knew well and barely knew at all and, given the timing, ended more quickly than most showers. People needed to go to work, parcels had to be delivered, offices had to open, and by eight, only Claire, Henry, and I remained in the Market. My father and Priscilla were heading downtown. There were monuments to visit and museums to explore. Claire invited them to dinner and expressed, several times, how pleased she was to see them.

I was at work on a bitterly cold afternoon a week after Thanksgiving when Melissa called. "I'm taking Mom to the hospital—it's time. See you soon."

I suppose I could have called Dr. Bingham and boarded Flynn but called Maurice instead. Thankfully, he was home with Celia and more than happy to care for Flynn. I told him the hiding place for the key to the front door, explained Flynn's rather substantial feeding habits and walking needs, thanked him, and bolted out the door.

~

It was one week after our son, Benjamin Beaumont-Pratt was born. We were as close as any couple I've ever known—and completely exhausted new parents. That Claire had been through this before with Melissa and her son did not make it any easier.

Everything was new for me. On several occasions I was terrified I had done something wrong, and on other occasions felt surges of love for our son unlike anything I had experienced before. Of all the things that happened during that time, the one that surprised me most involved Flynn.

As you may recall, among many other things on Flynn's list are small children. He was known to bark and occasionally snap at a child, although he reserved more aggressive attacks for bicyclists and people on stilts or with hats or beards.

Claire and I discussed the possibility that Flynn would have to be kept entirely separate from our son. I considered the difficult but quite possible option that a time might come when Flynn would have to leave, perhaps to live with Maurice and Celia.

On the day we brought home our son from the hospital, Flynn was lounging in the living room along with Melissa—and this will not surprise you—Alex, Maurice, Celia, and Henry. This was our family and, as families do, they had shown up.

Holding our baby carefully, Claire walked to Flynn and said, "Flynn, this is Benjamin." She patted him at length. I held my breath. Maurice and Alex stood next Flynn, ready to pounce but pouncing was not necessary. Flynn looked up, his wagging tail sweeping a small section of the floor, licked Claire's outstretched hand, and then drifted back into a happy sleep.

Claire kneeled even closer to Flynn, lifted his soft substantial ear, and said: "You are now the family dog, Flynn." Benjamin yawned one of those priceless, sweet-smelling infant yawns, and closed his eyes.

A few minutes later, I watched the entire group, a parade of my beloved friends, follow Claire as she carried Benjamin to the bassinet set up in the dining room. In the silence that followed, it dawned on me: What I've shared with you has been, in meaningful part, a story about home. As I have mentioned earlier, I don't mean home in the common context of housing or shelter, but in that broad, vital, primitive way the term is best understood, home as a place of acceptance, that safe, simple, essential center where you can always return.

~

Just after seven on a Thursday night in mid-December, Wallace, the afternoon proprietor, turned over the keys to Henry and left the American Market. Alex, Maurice, Celia, and Henry straightened up the store, swept, vacuumed, and wiped down surfaces, turned on some music and placed the food they brought on the table. Claire and I arrived about a half hour later and, with our son wrapped in a blanket that we received from Priscilla (an heirloom of sorts that had been in her family for years), introduced Benjamin to the American Market.

There was a platter of roasted chicken in the center of the table surrounded by cornbread, Henry's specialty, a mac and cheese Celia made that afternoon, two large tossed salads, a green bean and mushroom casserole, fruit bowl, mashed potatoes, gravy, an apple pie, and a plate of brownies.

There is something special about chicken. I recognize this may not be true for everyone, but for me and I assume for many others, the smell of a properly roasted chicken induces a sense of comfort and familiarity. As the steam rose from the platter in the center of the table and people began to fill their plates, I had the most powerful sensation that this place, this convenience store, the American Market, would be part of me forever.

Epilogue

One morning, some months after Benjamin's arrival, Maurice looked up from the table and, for no particular reason, announced: "Wishing to be friends is quick work, but friendship is a slow-ripening fruit." When he attributed this quote to Aristotle, Alex pfff'ed him and said that nothing attributed to Aristotle could be traced to Aristotle or any reliable source. The quote, Alex stated with superficial confidence, was probably a line from one of Willa Cather's lesser works—and that comment caused Maurice to double over in laughter.

The discussion covered several mornings and was one of Claire's favorites. Neither had real facts and both defended their positions lightly at best. It was a disagreement bounded by affection, not discord or pride. We did not delve into history to resolve the dispute. Aristotelian or not, we had become the truest of friends.

Life at the American Market went forward with Benjamin making regular appearances to the delight of his proud parents and, of course, Henry. It was Henry who, for reasons he never shared, thought Claire and I a good match, and Benjamin was the proud consequence of that insight.

About a year after Benjamin was born, Henry announced that he planned to return to Burma to inter Simone's remains in a family plot. Burma, as Henry told us in several different ways, was still an unpredictable place, but he was determined. We tried to dissuade him from going but to no avail. In the end, we—all of us, Alex, Maurice, Celia, Claire, and I—decided that we could not let Henry go alone, but that is a story for another time.

Next, the poem. The verse that moved Milton Thurber to take on Alex as a client of Alpine Equinox seemed like something you might also want to see—and so here it is as well:

Write What You Know?

Alex Roman

I knew my great uncle (a man of distinction),
But you'd rather hear about thundering skies
Piercing black rain that saturates mountains
And slickens the surface so no one can stand.

She fell with the calf on her way to the pick-up,
Old cherished pick-up, her red metal lover
When lightning illuminated help that arrived.
He appeared on the hillside, stable and solid,
Firm on a night when traction was scarce.

Together they found an ancient plaid blanket,
Folded and waiting on her leather front seat,
A woolen embrace to cover the brown calf
Soaked through and shaking, now held to his chest.

While it's presumption, I think you'd select
The fate of the couple, the calf, and the pick-up
Over details of my encounter with my dental hygienist,
A pale bland hygienist who flossed and then plotted
With the office administrator to reveal baseless suspicions
Of marginal incompetence of the newly hired doctor.
I know this story far too well.
And God spare you from what I know.

Consider instead the pick-up and blanket
The calf that was saved and the warmth
That evolved from the storm on the hillside
That silently joined them, salvation partners.

This is about you, your rare and few moments
Stolen from footpaths your life has worn deep,
Quietly separate from life's dry routines
We owe you a difference, not more of the same.

Isn't it better to be one with the pick-up,
With the calf and the lovers on the side of the mountain
At sunrise in silence as new life begins,
Than stuck with the likes of the cloying hygienist
God save you, indeed, from all that I've known.

One other matter—I figured you still might be wondering whether I told Maurice, Celia, Alex, Henry, Lieutenant Cavise, Claire, or anyone else about the meeting I had with Simone shortly before she took her life and the role played surreptitiously by Lucy Vredeesha. If there was anyone on the face of the earth with whom I might share this information, it would be Claire. I know her better and trust her more than anyone I have ever known. Even so, there is something sacred about a dying wish, a secret told to me in confidence as a lawyer.

It is more than a simple truth that some things are best left unsaid. Regardless of the choices one makes, we all have the right to some modicum of peace in our lifetime and certainly the hope that we will rest in peace at the end of our days. I believe Simone will do so best with her secret forever secure.

Discussion Guide

I hope you have enjoyed *Sunrise at the American Market*. It was not my intention to answer every question raised by the plot or the characters. Instead, I hope the book will provoke discussion in a number of different areas. For those interested in a discussion of some of the issues the novel raised, consider the following discussion and questions:

1. Friendship

The epigrams in the front of the book suggest that, among other things, this is a story about friendship. As Alex noted at one point, despite the friendships that develop, the characters in the novel are not always particularly nice. Moreover, at least at the outset, there is an effort to avoid or limit any inquiry into life outside of the Market. Do these factors make friendship more possible? More artificial? More sincere?

There are endless options for those interested in reading more about this topic. To be clear, I am not comparing my work to the books that follow—I am only suggesting that the friendships they describe are worthy of study and reflection. Each book in J.K. Rowlings' Harry Potter series can be seen as a beautiful study of friendship. Nick Carraway's relationship with Jay Gatsby in Fitzgerald's *The Great Gatsby* is likewise a remarkable and telling exploration into one of the most famous friendships in all of literature. Other familiar works you may have read are equally evocative: E.B. White's *Charlotte's Web*; Mark Twain's *The Adventures of Tom Sawyer* and *The*

Adventures of Huckleberry Finn; Ann Patchett's *Truth and Beauty*; John Steinbeck's *Of Mice and Men*; and *The Kite Runner*, by Khaled Hosseini.

The intensity of friendship is hard to overstate. For example, when Alex tells Maurice he does not want to be politicized at the Market and therefore will not sign Maurice's no-growth petition, in the same breath he tells him he would lay down in front of a train for him. While I hope Alex was speaking metaphorically, the depth of their friendship was something I wanted to develop.

The more I've thought about this topic, the more I've realized that it is perhaps the most common theme in all of literature. From *Sisterhood of the Traveling Pants* by Ann Brashares to Stephen King's *Stand by Me*, writers and cinematographers explore, luxuriate, rely, and push the boundaries of friendship.

At times, the line between friendship and family is either hazy or simply disappears. Consider the easy use we make of the distinction between families of birth and families of choice, the latter being those we marry and those who become our closest and life-long friends. Other than genetics, how are they not family? I recognize the ancient truth that blood is thicker than water (rumored to have first been written in Sir Walter Scott's novel *Guy Mannering*—but I am sure there are earlier articulations), but writing this book—and perhaps reading it—might allow for a re-examination of that premise. Consider, for example, the following: Is Charlie's relationship with his brother, Wes, more meaningful than his relationship with Maurice?

2. Change

This is also a book focused on change. At many points in the story, the characters speculate on the importance and difficulty of change. How is the challenge of change expressed in the story? Do the characters experience real change or simply an evolving capacity to accept differences in others?

Like friendship, the topic of change has been part of literature since the beginning of the written word. Growth and transformation are the subjects of everything from ancient Greek literature and Shakespeare to almost all of popular fiction and, of course, to entire sections of bookstores and online literature devoted to "self-help," a term that means, if anything, assisting with the process of change.

As with many of the topics in this novel, I do not suggest that I am the first to realize the presence of such fertile human challenges. Instead, I simply wanted to tell a story that reflected a special set of circumstances applicable to a unique group of people to whom, at one level or another, you might be able to relate.

Change is at the heart of the Burmese fairytale Henry told Charlie. It is central to so many great works of fiction and nonfiction that I leave to you your favorites. Perhaps, like me, you grew up enchanted by Rudyard Kipling's *The Jungle Book*, or *Tarzan of the Apes* by Edgar Rice Burroughs, or any one of many, many books about children raised by a pack of wolves or brought up in the most primitive and harshest of circumstances, only to emerge later in life as fully-formed, sophisticated, and wholly civilized adults.

I think it is worth discussing, if you are up to it, the capacity for human change. Such a discussion can easily go along with the capacity for forgiveness and for full human transformation.

3. Henry's View of Life and Death

From the opening scene forward, the characters—particularly Henry—discuss their perspectives on the nature of life and death. This plays out in different ways in the story. How would you articulate Henry and Simone's view of the grander issues pertaining to our existence and our demise?

Beyond the Bible, the Torah, and the Koran, there are thousands of books devoted to these ultimate questions. If you are looking for something grounded in science, you might try *Death by Black Hole: And Other Cosmic Quandaries* by Neil deGrasse Tyson or, somewhere between science and fiction, *Contact* by Carl Sagan.

4. Compassionate Life Termination

The matter of compassionate life termination or assisted suicide becomes central to the story as Simone's condition deteriorates. Though she is seemingly at peace with taking her own life or having another assist in that process, her perspectives are not universally shared.

The story is an opportunity for you to think through and discuss this difficult and powerful set of questions. Do we have the right to control the end of our lives? There are arguments that run in many directions—which seem right to you? How should the legal system function when such fundamental decisions are in play? For those who are interested, you might take a look at the Washington statute that permits assisted suicide, Washington Death with Dignity Act, Wash. Rev. Code Ann. §§ 70.245.010-70.245.904 (West 2009). In addition, here are some resources for further study: George P. Smith, II, *Refractory Pain, Existential Suffering, and Palliative Care: Releasing an Unbearable Lightness of Being*, 20 Cornell J. L. & Pub. Pol'y 469 (2011); Margaret K. Dore, *Physician-Assisted Suicide: A Recipe for Elder Abuse and the Illusion of Personal Choice*, 36 Vt. B. J. 53 (2011); Edward Rubin, *Assisted Suicide, Morality, and Law: Why Prohibiting Assisted Suicide Violates the Establishment Clause*, 63 Vand. L. Rev. 763 (2010); Annette E. Clark, *Autonomy and Death*, 71 Tul. L. Rev. 45 (1996); DeWitt C. Baldwin, Jr., *The Role of the Physician in End of Life Care: What More Can We Do?* 2 J. Health Care L. & Pol'y 258 (1999); and John Finnis, *The "Value of Human Life" and "The Right to Death": Some Reflections on Cruzan and Ronald Dworkin*, 17 S. Ill. U. L.J. 559 (1993).

5. Unwanted Medical Confinement

At another point, the novel raises the issue of unwanted medical confinement. Simone's plea to spend her remaining time in her own home seems irresistible. While it may appear to be a simple issue, it is not. Some of the root questions are the same as the problems raised above regarding assisted suicide and involve one's perspective on individual autonomy. What are the arguments, pro and con, for compulsory confinement regarding essential medical care?

As you discuss this, consider the dilemma doctors and hospitals face: As Charlie suggested, if they keep a patient against her or his will, they may be sued for false imprisonment. If they release a patient in need of medical care and the patient deteriorates or passes away, they run the risk of being sued for medical malpractice. Many law students are first exposed to this topic in *Big Town Nursing Home v. Newman*, 461 S.W.2d 195 (Tex. Civ. App. 1970), or *Pounders v. Trinity Court Nursing Home* 265 Ark. 1, 576 S.W.2d 934 (1979). More recent case law recites essentially the same standards, see, *e.g.*, *Berryhill v. Parkview Hosp.*, 962 N.E.2d 685 (Ind. Ct. App. 2012), derived from the Restatement of Torts. *Restatement (Second) of Torts,* § 35 (1965) (requirements for a false imprisonment claim).

6. Same-Sex Marriage

The next two topics fall under the category of marriage but involve very different questions.

In the most direct way possible, this story raises issues involving same-sex marriage. Jennifer and Samantha's spectacular wedding provides an opportunity for a discussion of some of the issues involved. While many of the guests can do no better than participate in a shouting match, it is worth spending time to sort through the different positions on this matter. As this book goes to press, the Supreme Court handed down the landmark decision, *Obergefell v. Hodges*, 576 U.S.__; 135 S. Ct. 2584 (2015) (http://www.supremecourt.gov/opinions/14pdf/14-556_3204.pdf), holding that marriage, including same-sex marriage, is a fundamental right and, accordingly, same-sex couples cannot be denied the right to marry in *any* state.

On this topic, see generally: John Corvino & Maggie Gallagher, *Debating Same-Sex Marriage* (2012); Michael Klarman, *From the Closet to the Altar: Courts, Backlash, and the Struggle for Same Sex*

Marriage, (2012); Dave Gram, *Vermont Legalizes Gay Marriage, Overrides Governor's Veto,* Huffinton Post (May 8, 2009), http://www.huffingtonpost.com/2009/04/07/vermont-legalizes-gay-mar_n_184034.html; Darren Bush, *Moving to the Left by Moving to the Right: A Law & Economics Defense of Same-Sex Marriage,* 22 Women's Rts. L. Rep. 115, 137 (2001); Lyle Denniston, *Analysis: Paths to Same-Sex Marriage Review (Updated),* SCOTUSBLOG (Nov. 7, 2014), http://www.scotusblog.com/2014/11/analysis-paths-to-same-sex-marriage-review.

7. Traditional Marriage

Unlike Jennifer and Samantha, there is no controversy about the legality or general acceptance of a marriage that might take place between Claire and Charlie. The issue they face is whether to marry at all. While Charlie seems intent on a traditional marriage, Claire, for many reasons, is uncertain.

Claire is not alone in questioning this ancient and fundamental institution. Consider the following questions: Is marriage outdated? Essential? Legally required? Morally critical? In need of reform? In need of protection?

Proponents of the traditional understanding of marriage are not shy in expressing their views on the importance of marriage: "Marriage, a sacred institution supported for thousands of years, has been, and must continue to be, a solid building block for our country." Troy King, *Marriage Between a Man & a Woman: A Fight to Save the Traditional Family One Case at a Time,* 16 Stan. L. & Pol'y Rev. 57, 71 (2005). Others have a very different perspective: "The time has come to abolish civil marriage. Such abolition would recognize [that] marriage today plays a reduced role in our law and culture. Abolishing ... would also strengthen marriage by encouraging competition among alternative versions [and] by eliminating the political strife inherent in government propounding a single legal definition of marriage...." Edward A. Zelinski, *Symposium, Abol-*

ishing Civil Marriage: Deregulating Marriage: The Pro-Marriage Case for Abolishing Civil Marriage, 27 Cardozo L. Rev. 1161, 1219 (2006).

8. Professional Identity

One of the themes running through the book involves Charlie's professional identity. He suggests he was pushed through the educational process leading to his status as an attorney. It is not surprising, therefore, that there are times he seems highly resistant to that role. There are other times, however, when he embraces his status as a lawyer.

Charlie characterizes himself initially as a "reluctant lawyer," raising questions common to a number of professions. There is an expectation in the Market that when anything comes up tangentially involving a legal matter, Charlie should be able to transform to the role of an attorney—and quite obviously, this makes Charlie uncomfortable. At some point, Charlie, like most lawyers, doctors, architects, and other professionals must wonder whether having the privileges of professional status implies a continuous responsibility to be in role. What are your expectations of professionals—do they have a duty, no matter the time or place, to provide the kind of aid, advice, or assistance they are licensed to render?

A few pieces on professional identity for lawyers may be helpful in thinking this through: Fred C. Zacharias, *The Images of Lawyers*, 20 Geo. J. Legal Ethics 73 (2007); Deborah M. Hussey Freeland, *What is a Lawyer? A Reconstruction of the Lawyer as an Officer of the Court*, 31 St. Louis U. Pub. L. Rev. 425 (2012); Jerome M. Organ, *What Do We Know About the Satisfaction/Dissatisfaction of Lawyers? A Meta-Analysis of Research on Lawyer Satisfaction and Well-Being*, 8 U. St. Thomas L.J. 225, 271 (2011).

9. Urbanization

For Maurice and Celia, this story raises difficult questions of land use and suburban growth. Jackson Park, like hundreds of older municipalities that thrive on the edge of large cities, is ripe for development and also at risk of losing its small-town character. Consider its unique legal structure—Jackson Park has an elected Town Council that votes on zoning and other land use matters. Should zoning decisions be political questions? In their fervor to protect the present, are Maurice and Celia actually stuck in the past, unwilling to embrace change—or are they right to oppose every new building or project proposed?

Decisions on the use of land raise economic, constitutional, and philosophical questions. If Maurice and Celia have their way, is the failure to permit development a "taking" from a constitutional point of view?

A few sources in the area might help with this inquiry: William A. Fischel, *Zoning and Land Use Regulation* 407 (1999) (Zoning decisions are "embedded in local government politics"); Kenneth A. Stah, *The Artifice of Local Growth Politics: At-Large Elections, Ballot-Box Zoning, and Judicial Review*, 94 Marq. L. Rev. 1 (2010); Frank J. Popper, *The Politics of Land-Use Reform* 52 (1981); Mary Dawson, *The Best Laid Plans: The Rise and Fall of Growth Management in Florida*, 11 J. Land Use & Envtl. L. 325, 328 (1996) (favoring local politicians making land use decisions). Finally, if you are interested in my compilation of a discussion of similar land use legal issues, you might read my novel, *Bordering on Madness: An American Land Use Tale*, and the fully documented *Companion to Bordering on Madness* (with Salkin and Avitable), both published by Carolina Academic Press.

10. Prejudgment

I began this book writing character studies, but as the manuscript took form, the characters changed, in some instances significantly. Perhaps the most notable of those changes and the most complex of those studies involved Henry. The complexity grew from a realization I made regarding the great differences that exist between those who run convenience stores.

While some proprietors fit the model used initially for Henry (the honest and grateful newly-arrived immigrant), many do not. With rudimentary field work (a fancy term—my research involved going to a number of convenience stores and speaking with the people behind the counter), I discovered that those who own and operate such stores, to the person, had interesting stories, complicated lives, and far more to offer than I would have guessed before I started this project. Some had PhDs, others advanced degrees in science and engineering; still others are entrepreneurs owning more commercial properties than Maurice.

This raised for me a set of fairly traditional questions: What assumptions do we make about those around us and how much are those assumptions based on role, job or profession, appearance, or speech? Without putting too fine an edge on it, how much do we engage in the kind of controversial profiling that is done in some areas of domestic security (*e.g.*, airport passenger screening) and law enforcement?

If you are interested in learning more about this, consider Kristina M. Campbell, *(Un)Reasonable Suspicion: Racial Profiling in Immigration Enforcement After* Arizona v. United States, 3 Wake Forest St. J.L. & Pol'y 367 (2013); Stephen Rushin, *The Legislative Response to Mass Police Surveillance*, 79 Brooklyn L. Rev. 1 (2013); Jason A. Nier et al., *Can Racial Profiling Be Avoided Under Arizona Immigration Law? Lessons Learned from Subtle Bias Research and Anti-Discrimination Law*, 12 Analyses Soc. Issues & Pub. Pol. 5 (2012); R. Richard Banks, *Beyond Profiling: Race, Policing, and the Drug War*, 56 Stan. L. Rev. 571, 575-76 (2003). At a more direct level, give some thought to how you assessed Henry and Simone. How, if at all, did learning about their past change your views on them? How did learning about their home affect your perception of them? Next time you go into a convenience store, ask yourself what assumptions you are making about the employees—you might find it an interesting experiment.

11. The Lottery

At a number of different points in this story, I made reference to the lottery. Were you surprised to learn that more than half the population plays the lottery from time to time (most play casually—but some, like Alex, to great excess)? Could you accept Alex's condition as a diagnosable medical condition activated, in part, by his economic situation? In the most recent DSM, gambling is defined as a medical condition (a behavioral addiction) that requires and can benefit from conventional treatment. *Gambling Disorder*, Diagnostic and Statistical Manual of Mental Disorders, DSM-5, Section 312.31 (2013). For contrast, *see* Henry R. Lesieur & Robert L. Custer, *Pathological Gambling: Roots, Phases, and Treatment*, 474 Annals Am. Acad. Pol. & Soc. Sci. 146, 147–48 (1984).

Should states be allowed to sponsor activity that plays into a common addiction and costs those who can least afford it to lose meaningful amounts of money over an extended period of time? Keep in mind that, like a casino, when it comes to the bottom line with lotteries, the state always wins. Roger Neumann, "Lottery brings tide of gambling addicts," Lohud.com (Jan. 28, 2007), http://www.lohud.com/article/20070128/NEWS05/701280397/<d>Lottery-brings-tide-gambling-addicts.

You might look at *West Virginia Ass'n of Club Owners & Fraternal Servs. v. Musgrave*, 553 F.3d 292, 301 (4th Cir. 2009), for a recognition of the balance between raising public revenue through the lottery and the hazards of gambling addiction.

12. Dogs

Lastly, there is the matter of Flynn. From Ulysses' faithful dog, Argos, in Homer's *Odyssey* to thousands of more recent titles, much of the fiction we enjoy celebrates or includes meaningfully our furry, faithful, and loyal friends. While I am not an anthropologist or paleontologist, there is ample data showing that dogs have lived among us, both for companionship and as guardians of our dwellings, for at least the last 12,000 years. Joshua Mark, "Dogs in the Ancient World," http://www.ancient.eu/article/184/ (June, 2014). With that history, it should come as no surprise that there can be a fine line between pathological anthropomorphizing and affectionate characterization of our canine companions. How did you respond to Flynn—was that fine line maintained or crossed in the story?

What follows is a very short list of novels where dogs play a central role: John Grogan, *Marley & Me*; Garth Stein, *The Art of Racing in the Rain* (one of my favorites); William Armstrong, *Sounder*; Fred Gipson, *Old Yeller*; Mark Haddon, *The Curious Incident of the Dog in the Night-Time*; Stephen King's frightening *Cujo*; and of course, John Steinbeck, *Travels with Charley* (the poodle, not the Pratt).

Author's Note

Sunrise at the American Market is a work of fiction. It derives in part from my experience at the One Plus Convenience Market, a convenience store that once graced Norfolk Avenue in Bethesda, Maryland. It was my pleasure to get to know the proprietors of the market, Sophat Chhum Or and his wife, Min Keth Or. Sophat and Min are survivors of the killing fields in Cambodia. I hope one day they will have a chance to share the details of their history. It is an amazing story—but it is their story, not mine. In the novel you've just read, Henry and Simone were inspired by Sophat and Min Keth, but beyond the roughest contours in their distant past, like all the characters in this book, they are fictional creations.

About the Author

Andrew F. Popper is the winner of various awards, including the Maryland Writers Association Prize for Mainstream Fiction, the American Bar Association Robert McKay Award for Excellence in Tort Law, the Guttman Casebook Award, and the American University Scholar-Teacher of the Year Award.

He has taught for the last three decades at American University, Washington College of Law and is the author of more than 100 books, articles, papers, poems, and public documents. His books include, *Rediscovering Lone Pine*; *Bordering on Madness: An American Land Use Tale*; *Administrative Law: A Contemporary Approach* (with McKee, Varona, and Harter); *Materials on Tort Reform*; and, *A Companion to Bordering on Madness: Cases, Scholarship, and Case Studies.* His articles appear in journals published at Harvard University, Northwestern University, Marquette University, Catholic University, DePaul University, University of Kansas, and a number of other institutions.

He has served as a consumer rights advocate and *pro bono* counsel for the Consumers Union of America, testified before Congressional committees on more than 30 occasions, and authored *amicus curiae* briefs before the United States Supreme Court. Prior to coming to the Washington College of Law, he held the MCLA Endowed Chair at the University of Denver. Before going into teaching, he practiced law in Washington, DC.

About the Cover Artist

Lesley Giles was educated in London at Royal College of Art, Goldsmiths College of Art, and Kensington & Chelsea College. Spanning more than a quarter century, her remarkable works have been displayed in China, France, Great Britain, and the United States. In addition, her art work is in numerous books and periodical articles. A sampling of her unique and striking artistry as well as her contact information are available on her website, http://www.lesleygilesart.com/.

Acknowledgments

My deepest thanks to Catherine Riedo, Ashley Hoornstra, and Nicolas Mansour for their remarkable assistance and to Dean Claudio Grossman for his unfailing support. I would also like to thank my daughter, Katherine, for her help and encouragement and the following generous readers and editors: John (from C.T.), Linda (from N.C.), from Yorktown: Bob, Lanny, and George, and from Washington: Amanda, Chip, Janie, Anne, Elliott, Cindy, Paula, Mary-Kate, Krystal-Rose, and Billie Jo. Finally, I would like to thank the students at the Washington College of Law who generously volunteered their time to proofread and suggest edits.

Attribution

I am the copyright holder on both poems in this book. "The Painter from Acumbaro," 2011 © Andrew F. Popper, appeared in an edited form in the *Tipton Poetry Journal*. A slightly different version of the poem "Write What You Know," 2012 © Andrew F. Popper, appeared under the name "More than You Know," in *Millers Pond Poetry Journal*.